IT WAS HIS FAVORITE TOOL.

It weighed more than a pound. Most of the weight was in an elaborately carved ivory handle. Its blade was six inches from the butt of its handle to its sharp tip.

He'd taken steel wool to it only the day before. He often did that with the tools of his profession. He took pride in them, considered them surgical instruments. He knew that without them, he could not be the best in his profession.

He stepped back and surveyed his work, his favorite ice pick in his large, beefy hand.

"That thing could kill you," someone said.

Of course he already knew that.

About The Author

MARGARET TRUMAN is the author of, among others, the novel *Murder in the White House; Women of Courage;* and the biography of her father, President *Harry S. Truman.* Arbor House has also published *Letters from Father: The Truman Family's Personal Correspondence,* edited, annotated and with an introduction by Margaret Truman. Born in Independence, Missouri, she now makes her home in New York City.

MURDER
ON CAPITOL HILL

by

Margaret Truman

WARNER BOOKS

A Warner Communications Company

WARNER BOOKS EDITION

This Warner Books Edition is published by arrangement with
Arbor House Publishing Company, Division of The Hearst
Corporation, 235 East 45th Street, New York, N.Y. 10017

Warner Books, Inc.
666 Fifth Avenue
New York, N.Y. 10103

W A Warner Communications Company

Printed in the United States of America

First Warner Books Printing: *February, 1984*

10 9 8 7 6

*For my husband, Clifton Daniel,
and my sons Clifton, William,
Harrison, and Thomas*

One

It was his favorite tool.

It weighed more than a pound. Most of the weight was in an elaborately carved ivory handle. Its blade was six inches from the butt of its handle to its sharp tip.

He'd taken steel wool to it only the day before. He often did that with the tools of his profession. He took pride in them, considered them surgical instruments. He knew that without them, he could not be the best in his profession.

He stepped back and surveyed his work, his favorite ice pick in his large, beefy hand. He was not what most people would envision a sculptor to be. There was nothing artistic about him. He was broad and lumpy and very Scandinavian-looking. His large head was bald, with the exception of a soft fringe of blond and gray hair over his ears and an unruly tuft of it spiraling up from the center of his dome.

Just a little more, he told himself as he stepped forward, weighed the ice pick in his hand, then chipped away on the right side of the work. As long as he'd been sculpturing ice he'd never gotten over the joy of feeling the pick ram home at precisely the right spot. He could sever a block of ice in seconds with the pick or, as was now called for, could gently and deftly shape a corner, deepen relief on an ice portrait, turn frozen water into whatever he wished.

Again, a step back to gain perspective. Good, he told himself. Just one more spot.

"Looks good," an employee of the restaurant said from behind him. The voice distracted him. He jerked his head and felt the point of the pick break through the skin on his left thumb.

"Damn it," he said as he looked at his hand. It wasn't much of a wound, just a small hole in the skin from which a tiny bubble of blood welled up.

"I'm sorry," said the restaurant worker.

The ice sculptor laughed and shook his head. "I haven't stabbed myself in years." He placed the pick on the table. His own blood was on its tip. "I'm done anyway," he said as he sucked blood from his finger into his mouth and packed up a black bag in which he carried the tools of his trade. "Like a surgeon's bag," he often said about it.

He took one final look at his work, then turned and walked from the large banquet room.

"He forgot his pick," the restaurant worker mumbled to a co-worker who'd just come from the kitchen. "No wonder. He stabbed himself."

The other young man looked down at the pick and said, smiling, "It's a good thing he didn't stab himself in the wrong place. That thing could kill you."

Two

Senator Cale Caldwell entered the Senate Dining
Room at precisely twelve noon. He liked being early
for lunch because it meant that his favored table, in a
far and secluded corner and affording a view of everyone who came and went, would be available. He could
have demanded that the table be set aside for him no
matter what hour he arrived, just as others did, but
never had, which endeared him to the dining room's
staff and management. Not that Cale Caldwell was
without appreciation for the perks that accompanied
his position as Senate Majority Leader and chairman
of the Senate Appropriations Committee. He enjoyed
them along with the rest of his colleagues. It was just
that he liked being liked by those who served him,
especially in restaurants, which, he sometimes speculated, probably resulted from having waited tables to
help put himself through the University of Virginia
Law School.

"Senator Caldwell," the assistant restaurant manager said, "you're looking splendid today."

"Thank you, Charles, I feel splendid. But then again,
I always do once the first fall snap hits. What's for
lunch?"

"Vermont Day, senator."

"Really? Do I have to have pancakes and maple syrup?"

Charles laughed. "Of course not, senator." He consulted the menu he carried. "We have a boiled dinner, beef pudding and lime-baked chicken."

Caldwell moved into the dining room and headed for his table, muttering as he went, "I've never understood why we have to have every day devoted to one damn state or another. Any bean soup?"

"Yes, sir. Will you be alone?"

Caldwell pulled out a chair. "No, my son is joining me."

"Very well. Your usual?"

"Please."

He adjusted his legs beneath the table, pulled up one long black sock that had drooped and placed a white linen napkin on his lap. He noticed a white speck on the lapel of his dark blue suit and brushed it away. Cale Caldwell was known as one of the best-dressed men on the Hill. A local columnist repeatedly placed him at the top of her yearly best-dressed list. He hadn't the money while a student to afford nice clothes and was constantly embarrassed around his more affluent classmates at the University of Virginia. Once he'd graduated and had begun his rise in law and politics, his clothing had become almost an obsession with him.

He waved to a senator at another corner table who'd been served a large platter of cold shrimp, which the lawmaker had flown in fresh daily and that was stored for him in Senate refrigerators. The chef had prepared a special sauce for the shrimp and had garnished the platter with tomatoes, radishes and cucumbers. Because the senator provided his own shrimp, he was never charged for lunch. Rank—and homegrown fish—had its privileges.

Charles returned with a Virgin Mary—liquor was not served with lunch in the Senate Dining Room. "Here's to you," Caldwell said, raising his glass.

"Here's to the Redskins," Charles said. "They won last night."

"I know, my son and I were there. Hell of a game." He spotted his son standing in the doorway, stood and waved him to the table.

"Good game, wasn't it, dad?"

"Yes, it was. Did you make your appointment this morning?"

"Sure. I think he'll go with me. I could use another client."

They ordered, bean soup for the senator, chicken for his son. When their appetizers were served, Caldwell asked, "Have you heard from your brother?"

His son shook his head and started on the salad. His father watched him. They looked very much alike, both tall and rangy and with full heads of hair, although Cale, Sr.'s had turned completely silver. Both had green eyes and aquiline noses. Cale, Jr., had followed in his father's educational footsteps and had graduated from law school at the University of Virginia. After working in two prestigious law firms, one in New York, the other in Washington, he'd set up his own practice which, as it developed, had turned increasingly into a lobbying activity. He had three industrial trade associations as clients, as well as a conservative foundation that was dedicated to social change through political efforts. Both knew that the senator's lofty position on the Hill helped to attract clients to the son's office, and they carefully avoided any overt use of that competitive edge.

"Tell me about the new client," the senator said.

"Not much to tell. Small trade group representing a loose group of U.S. watch manufacturers. They want trade restrictions with Japan, that's all." His laugh was sardonic. "Same thing happened this morning as always happens. Because I'm a Junior, they assume I was the first-born. Had to tell 'em it isn't true. Why they even bring it up is beyond me."

His father smiled and wiped his mouth. He'd wanted to call his first-born Cale, Jr., but had given in to his wife's wishes that their first son be named after her father, a distinguished and wealthy Virginia land-holder and industrialist whose roots went back to Jefferson, and whose name had been Mark Adam. So their older son had been named Mark Adam Caldwell. Two years later their second son was born and the father's name Cale was bestowed on him.

The elder Caldwell finished off his lunch with rum pie. His son declined dessert. "Seeing anyone special lately?" asked the father.

Another nonverbal denial. The younger Caldwell resented his father prying into his social life. Neither brother had ever married, although Cale, Jr.'s social life was an active one. He was a prized eligible bachelor in a city crawling with unattached women, and was often seen at dinner parties and quasi-official Washington social gatherings and fund-raisers on the arm of a beautiful woman. Surprisingly, it was his father who most often expressed a desire that his son settle down and begin raising a family. Veronica Caldwell seemed to enjoy her younger son's free and easy movement through the city's social circles and often laughed at her husband's protests.

"Are you bringing someone to the great party your mother is throwing for me night after next?"

"I don't know, dad. I'll be there. Isn't that enough?"

The senator glanced around to see whether anyone else had caught the hostility in his son's voice. He leaned across the table. "What the hell is eating you?"

"Nothing. I happen to think it's great mother is doing this for you, but what I hear are sarcastic comments. You ought to be happy that she loves you enough to turn herself inside out to honor you—"

"I know, I know," he said, half meaning it, actually more anxious to change the tenor of their conversation than anything else. He knew his son was right. Although he didn't have any particular love or appreciation for the arts, he'd worked hard within various committees to increase that portion of the federal budget allocated to creative and performing endeavors, all very dear to his wife's heart. That year it had reached a level unparalleled in history, and a sizable hunk of it had gone to the Caldwell Performing Arts Center.

Were Cale Caldwell a man of lesser stature, and were his reputation for honesty and integrity not as firmly established, eyebrows might have been raised. Actually, his wife's passion in life, the center, had received what could only be considered a fair share of the pie. It had applied for the funds through normal channels, with her close friend Jason DeFlaunce spearheading the drive on her behalf and her board of directors. A simultaneous and energetic private fundraising campaign within Washington's society and artistic communities had brought in large amounts to supplement the federal grant. All in all, the financial picture at the center had never been brighter, and Veronica Caldwell was the first to acknowledge that her husband's efforts in Congress, and having his name attached to the private fund drive, had played a major role. Which was why she'd insisted on hostessing a party for him two nights from then in the Senate's largest private dining room. Attending would be an assortment of her associates from the center, some of Cale's closest friends, his family and, in the interest of continuing publicity, selected members of the print and electronic media.

They left the now-crowded dining room, stopping at a few tables on their way for Caldwell to greet a friend and to introduce his son. Finally, they reached the corridor.

"Where are you off to now?" the father asked.

"The office, and I have an early dinner engagement."

"A client?"

"Yes."

"I have a committee meeting, a couple of votes and a doctor's appointment this afternoon. Wish you were free tonight. I know your mother would like to have you for dinner. She hasn't seen you in a while."

"She's going out for dinner, then to the center."

"Oh."

"I called her this morning."

"Oh."

They took a few steps before Cale, Jr., said, "Dad..."

Caldwell stopped, looked at his son.

"Are they still planning a hearing on religious cults?"

"Hard to say...Senator MacLoon seems against it—"

"Couldn't *you* do something to kill it?"

Caldwell raised his eyebrows. "It's not exactly my concern—"

His son's face hardened, his mouth tightened. When he put on that expression he looked like his mother when she was upset or angry, and Cale Caldwell had always intensely disliked that expression on both of them. The son broke in, "It *is* your concern, it's all of our concern."

"Come for dinner some night and we'll discuss it. I'm late for my meeting."

"You don't really care—"

Caldwell glanced around. His son's voice had risen. "We'll discuss it at home, where it belongs. Well, thanks for coming, I enjoyed lunch."

"Yes, well, so did I...I'll see you at your...testimonial."

His father looked at him, wondering if he only imagined a tinge of sarcasm.

Three

Lydia James was grateful the performance was over. She'd never particularly appreciated Haydn, though she did admire some of his symphonic works like "London" symphony Number 101 that mixed a rondo with a variation form.

She glanced across the partially filled hall at the recital's sponsor, Veronica Caldwell, wife of the Senate Majority Leader and Lydia's friend, whose face reflected her intense enjoyment of the evening. Veronica was partial to string quartets.

"Bravo," Veronica called out as she stood applauding. The members of the string quartet, who'd just completed Haydn's "Razor" Quartet—the composer had given it to an Englishman in exchange for a new razor—stood and bowed.

The man next to Lydia sighed and scratched his Adam's apple. "The best thing that ever happened to Haydn was meeting Mozart. Everything he composed improved after that."

Lydia smiled and placed her hand on the arm of Clarence Foster-Sims. Among other things, he'd been her last piano teacher before she gave up her early dream of a performing musical career for the more pragmatic one of law, at which she was damn good. She'd once blamed him for being so tough on her that he'd undermined her, but finally she was able to acknowledge that his demanding, caustic approach had helped make her a brilliant lawyer instead of a so-so piano player.

The sparse audience stood and filed into the lobby. Foster-Sims excused himself, and Lydia watched his tall, angular frame, from which a brown tweed suit hung loosely, slice through clusters of people to the men's room. A handsome self-possessed man, she thought. No use denying it, she was very attracted to him—

"Lydia…"

She turned to face Veronica Caldwell.

"Oh, hi, Veronica. I enjoyed it very much."

"So did I. Every time I listen to Haydn I'm more aware of how he must have suffered being married to that awful woman…You look lovely."

"Thank you." Lydia appreciated the compliment. She didn't feel lovely. It had been a long hard day at the office, and she'd barely had time to brush her hair and change into a beige linen suit before Foster-Sims had picked her up.

"Is Cale here?" Lydia asked, referring to Veronica's husband, the Senate Majority Leader. She would have been surprised if he were. Cale Caldwell was not a concertgoer, although he was dutifully supportive of his wife's involvement in the arts, and of the center that carried their name.

Veronica waved to someone across the lobby, then said, "No, he went to some game…baseball, football, I'm not sure."

"Ready?" Foster-Sims asked Lydia as he squeezed through the crowd and came up to her side.

"I think so."

"Good. Let's stop off for a brandy. Haydn's so damned dry, I work up a real thirst listening to him."

"Bull, but okay…Good night, Veronica," Lydia said.

But before they could escape, Jason DeFlaunce came

up, decked out in a green velvet jacket, an open white shirt, brown-and-green paisley ascot, wrinkled gray slacks and brown molded shoes. Lydia had never particularly liked Jason. Too *much*...Still, he was well-known in Washington's so-called creative community as someone who could get things done. Which was to say an ability to raise money for the arts, which Veronica Caldwell especially appreciated. Jason was also, to some, witty and well-connected. Foster-Sims had once labeled him an unregistered lobbyist—"unregistered whore" was actually what he'd said. Clarence had strong opinions.

"Hello, Jason," she now said. "You look...well."

Eyebrows arched. "Actually I haven't been feeling all that well, Lydia. I suspect I'm terminal."

"I'm very sorry to hear that," she said with a straight face. Jason extended his hand to Foster-Sims, who seemed to examine it before shaking. "Let's *go*," he said to Lydia.

She nodded. "Well, see you soon, Veronica, and my best to Cale."

"I'll tell him if I ever see him. Being married to a United States senator is no bed of roses, or petunias for that matter...By the way, Lydia, you will be at Cale's testimonial, won't you?"

"Of course."

"You, too, Clarence?"

"I wouldn't miss it." Unless he could figure out an excuse, which he doubted.

Lydia and Clarence went to a bar in the Hotel Madison where they ordered brandy—Hennessy for him, Rémy Martin for her. The bar was virtually empty as they settled into a corner booth, sipped from their snifters.

Lydia broke the brief silence. "I felt sorry for Veronica tonight, Clarence."

"Why?"

"Oh, I don't know. I like her very much, always have. She's been through so much, in spite of her money and

(17)

marriage and success. I always sense a kind of sadness in her."

"I guess...but I find it hard to get too worked up about it."

She forgave him that. Beneath his gruff cynical hide was a warm, caring man with a will of iron, but a limited tolerance for fools and pompous asses, of which Washington had more than its share. He was also frighteningly no-nonsense about himself.

Four years earlier he had decided that he'd wasted his life since the age of four playing the piano. He made up his mind never again to lift the lid of his Steinway, and had obviously stuck to it, no matter how drunk he might have been when making the pledge. But he'd been an inspired teacher, and many of his pupils had gone on to impressive careers. He'd simply decided that he didn't have concert talent, and teaching others who had it was the best he could do. She respected, admired him, and maybe was a little in love with him. She wasn't sure...

A man at the bar openly admired her, which she told herself was standard operating procedure for most men at bars, especially after too many drinks. Still, she didn't dismiss it. Lydia had just turned forty. She'd been married once, but that was when she was twenty-one. It had lasted two years. She'd met her husband in music school, where he was a promising string player.

Actually, she rather liked the way she looked, realizing that she'd been blessed with good genes that provided a tall, supple, full female body that she kept in condition through a regular exercise regime—nothing fanatical, just consistent.

Lydia and Clarence shared a Scottish heritage. Her bloodline went back to Inverness, his to the more southerly Edinburgh. No one ever doubted that he was a Scot, with his fair skin. She, on the other hand, was surprisingly dark, and was taken for Jewish or Italian at times. Her hair was a thick, black mane, and there was a duskiness to her complexion that came from the French ancestry in her family.

She took another sip of her brandy. "Know what I'd like to do, Clarence? Hear some jazz." She'd developed an interest in jazz years ago and had become an avid record collector. She'd tried to convince Veronica Caldwell that jazz was America's only true art form and that it deserved time in the art center's performing schedule, but Veronica was a slow convert. "Come on, Monty Alexander is playing at Blues Alley."

And so they went to the jazz club in Georgetown and took in a full set before he delivered her to the nearby brownstone she'd purchased four years earlier.

"Coming in?" she asked.

"Well, my back is acting up and—"

"Oh shut up and get in here."

"Ah, modern woman." And taking her in his arms, he added to himself, God bless 'em...

Early the next morning, just before she showed him out, she extracted his promise to take her to Senator Caldwell's testimonial party.

Nodding unhappily, he kissed her, and said, "Well, they always told me everything has its price," then escaped before she could beat him about the head and ears.

Leaning against the closed door, she had to smile. It had been a very good night. With a good man. Life could be worse...

The day of the big party proved out the truth of Lydia's thought. It had been a long frustrating day at the office with a client who she almost felt like prosecuting instead of defending. A real hardhead who seemed determined to defeat himself... As she drove home she realized she'd barely have time to get ready before Clarence picked her up for the Caldwell party.

She raced into the house, tossed off her clothes, showered, dried herself and went to one of two closets where she chose a sleek, butterscotch evening dress that dipped at the bosom and was lower in the back. She applied lipstick only, pulled her hair back into a chignon and attached a single gold strand around her neck. The clock at her bedside said 6:15. Fifteen minutes. *Good Housekeeping, Esquire* and *Newsweek* had arrived in the mail and she scanned their covers. One of the blurbs on *Good Housekeeping*'s cover told readers that inside they could read an interview with "Washington's First Lady of the Arts, Veronica Caldwell."

She was turning to the first page of the Caldwell interview as her door chimes sounded and she went to the door.

"Hi, I was just about to read an interview with Veronica."

"Bring it with you," he said. "Read it in the car. Then you'll be loaded for knowledgeable chitchat."

"Oh, shut up," she said, and smiled. But she did as he suggested and read the interview as Clarence drove them to the party.

He found a parking space after circling the block twice, came around and opened the door for her.

"By the way, you look lovely," he said as they crossed the street and headed for the Senate Building.

"Thank *you*, sir," and she meant it. Loved it.

"So what did the article have to say about Veronica?"

"It talked about the center, her role as a senator's wife and as a mother, her hopes for the future of the arts in America, you know, that sort of thing. The photographs are terrific."

"Terrific...Well, I hope we have better luck than the last time I went to a reception here...the host was drying out and a godawful nonalcoholic punch was served. I think it was a Kool-Aid base."

"I bet it was a short reception."

"Very short."

He stopped halfway up the steps, looked at her and repeated how well she looked. But in his head was the dream he'd had the previous night. Of course it was only a dream, but in it she'd died...They were at a party and all of a sudden it was a wake. He'd walked up to the coffin and there she was in a dress sort of like the one she was wearing now, a rose in her hands and a horribly tranquil expression on her face.

He took her arm firmly and led her up the steps. What the hell, a bad dream was a bad dream...don't impose it on Lydia, or take it seriously. He'd better stop snacking before bedtime...

Lydia looked at him. "Is anything wrong, you look sort of strange." She seemed to shiver beneath the white woolen shawl she wore over her shoulders, and Clarence felt it. Or was he the one?

"No, don't be silly, everything's fine," he said, "except it's getting chilly." He put his arm around her. "It's the wind. We'll be inside in a moment."

Four

Charles was putting his final touches on preparations for the Caldwell reception, working closely with Veronica Caldwell through her representative Jason DeFlaunce. Under ordinary circumstances, Charles disliked dealing with Senate wives; they were too quick to invoke proxy power of their husbands. In the case of the Caldwell party, though, he wished it had been Mrs. Caldwell rather than DeFlaunce he'd had to deal with. He found DeFlaunce obnoxious. But since the senator's wife evidently had great faith in the man and had given him carte blanche as far as preparations were concerned, Charles had little choice but to grimace and bear it.

The guest list contained 120 names. The decision was to keep it simple with an abundance of hors d'oeuvres and canapes.

The center of attraction was a large ice carving in the shape of the senator's home state of Virginia. Charles had suggested a sports figure, perhaps a football player about to throw a forward pass, but the idea had been vetoed, not surprisingly, by Jason. An ice carver well-known to Washington's society set had been brought in to accomplish the sculpture and had done a remarkable job: it stood five feet, glistening beneath red and blue pin spots.

On another table was a tall shrimp tree that Charles had personally built a year ago from a discarded silver service. He'd ordered fifty pounds of jumbo shrimp, ten per guest. Each of the four graduated levels of the tree was edged with shrimp and lemon wedges, and shrimp skewered with frilled toothpicks were heaped on each silver disk. The shrimp had been soaked in an imported beer and a herb-and-spice mixture prior to deveining and shelling, then sprinkled with lemon juice before being placed on the tree. A cocktail sauce was in a silver bowl at the tree's summit.

"I love it," Jason said to Veronica as Charles applied the finishing touches.

"It's just magnificent," she said. "Bravo to you and yours, Charles."

"Thank you, Mrs. Caldwell. I hope the senator will be pleased."

The room had been divided with folding green screens to provide a better flow between beverage and food areas. One of Washington's top society pianists arrived early and fastidiously wiped down every inch of a grand piano with a soft cloth he'd pulled from a Gucci attaché case in which he carried the sheet music to standard show tunes.

As the first guests arrived Veronica excused herself from Jason and Charles to greet them. Lydia and Clarence were among the first, and after briefly chatting with their hostess they gravitated toward the nearest bar.

"Okay, I'm ready to leave," Clarence said after getting a brandy. It was his standard refrain immediately after arriving at just about any such soiree.

"Look," Lydia said, ignoring him and nodding toward the door. "I may be wrong but I think that's Mark Adam Caldwell."

"So?"

"So, Clarence, if it is, Veronica has pulled off a coup

of sorts. Mark Adam is, after all, the wayward son, Peck's bad boy, the black sheep of the Caldwell clan."

Clarence looked at the young man who'd entered the room. His first thoughts were that if he were a Caldwell son he'd been the product of Veronica Caldwell and a stranger, or Cale Caldwell and a stranger. Or...He looked nothing like the others in the family, had none of their unmistakable patrician features. Nor was he as tall as even his mother. He had a bull-like neck that barely provided separation between his head and wide, thick shoulders, the product of years of ritualistic weight lifting. Dark eyes set in small sockets were in constant motion, like tiny ball bearings swiveling about on a broad, fleshy face. His nose could have belonged to a professional prizefighter. His head was clean-shaven, and he wore an ill-fitting tan suit. The collar of his shirt dug into the folds of his neck, and his tie barely reached his distended belly.

"I knew him," Lydia said, "before he went off the deep end and joined that weird cult in Virginia."

"It was quite an embarrassment to his father, wasn't it?"

"It still is. Veronica says Cale's never forgiven him. I'm amazed he's here. I thought he'd been disowned."

"Maybe the mumbo jumbo has worn off. Prodigal son returns, asks forgiveness of his father. Will he forgive him?"

Lydia shrugged. "Who knows...Veronica got him here, and I can only assume that Cale will be pleased to see him."

They watched Mark Caldwell go to a secluded corner of the room, lean against the wall and watch sourly as his mother greeted her guests.

"Why don't you go say something to him?" Clarence suggested. "He looks pretty miserable."

She did. "Mark Caldwell?" Lydia said as she approached him, hand out.

He scrutinized her, she thought, like a cornered animal might a potential enemy.

"I'm Lydia James. Remember me?"

He obviously didn't, but went through the motions of shaking her hand. A long awkward pause. Finally she said, "Quite a night for your father."

"I guess so. Excuse me, I want to get something." He went quickly to one of the bars and ordered a Seven-Up.

Lydia returned to Clarence. "That was quick," he said.

"He never was very talkative. Sort of nice, though. I hope he puts things together and gets out of that awful cult. It's scary what they can do to a person who's susceptible to control. You'd think after Jonestown and all the exposés, but they go on. My God, even the daughter of the senator who was killed there went and got herself a guru..."

More guests arrived, some of whom joined Lydia and Clarence, but Lydia's attention was focused on Mark Caldwell, who'd gone back to his corner. She felt sorry for him, wanted to break away and try again to put him at ease. She didn't. Along with her sensitivity to his discomfort was an apprehension about Cale Caldwell's entrance and his reaction to seeing the son he'd washed his hands of years ago.

Moments later, the Senate Majority Leader came through the door looking every bit the part of a successful and powerful senator. His face, tanned the year round from a sunlamp in the Senate barbershop, provided a healthy, handsome scrim for a wide, dazzling smile. As usual, he was dressed immaculately in one of a dozen suits he kept in his office to change to for nighttime activities. He kissed his wife, slapped a Senate colleague on the back and waved to well-wishers across the room.

The pianist immediately launched a medley of "man" songs—"Man of La Mancha," "The Man I Love," "My Man"...Guests pushed toward the door to greet the guest of honor. Lydia glanced over to where Mark Adam Caldwell stood, saw that he'd made no move toward the door, that his sullen expression hadn't changed.

Senator Caldwell made his way through clusters of people and now came up to Lydia and Clarence. "Hello, Lydia," he said, kissing her on the cheek. "Mr. Foster-Sims, glad you could come."

Someone touched him on the back. He turned, and as he did he spotted his son for the first time. Although Lydia could not see his face because his back was to her, the tightening of his body was evident. His shoulders hunched up, veins at the side of his neck bulged. His wife came up to him with their other son, Cale, Jr., on her arm.

Charles handed Caldwell a drink.

"Thank you, Charles," he said, never taking his eyes off Mark Adam. Veronica looked at Lydia, smiled, then said to her husband, "Well, go on and say hello. He's here to pay tribute to you too. Please, just go over and shake his hand."

"Why is he here—?"

"I just told you..."

"I'm not sure I—"

"Cale, it wasn't easy for him to do it. Please, don't drive him away again."

Lydia's gesture was involuntary as she reached out and touched the senator's arm. When he turned and looked at her, she nodded her head, trying to encourage him to do as Veronica asked.

He took a deep breath, glanced at those around him, then slowly strode toward where his son stood.

Few guests were unaware of what was occurring in the corner between father and son. Lydia, Clarence, Veronica and Cale, Jr., said nothing as they watched the hesitancy with which the senator offered his hand to Mark, and the apparently reluctant acceptance of it. The senator seemed to want to move closer, to close the gap between them, but it didn't happen. They remained a few feet apart, hands clasped, their words inaudible to onlookers.

The pianist, who'd stopped playing for a few minutes, started again, which prompted an increase in conversation. The air was soon filled with the mosquitolike drone of party badinage.

"Shrimp?" Clarence asked Lydia.

She saw that a small group gathered around the shrimp tree was systematically stripping it of its shellfish leaves. "We'd better dive in," he said, "it's going fast." She nodded, gave a final look over her shoulder at Cale Caldwell and his son.

One of those at the shrimp tree was WCAP talk-show host Quentin Hughes, who was known in Washington party circles for his bottomless appetite for freebies. He'd stacked his plate with shrimp, smothered them with cocktail sauce.

"Hello, Quentin," Lydia said coolly. She'd known Hughes a number of years, and twice had been a guest on his all-night radio interview and call-in show. She'd never particularly liked him—though she respected his professional talents—but could understand why a good many women did. He was very handsome, tall and erect, with good features and an intensity in his eyes that made people feel when he fixed his attention on them that they were the most important people in his life at that moment. This night he wore a double-breasted blue blazer that was nipped at the waist to show off his trim figure. His gray slacks were creased to a razor's edge, and a pair of black Gucci loafers had been shined to an appropriately dull sheen. He could, on self-demand, produce charm from every pore, especially when the conquest of a female was in the wind. Women liked men like that, even if they weren't good for them.

He smiled at her now. "Oh, Lydia James, girl barrister. How are you?"

She said just fine and introduced Clarence, who shook Hughes's hand, and for a moment his smug facade faded. "Are you still on the air, Mr. Hughes?"

Hughes smiled tightly, turned to Lydia. "You should come back on the show. You were a good guest, as I recall."

She shrugged. "Afraid I have nothing very exciting

to talk about these days, nothing like when I was in criminal law. The world of FCC license applications is hardly the stuff exciting radio shows are made of."

"I take care of the excitement," Hughes said as he crammed two shrimp into his mouth, sauce dripping to the floor.

Wilfred MacLoon, the senior senator from Utah, who happened to have an intense personal and political dis- like for Cale Caldwell but whose wife was an active member of Veronica's board of directors at the perform- ing arts center which, to Caldwell's chagrin, frequently brought MacLoon into their social life, had already had too much to drink. He swayed as he spoke with a couple near Lydia..."I never could stand Virginia," he was saying. Lydia thought he was talking about someone with that name, then realized he was referring to Cald- well's home state. "I was in the Navy there. Hellhole of the world. Backward damn state if I ever saw one."

As MacLoon rambled on, Lydia recalled the origins of the MacLoon-Caldwell hostile rivalry. There had been numerous incidents during their long and often parallel careers in the Senate that had caused sparks to fly, but none turned out to be as volatile as the recent, intense controversy over the placement of the most ex- pensive and elaborate missile defense system ever con- ceived by any government. MacLoon had fought long and hard to have Utah chosen as the site for its con- struction. It would mean a huge infusion of money into his state, and some people felt that his political future depended on how successful he was in bringing home, so to speak, the bacon.

Not only was Caldwell against Utah as the site, he was opposed to the missile system itself from its con- ception. Debates, increasingly heated, had gone on for nearly a year; now the issue was close to a vote. Smart money was on Caldwell and his troops. He was, after all, Majority Leader.

This dispute between Senators Caldwell and MacLoon had overflowed into the public arena, had been the subject of newspaper headlines and television news reports. Once the two of them had actually gotten into an arm-waving argument on the front steps of the Senate and nearly came to blows...

MacLoon's voice was getting louder. His wife tried to pacify him, but her efforts only resulted in infuriating him. He walked up to the ice sculpture. "Right there," he said, pointing to the right side of the sculpture where Newport News was located. "One hell of a hellhole, but then again, what would you expect considering who it sent to us."

MacLoon then casually picked up the ice pick left behind by the ice sculptor, aimed it at a corner of the sculpture.

"For God's sake," his wife said as she led him away.

"Don't overreact, darling," he said. "Just a joke. I'm not, after all, an idiot. Only idiots act out what they feel. Didn't you tell me that once?"

"I did," she muttered, "and I'm telling you again."

"No sweat, my dear. I just thought a little drama might go a long way in a good cause. Not to worry." And suddenly he seemed very calm and rational....

"Time to escape," Clarence said.

"Not just yet," Lydia said. "Veronica would be disappointed—"

"Would dinner at the Adams interest you?"

"Yes, but not so much that I'd leave this minute. Another half hour, please, Clarence."

"All right, but I'll need fortifying. Can I get you something?"

An easy way out, she thought, because at that moment Mr. Wonderful...just ask him...Quentin Hughes was putting down his empty plate on the table and in his charming fashion saying to Lydia, "Who invited the weirdo?" He nodded toward the corner where the two male Caldwells had attempted their reconciliation. The senator was gone. Mark Adam was still there, eyes uneasily taking in the room before he pushed away from the wall and disappeared behind a wall of guests.

"I'm sorry, but the kid's a loser," Hughes said. "Anybody who gets involved with those cults is playing with a half a deck to begin with. How come he's here?"

"To say hello to his father, I believe."

Hughes shrugged and his eyes went to the dip in Lydia's neckline. "You look especially well tonight, counselor. In fact, the best-looking woman on the ranch. Free for dinner, by any chance?"

"Sorry...I'm with Mr. Foster-Sims—"

"Who's old enough to be your father. Actually, I thought he was."

"Excuse me."

He took hold of her arm. "Oh, come on. I was, in my feeble fashion, trying to pay you a compliment—"

She ignored him and went to where Clarence stood behind the piano player.

"Maybe I should start playing again," he said to her. "Then I could get to attend all the swell Washington parties."

"Snob," she said into his ear.

"A privilege of age. You have fifteen minutes."

"I'm ready now, I guess. God, I detest men who undress you with their eyes."

"Hughes?"

"Yes."

"I noticed...You know, I'd never admit it to him but I still sometimes listen to him when I can't sleep. He's provocative and can usually get something out of his guests. Basically, though, he's a variety of rat..." His face suddenly lit up as he spotted Boris Slevokian, a violinist. Clarence had once been Boris's accompanist and they'd made several world tours together.

"Come and say hello to Boris," Clarence said.

"I'll be over in a moment. I want to talk to Veronica about something."

Clarence headed for his friend and Lydia scanned the room for her hostess but couldn't find her. Nor those most likely to be with her—her husband, their sons or Jason DeFlaunce. She started to ask someone, when Senator Caldwell suddenly appeared from behind one of the green folding screens. His face, no longer reflecting his earlier ebullience, was set in a tight angry mask as he pushed through a small cluster of guests and disappeared behind another screen that separated the desecrated shrimp tree and melting ice carving from the rest of the room. A waitress was in the process of dismantling the silver tree.

Lydia looked toward the door. Clarence and Boris had disappeared. She decided to ask Cale Caldwell if he knew where his wife was. She managed only a few steps toward where she'd last seen him when she was intercepted by the director of one of Washington's semiprofessional repertory theaters full of the good news that Veronica and her board had given them the green light to stage a production at the center. Nodding and trying to move off she saw Quentin Hughes emerge from behind the screen she was headed for and move toward the door. "Excuse me, I..."

Two Irishmen had encouraged Hughes to play "Danny Boy," and they now sang loudly out of tune with each other and their accompaniment.

Lydia finally excused herself and took another step toward the screen—and stopped short as the sound of a female voice cut through the party cacophony. It was a scream, a cry for help. Then a second scream, even louder. The singing cut off, the chatter died. All eyes looked in the direction of the screen as a third and final scream slashed at everyone within earshot, made them immobile like players in a game of statues.

Lydia, finally out of her trance, moved around the screen. At first she saw only the source of the sound, the young waitress who'd been removing the shrimp tree. Her eyes were open wide, fixed on the floor, her fist against her mouth, as though to stifle another cry.

Lydia followed the direction of the waitress's stare to a pair of highly polished men's shoes and two neatly creased trouser legs extending from behind the table.

Lydia forced herself to the waitress's side, where she could share her view. There, on the floor, his eyes open to their widest, his mouth twisted as though trying to say something, was the Honorable Cale Caldwell, the

Majority Leader of the Senate of the United States. Water from the melting ice sculpture of his beloved home state of Virginia dripped onto his forehead. His red-and-blue striped tie was still neatly in place beneath a buttoned suit jacket. He looked so typically *neat*.

Except for the oozing, spreading red stain coming from where an ice pick had been rammed through his chest, just above the button of his suit jacket.

The waitress gave up to unconsciousness, pitched forward and landed across the senator's legs.

Lydia turned to those who'd crowded behind the screen and said what was all too obvious.

"He's dead. My God, he's dead."

Five

Clarence, Lydia, Boris Slevokian and one of Cale Caldwell's Senate aides, Richard Marvis, were seated in Clarence's apartment. It had taken until one in the morning before the Washington Metropolitan Police Department had allowed the guests to leave.

Now, the initial shock over, Lydia could allow the tears to come as she sat in a corner next to a massive copper bust of Bach.

"No, I'm all right," she said to Marvis as he came over to comfort her. "Thank you."

"I do not believe this," Boris said. He'd retained most of his Hungarian accent even though he'd been in the United States for more than thirty years. Now he paced the room, hands clasped behind his back, perspiration on his bumpy, broad forehead glistening in light from pin spots used to illuminate Clarence's numerous works of art. "It was like being back in a communist country the way the police treated me. I felt like a prisoner. They told me that I am not to leave the city until they question me again. Question *me*."

"It's procedure, that's all," Dick Marvis told him. "After all, as far as they're concerned, anyone at the party *might* have done it."

"Poor Veronica," Lydia said.

"The doctor seemed to have things under control," Clarence told her. "I'm sure she's been sedated and is resting...she has her sons—"

"God, Clarence, how much should a person be asked to take? First Jimmye, now this."

"Jimmye? Oh, yes...how long has it been, two years?"

Jimmye McNab had been raised by the Caldwells since infancy, following the simultaneous death of her parents in an automobile crash. Jimmye's mother and Veronica had been sisters, and the suddenly orphaned child had promptly been taken in by Veronica and Cale Caldwell to be raised as one of their own. She'd never been legally adopted, for reasons unknown to Lydia. What she did know was that approximately a year before Jimmye was found bludgeoned to death in a park in downtown Washington, she'd broken with her surrogate family and had seen little of them.

At the time of her death, Jimmye was also one of Washington's most visible and respected TV journalists. She'd uncovered and broken numerous important stories in the nation's capital, and there had been talk of a network tapping her for a top anchor spot in which her natural journalistic ability and exciting good looks would be put to more solid commercial use.

"I'm afraid," Lydia said, "that I thought of Jimmye when I saw Cale on the floor. I remember talking to Cale and Veronica right after Jimmye died. They tried to be so strong, but you knew what they were going through. Veronica's too decent to have such a dreadful thing happen *twice*."

He'd brewed a pot of coffee. "We'll all feel better after this. It's two in the morning."

"Why?" Lydia asked of no one in particular. "Why would someone kill him?"

"That's the MPD's problem," Marvis said. "But anyone in the public eye makes enemies."

"You worked with him," Lydia said. "Do you know

of anyone who could hate him enough to *stab* him to death?"

Marvis shrugged. "He had his enemies but no more than any other man in a leadership position. I suppose Senator MacLoon led the pack." He lit a cigarette, crossed his legs. The smoke drifted in Lydia's direction, making her want one too. She'd stopped smoking ten years ago, and although the craving had long since disappeared, there were times like this when it came back with a wallop.

"Being killed at a party certainly compounds the MPD's job," Clarence said. "How many guests were there, two hundred, maybe more? All at least theoretical suspects."

"Not *all*," Boris said. "I did not even know the man."

"You'd met him, hadn't you?" Lydia asked.

"No. His wife, yes, when I gave a recital at her theater. Him, no. I am an apolitical man, I have no interest in politics or men who practice it. Art and politics are not compatible."

Foster-Sims noticed that Lydia had wrapped her arms about herself. "Are you cold?" he asked.

"Yes."

"I'll get you something." He returned with a white cardigan sweater and draped it over her bare shoulders.

"I think I'd better be heading home."

Marvis checked his watch. "Me too. If I thought working for Cale Caldwell was a busy job before, I can picture what this morning will be like."

Lydia looked at him. "I was surprised that you weren't at his office, Dick. It must be alive with press—"

"That's Joe Borgen's territory, he's the press aide. I'm strictly a legislative type...sorry, but that's Washington..."

He stood, nodded to Lydia. "If there's anything I can do, please call. I know you were a particular favorite of both the senator and his wife."

"Most upsetting," Boris said after Marvis had left. "A party in a man's honor terminates in his murder.

If man listened more seriously to music perhaps he would not be so much the savage. I must be going." Boris pulled a black tam from his jacket pocket and yanked it down over his large head, took black leather gloves from the other pocket and slipped them over thick stubby fingers that seemed never to have been meant to caress a violin yet did so with grace and precision. "Good night," he said, bringing his heels together and bowing to Lydia. He shook Clarence's hand, spun around and departed with great flourish.

"Talented yet so boring," Clarence said as he sat on a couch. "Sit down," he said to Lydia, who stood in the center of the room, eyes focused on twinkling lights visible through the window.

"I'm really beat, Clarence, I guess I'll be leaving."

He shook his head, patted the couch next to him. "Stay a few more minutes. It'll do you—and me—some good to talk. What do you think about it?"

"Think about it? What could I possibly think about it?"

"Look, I know you're upset. But I also know your brain is working overtime. All these years of law plus the mathematical mind of a musician can't be completely overridden by emotion. So...who killed Cale Caldwell?"

"Boris," she said as she sat next to him.

He smiled. "Know what I think? I think Mr. Charm, Quentin Hughes, should have been the one with the ice pick in his chest. Did you see him? The minute he realized what had happened he was on the phone calling in a report to his studio. What a ghoul."

"He'd say it was being professional—"

"Also disgusting...what was Caldwell working on lately?"

"In the Senate? The missile system, a new budget, I think. I meant to ask Dick Marvis about it. I do know he'd been under the gun to resign from chairing the Appropriations Committee on the Interior and Related Agencies because of the pressures of being Majority Leader. I got a feeling from Veronica that he wanted to, but that she'd convinced him to stay with both posts. From her perspective, I suppose the committee is more important than being Majority Leader. Arts funding rides along on what comes out of that committee, especially since Cale also sat on the House-Senate conference committee that made the final cuts. Her husband is the most important member of Congress when it comes to funding the National Endowment on the Arts and the Humanities—"

"Was."

"Yes...You can only speculate on what happens now. Will MacLoon is in line for that committee chair, and you know what he thinks of federal funding for anything besides cars, guns, steel and the right labor unions...God, I'm so damn tired..."

"I know...but it's interesting...trying to solve a murder like this is sort of like resolving a chord."

"What?"

"Like the cycle of fifths. A G can go nowhere but to C. To get to G you start with D. And only an A can lead to a D."

"Lordy, Clarence, let me close my eyes for a minute." She put her head on his shoulder, and he put his arm around her and held her close. He glanced down at the beginnings of her breasts above the neckline of her evening dress, felt a familiar response and shifted his legs. Tonight was distinctly not the night for romance.

Fifteen minutes later, when he was sure she was sound asleep, he gently shifted so that she could stretch out on the couch. She'd removed her shoes earlier in the evening. He straightened out her legs and adjusted a throw pillow beneath her head. She opened her eyes, smiled, closed them again.

He took a comforter from a closet and placed it over her, turned off all but one lamp, ignored the urge to carry her to the bedroom and went there himself and slipped into bed. Sleep eluded him for nearly an hour. Just as it did arrive, he was jarred awake by the ringing of a phone on his night table.

"Is Lydia James there?" a male voice asked.

"Who the hell is this? Do you know what time it is—?"

"This is Cale Caldwell. If Ms. James is there, please put her on."

"Cale Cald...? Oh, his son. Yes, just a moment."

Lydia took the call in the living room. "Yes, Cale, hello, what...when?...I don't know, I...all right, of course, tell your mother that I'll be there at ten. Is ten okay?...How is your mother?...I'll see you at ten...goodbye."

"What was that all about?" Clarence asked after she'd hung up.

"Veronica wants to see me. I hate to face her, Clarence, really dread it. Do you have any coffee left?"

"I'll heat it."

"I'm sorry I fell asleep on you." She went to the bronze bust of Bach and absently ran her hand over its surface.

"What are you thinking?"

"About your cycle of fifths. I was wondering what key this has all been written in, and what, to belabor a metaphor, the final chord will be."

"Major, not minor. Bet on that."

"Or a deep blues," she said.

"Yes, maybe that too. I'll put the coffee on."

Six

Lydia, in her office, pulled papers from a file folder about a client's application to the Federal Communications Commission for a license to operate a radio station he and a syndicate were trying to buy.

She sat back and rubbed her eyes. Her secretary took the file from her. "Everybody seems to be buying radio and TV stations."

Lydia smiled. "Maybe it's because having a broadcasting license is, some say, a license to steal."

Lydia went to a window that overlooked F Street. She'd been practicing communications and copyright law for six years, but had only moved into these new offices six months before. Her practice had grown, and with it her reputation. She'd gotten into her specialized field after working in a firm that practiced general law, and her background as a public defender had helped her to become one of the firm's most able and desired trial attorneys.

She'd then begun dating a recently divorced man who owned a string of suburban newspapers and two television stations. He asked her to handle some matters before the FCC. She ended up diving into the intricacies of the FCC and broadcast licensing and found herself fascinated with them. Result—she took a job with one of Washington's most prestigious communications firms, then branched out on her own...

She answered her intercom, was told someone who'd broken an appointment had arrived and wanted to speak to her.

"Tell him I'm sorry but I'm on my way out." She slung a leather purse over her shoulder, pushed some papers into a pile on her desk and left the office.

She got into a new metallic blue Buick Skylark she'd taken delivery on only a month before and headed for Mount Vernon, Virginia, former home of George Washington and of the late Cale Caldwell. The day had dawned gray; a weatherman announced over the radio that the likelihood of showers was sixty percent during the day and forty percent at night.

She crossed the Rochambeau Memorial Bridge and continued south, past National Airport, the Potomac on her left. Rock music came from speakers mounted in the rear deck of the car, and she twisted the dial until she found WCAP's assigned frequency. After two commercials, a newscaster said, "Good morning, this is Harold South with the news. I'll have the latest development in the bizarre murder of Senate Majority Leader Cale Caldwell right after this..."

Sixty seconds later he was back. "All Washington was shocked last night when the body of Senate Majority Leader Cale Caldwell was discovered stabbed to death at a party given in his honor by his wife. Our own Quentin Hughes was a guest at that party and filed this report by phone immediately after the murder."

Hughes's voice then came on. Usually he spoke slowly and deliberately. This time the urgency was unmistakable.

"...An incredible thing has happened right before my eyes, ladies and gentlemen. I'm Quentin Hughes, and I'm standing directly outside a large party room in the Senate Building where I've been attending a party in honor of Senate Majority Leader Cale Caldwell. The party was given by his wife in appreciation of his undying efforts on behalf of the arts in America..." Pause for effect. Then, "Undying? Unfortunately, that's not the case tonight, ladies and gentlemen. Just moments ago a waitress discovered the senator's body behind a screen. He's apparently been murdered with an ice pick that, we believe, was used to carve a large ice sculpture of his home state of Virginia."

A pause in the background. Hughes again. "I don't know how many people are here, probably two hundred. Which means every one of them, including, I suppose, this reporter, must be considered a suspect..."

Hughes's tape ended and the local newscaster led into an interview with Horace Jenkins, deputy chief of police of Washington's Metropolitan Police Department.

"Any leads?" the interviewer asked.

"No, none yet," Jenkins told him. "It's a complicated case, so many people had access to the victim just prior to his death. We established the identities of all of them last night and are in the process of interviewing them on a systematic basis. I've assigned every available officer to this case—"

"What about *motive?*"

"If we had a motive, sir, it wouldn't be so complicated," Jenkins said. Lydia couldn't help but smile. Jenkins had undoubtedly been up all night and was under intense pressure. She'd known him ever since she'd been a public defender. Personally, she liked him, found his direct, cantankerous personality refreshing in a city noted for its lack of candor and guts. She'd also learned the hard way that beneath his lone-hand approach beat the heart of a survivor who knew when to play the game, and when to disdain it. It was, went the rumor, Jenkins who provided a pipeline between the MPD and the FBI for reports of indiscretions on the part of official Washington—especially its more pretentious members. It had gone back to Hoover's days as FBI director, and it was these MPD reports that had provided much of Hoover's incredible files that were often used to keep certain enemies at bay. Jenkins denied that he or his department was involved. Lydia—

and others—knew better. So while Jenkins was several cuts above the ordinary in his field, he was, she reminded herself, no Little Boy Blue.

The final segment of the report about the murder involved two of Caldwell's Senate colleagues. One said the expected about the nation having lost a valued, beloved public servant and so forth.

The second said, "Although a murder is a matter for the police, I intend to call upon the Senate to launch its own investigation through a special committee formed for that purpose. It's *our* house that has been the scene of this unconscionable act of violence, and the American public deserves and expects that same house to do its own cleaning."

A commercial for floor wax followed.

Lydia reacted, at the moment, more to the first comment than the second. She would soon learn how wrong she was...She passed the Appomattox Memorial and turned off onto the Richmond Highway...Cale Caldwell was dead—that was the hard reality. All right, face it...and the new reality of needing to find out who'd rammed the ice pick into his chest, and why. Or vice versa. *Why* would find *who.*

An announcer broke into her thoughts to say that Quentin Hughes had just completed a phone interview with Veronica Caldwell. Lydia was astonished. So soon...?

"This is Quentin Hughes, who was at the scene of Senator Cale Caldwell's murder. I have on the line the widow of the late senator, Veronica Caldwell, who is almost as well-known as her husband for her work in fostering the arts, here in Washington and across the nation. Mrs. Caldwell, allow me to express my own personal sympathy to you."

"Thank you, Mr. Hughes." Veronica's voice seemed to possess remarkable control. Well, Veronica Caldwell was a very strong woman, blessed with hearty pioneer stock going back generations. Still...

"I know this is difficult for you, Mrs. Caldwell, but

as a reporter I must ask you whether you have any idea who might have killed your husband—"

"No, I'm afraid not. He had so few enemies... for a man in his position. I will say this. I will not rest until his killer has been identified and punished. It was the act, surely, of a twisted person. An evil person. I refuse to use the term sick because that would be unfair to those who truly are emotionally ill."

"The nation mourns with you, Mrs. Caldwell," Hughes said, "just as it did when tragedy struck at your family two years ago when Jimmye McNab was murdered. I hesitate to bring it up at a time like this but she was, after all, not only, in effect, your daughter, but a valued colleague of mine in broadcasting. That crime has never been solved, as we all know. Do you think the same thing might possibly occur in your husband's case?"

Lydia winced as she waited for Veronica's response. "No," she said, still apparently composed, "that will *not* be the case, I assure you. Jimmye's file is still open, but my husband's will be closed when his murderer is brought to justice... Excuse me, I really would prefer not to talk any more about this. I'm sure you understand what a shock this has been—"

"Of course, Mrs. Caldwell. How are your sons taking it?"

"As might be expected. They loved their father very much." She hung up.

Astonishing, Lydia thought. Both Hughes's irrepressible rushing in where good taste would restrain anyone else, and Veronica's willingness to be interviewed so soon after...

The Caldwell estate was located four miles from the historic Mount Vernon home of George and Martha Washington. Although not nearly as old as Washington's home, which went back to 1743, the architect for the Caldwell house had undoubtedly been influenced by it. The Caldwell residence was a wide, handsome, stately two-story residence set on thirty acres of meadowland and wooded tracts, and was reached from the highway by a long, winding macadam road.

As Lydia approached the entrance to the estate, she saw a dozen cars and vans parked on the shoulder, including two highway patrol vehicles, their lights flashing from their roofs. Two vans bore the call letters of area television stations. Lydia recognized a reporter from the *Post,* another from an all-news radio station.

She joined the line of parked cars, got out and walked to where a beefy state patrolman stood in the middle of the road leading to the house.

"Yes, ma'am?"

"I'm Lydia James. Mrs. Caldwell is expecting me."

A patrolman checked with his walkie-talkie, then told her she was cleared to go in. She went to her car, carefully steered it between the other vehicles and turned onto the access road. As she looked in the rearview mirror and saw the disappointed faces of the reporters clustered about who'd been denied entry, she understood their frustration. They had a job to do too. Judging from the patrolman's call, the exquisite Jason DeFlaunce was very much involved in shielding the family from the press; Lydia decided she'd suggest that some sort of public statement might be in order to satisfy the media. Otherwise they'd go off half-cocked and create their own stories based mostly on rumor and half-truth.

Another state patrol car sat in front of the two-story white house, a patrolman behind the wheel, his long legs sticking out through the open door. Leaning against the fender was Jason DeFlaunce, turned out in a wheat-colored crew-neck sweater, gray slacks and loafers. Lydia parked behind the patrol car and rolled down the window as Jason came up to her.

"Hello, Jason. Veronica asked for me. How's everyone holding up?"

"Very well, although there are those moments when the Caldwell steel turns to jelly. Are those *media* people still out there?"

"Of course. I think they'd be satisfied with a statement

from a member of the family. In fact, I'd recommend it. No sense having them make up their own stories."

"The hell with them..."

Lydia got out of the car and started toward the house.

"Lydia, before you go in there's something you should know."

"What?"

A gust of cool wind whipped her hair across her face.

"Veronica wants the family kept out of this as much as possible...and bear in mind"—he took a few steps toward her—"this is not just *any* family, Lydia. This is the Caldwell family."

"I'm well aware of that."

A housekeeper opened the door and Lydia stepped into a large anteroom. A well-worn red-and-gold area rug partially covered wide floor boards that glistened with fresh wax. A long, cherry table along the wall to her left held a large silver bowl, nothing else. Above it hung an oil portrait of Veronica's father. A scarred, sturdy church pew was against the wall to her right. Next to it stood an elaborately carved clothes tree on which a woman's pale pink cardigan hung from a peg.

"One moment, ma'am," the housekeeper said.

Lydia watched her go through a wide archway and disappear to her right, which Lydia knew led to the living and dining rooms. A few moments later Cale Caldwell came through the arch, extended his hand. "Thanks for coming, Lydia. Mother is very pleased you're here."

"Cale, I'm—"

"Yes, I understand, it's an awful shock to all of us. Come on, mother is in the den."

The den was a large room just off the living room. A stone fireplace took up one entire wall, and a fire that had been recently stoked and replenished cast a flickering orange glow over the room.

"Lydia," Veronica said as she got up from a cushioned club chair in front of the fireplace. They embraced, Veronica clearly on the edge of tears.

They sat together on a couch from which Lydia could

see into the living room, where Cale, Jr., and a young woman stood next to a table. The woman was talking into a telephone, and although Lydia could not hear from that distance it was obvious that Cale was coaching her on what to say. The resemblance to his father struck her as remarkably strong at that moment.

"Who's that?" Lydia asked, indicating the woman on the phone.

"Joanne Marshall. She works for Cale in his office and offered to help out here. God, Lydia, will the phones ever stop ringing?"

"Probably not for a long time."

"Cale sometimes used to be critical of the press and I never really understood. Now..."

"I heard the interview you gave this morning to Quentin Hughes—"

"You did?" She seemed genuinely surprised.

"Yes. Frankly I was surprised you'd done it. And why him?"

"Well, he *has* always been a good friend of the center, promoting it, helping raise funds through his show...Did you know that Cale taped Hughes's TV show only last week?"

"No, I didn't...I thought Cale disliked Hughes."

"I suppose he did, but he agreed to do it because it was a chance for him to explain some new legislation he was involved with. I remember he said it went very well."

"When was it supposed to air?"

"This Sunday, I think. The program is on every Sunday morning, isn't it?"

"Yes."

A year before, Hughes had begun a weekly "public service" program on WCAP-TV. It ran for half an hour each Sunday morning and featured interviews with newsmakers in the Washington area. Ordinarily such shows were scheduled only to satisfy an FCC requirement that a station devote a certain percentage of its weekly programming to noncommercial, informational subjects in the "public interest." But because Hughes had a wide following, and because his abrasive, probing interview style often made sparks fly, the show had quickly gained a wide audience.

"I've agreed to be a guest," Veronica said, looking away from Lydia.

"About Cale's death...?"

"Yes... and other things."

Lydia tried to hide her dismay. "When are you doing it, Veronica?"

"Tomorrow. He's going to bring a mobile crew here. I think it's the best way, don't you, to put an end to all this media probing? Cale used to say that the best way to handle the press was to come out quickly, candidly and with strength before they had a chance to go off on the deep end by themselves. I'll do Quentin's program, answer all his questions truthfully and that will, I hope, be that."

Veronica's thinking made a certain sense to Lydia, even mirrored her own. What bothered her was choosing Quentin Hughes as her forum, giving him what amounted to an exclusive. Such a move would only anger the rest of the press and move them on to extremes to compete with Hughes. She tried to tell Veronica this.

"I don't want to talk about it, Lydia. Please. Jason is experienced in these matters and is handling everything where the press is concerned."

Lydia subsided, changed the subject. "Cale told me when he called that you wanted to see me. I'm pleased you feel you can reach out to me. I want you to know that I've admired, and liked, both you and Cale for a very long time. I'll do anything I possibly can to help. Just name it."

Veronica took a deep breath. "Then be special counsel to a Senate committee being formed to investigate Cale's murder."

Before Lydia had a chance to answer, Joanne Marshall from the next room came into the den and said, "Mrs. Caldwell, Senator MacLoon is on the phone—"

Veronica waved her hand. "Not now, Joanne. Tell him I'm resting and will return his call this afternoon...By the way, Miss Marshall, this is Lydia James, a very dear and old friend."

"It's good of you to be helping like this, Miss Marshall," Lydia said.

"I'm pleased to do anything I can. I didn't know the senator, but I have great respect for his son."

Lydia watched her sashay into the living room, a tall, willowy girl with a splendid figure she was obviously well aware of.

Lydia turned back to Veronica. "Before she came in you said something to me that I don't understand—"

"About the Senate committee? Yes, I'm pushing for it through some of Cale's colleagues. I don't think the American public will stand still for anything but an open examination of the facts. You know how the police are, Lydia, they'll bungle about, get into all sorts of irrelevant things about family and never even get to the root of things. Lord knows, it happened with Jimmye, and I won't stand for it again..."

"Well, Veronica, I can understand your concern, but it really is a police matter. I'm not sure that Congress has any business investigating a murder—"

"What about Jack Kennedy?"

"I'd say that was sort of different, Veronica. The Warren Commission was appointed by Lyndon Johnson and staffed from every branch of government—executive, legislative and judicial."

"No matter. Congress can appoint a committee to investigate anything it wants. I've spoken with people who assure me that it can, and that it *will* be done. As you know, the special counsel to any committee holds the key to its success or failure, to the way, in particular, that it conducts its business. I want someone in that job who *cares,* not only about justice but about human decency, feelings...I can't think of anyone I'd trust more with that responsibility than you, Lydia."

"I...I don't know what to say—"

"Just say that you'll do it."

"I can't say that right now. It's something I'd need to think about..."

Cale, Jr., entered the den and motioned for his mother to accompany him back into the living room. When she didn't move, he said, "Mother, please, it's important."

"Will you excuse me, Lydia?"

"Of course."

While Veronica was gone, Lydia wandered about the den, warming her hands by the fire, scrutinizing a cracked oil of Veronica's father and photographs of Cale Caldwell with President Kennedy and actress Helen Hayes, and of Veronica laughing at something the composer and conductor Leonard Bernstein had said.

Abruptly she felt terribly sad. She thought of the many evenings she'd spent in the den with the Caldwells and their friends—warm, casual moments full of laughter and good talk. There had been, of course, not such good moments too, like when the first son Mark Adam had dropped out of college to join that cult he still belonged to. The family's bitter disappointment about that often broke through. And of course Jimmye McNab's death had left a lingering hurt that, in spite of Cale's and Veronica's attempts to submerge it, never was really far from the surface.

Photographs of Jimmye that once hung in the den had been removed. The only tangible reminder that she'd been a member of the family was a leather-bound copy of the book she'd written about brainwashing and mind control that resulted from her research into the use of those manipulative techniques by government agencies.

Lydia took the book from the shelf, opened it and read the inscription scrawled on the title page: *For Mom and Dad, who chose to love and believe in me. Love, Jimmye.* She closed the blue leather cover and was about to replace the book on the shelf when Veronica came back.

"It was a good book, wasn't it?"

"To tell the truth, Veronica, I never read it. I always meant to get a copy but, like they say, the road to hell..."

Lydia sat on the couch, and Veronica went to stand at the window. "Winter again..."

"Soon...Veronica, I'll really have to think very carefully about what you asked—"

"Of course. Besides, I can't guarantee you'd be accepted as special counsel. I mean, I suppose someone could say you're not exactly impartial, being a family friend..."

"I could be, I think. I like to think I'm fair, and the family and I would share a desire to see justice done..."

Veronica smiled, came around behind Lydia and placed her hands on her shoulders. "Well, my dear, give it some serious thought. If you agree, I'll suggest you to the people who'll be spearheading the committee... Now, will you stay for lunch?" Veronica asked as she went to the door and observed Cale and Joanne in the living room.

"Thanks, no, I've got to get back to my office...God, I really admire your strength, Veronica. I doubt I'd have as much under the circumstances."

"We do what we have to do, Lydia. Besides, some of it's for Cale, and of course his brother...they deserve not to have me fall apart."

Lydia kissed her on the cheek. "I'll call you tomorrow." She left the house and got into her car. Jason was nowhere to be seen. The state patrolman nodded to her, went back to his newspaper as Lydia turned her car around and headed toward the highway.

Had she looked in her rearview mirror she would have seen Jason come around the corner of the house. He stood on the porch and watched her disappear into the grove of trees, then emerge on the far side. His boyish, handsome face framed by a helmet of loose, thick brown curls was now a tight mask of undisguised anger. He looked up into a slate gray sky, squinted against its uniform brightness, clenched his fists and entered the house.

Seven

At four o'clock the next morning Quentin Hughes glanced up at the clock in the studio from which he conducted his nightly radio talk show on WCAP. He'd dismissed that evening's guest moments before because he felt the show had bogged down, preferring instead to take calls from listeners during the final hour.

"To you after this spot," his producer said through the intercom.

Hughes looked at the multi-line telephone instrument on the table in front of him. All the buttons were lit, which meant that there were still people waiting to be heard. A red light flashed above a large expanse of window that separated the control room from the studio.

"Quentin, what ever happened with that Jimmye McNab murder? I never heard any more about it. That was two years ago, even more, huh?" said a caller.

Hughes pointed a long, slender finger at the control room. The caller was immediately cut off and a promo for an upcoming program played.

Christa Jones, his longtime assistant, watched Hughes lean back in his orange padded chair, close his eyes and run his fingers though long, floppy hair. She was sorry the caller had brought up the Jimmye McNab murder. Quentin Hughes didn't need any additional upset that night, and she knew that the mention of Jimmye's name would have that effect. She hesitated, then said to him through the intercom, "We can play that twenty-minute interview again you did with the guy from the National Rifle Association...you look beat."

Hughes didn't open his eyes. He remained silent until he realized that the commercial was coming to an end. "Yeah, do that," he said.

Hughes left the studio and went to the men's room, where he was obliged to listen to his own voice through the speaker in the ceiling. He hated his voice—high-pitched and undoubtedly grating to those who heard it. He knew he mispronounced too many words...he'd never finished high school. But because his voice was not out of the classic announcer's mold, and he tended to interview guests from very much the layman's perspective, he'd been very successful. He was known as a character, an original, an instantly recognizable voice in the night. Of course, the fact that New York had eluded him and undoubtedly always would at this late stage in his career caused him occasional anguish, but it never lasted long. At least he was king in Washington. In New York, unique as he was, he might well end up lost in the scramble.

The taped interview ended and Hughes closed the show.

"Feel like something to eat?" Christa asked.

"No, I'm for home. I'll call you at noon."

She watched him amble from the control room and disappear around a corner. What she felt at that moment was exactly what she'd felt for most of the years they'd worked together. In the very beginning, when she'd first been hired by him in Des Moines, things had been different between them. They'd been lovers. But that hadn't lasted long, and for the past fifteen years most nights ended up the way this one had—Quentin leaving the studio and she, after putting the night's materials away, going to her own apartment, where she would feed her cats, make herself something to eat and eventually fall asleep. Habit was her life...but it wasn't all that bad. What she'd had with this difficult, abrasive yet, in his fashion, consumingly committed man was something she'd never trade for one of those gray-suited gray men with brains and personality to match...

Eight

Lydia propped a bare foot up on a coffee table to begin applying polish to her toenails. She'd showered and washed her hair but had put off drying it until there was a commercial break in the golden oldie she was watching on TV. She wore a pink terrycloth wraparound that matched the towel she'd wound around her head.

Although it was Saturday, she'd woken up at her usual time, six o'clock, but had forced herself to stay in bed until eight. The week had drained her.

Caldwell's funeral had been on Friday, family only, reflecting the deceased senator's wishes. A memorial service at the Capitol was scheduled for Monday night.

Lydia had called Veronica on Friday morning. It was a hurried conversation because, in addition to the funeral, Veronica was taping Quentin Hughes's TV show that afternoon at her house.

"Have you given any more thought to my idea?" Veronica had asked.

"I really haven't had a chance, Veronica," Lydia had told her, which was true. There simply had not been enough time to make such a decision. She'd called Clarence and had tried to arrange time together to discuss it with him but he'd had to go to New York for a day and night, and the crush of business had kept her to her desk until almost midnight on Friday.

The commercial break she'd been waiting for arrived, and she turned on the hand-held dryer and directed the hot air over her head. When the film resumed, she clicked off the dryer and worked on her other foot.

Clarence's call coincided with the next commercial break.

"How are you? Clarence, I need to talk to you...are you free later this afternoon?"

"No, but how about brunch tomorrow?"

"Okay, I'd planned to go to the office early and catch up on paperwork but...oh, I meant to tell you. Veronica taped Quentin Hughes's show yesterday. It's on tomorrow morning. He was scheduled to run an interview with Cale but he's putting it off a week."

"She taped it yesterday?"

"Yes."

"The grieving widow..."

"Clarence, I know what you're thinking, but don't be so judgmental—"

"I'm not being judgmental, Lydia, I'm simply reacting to what seems pretty bad taste. What do you want to talk to me about?"

"I'll tell you tomorrow. Noon?"

"Meet me at the Four Georges. I'd pick you up but I'm being interrogated in the morning by someone from the MPD."

"They're coming to your house?"

"Yes. Your turn will come. I should be free by noon. See you then."

She lay back, extended her legs and scrutinized the work on her toes. The movie was no longer of interest to her. She thought about Cale's murder and Veronica's request that she become special counsel to a committee formed to investigate his death. She knew she had to face the possibility that the offer would become reality.

She went to dinner that night with an attorney she

(58)

dated from time to time. He suggested that they return to his apartment after dinner but she declined, mostly because she felt it wouldn't have been fair to him. Throughout dinner she'd had trouble concentrating on what he said. Invariably her thoughts came back to the Caldwell murder.

"Sure you want to pack it in so early?" her date asked as he escorted her to her door.

"Positive. I'm sorry, please understand."

"I'd hoped we could talk a little about Cale Caldwell's murder. I hesitated bringing it up at dinner because I was sure it was the last thing you wanted to think about."

Lydia kissed him lightly on the lips. "That was decent of you, Craig." He pulled her to him and deepened the kiss, the pleasure of it setting off in her a series of very mixed emotions. The comfort of his arms, his hardness, were undeniably welcome. She lingered there, her face pressed to his until finally she pulled away. "I'm really not fit to be with tonight, Craig. I loved dinner. Thanks for not pressing."

"You know me, Lydia, the last of a breed—chivalry above all else." He touched her nose. "Good night. I'll call you during the week..."

Lord, she thought, the perils of Lydia...

She was up at five and by six had finished off her third jogging lap around the Reflecting Pool in front of the Lincoln Memorial. She stripped off her blue sweat pants and shirt the moment she returned to her apartment; then went through a series of sit-ups, toe-touches and side-bends, followed by a lovely needle shower. She dressed in a gray turtleneck sweater, navy skirt that flowed loosely around her knees, brown calfskin boots and a muted blue tweed jacket.

She walked into her office, flicked on the lights and one of two television sets, removed the top from a container of black coffee she'd picked up on her way, leaned back in a leather chair and perused a client's file she hadn't had time to review on Friday.

A local newscast sandwiched between religious programs used as its lead the fact that no new developments in the Caldwell case had been reported. The announcer added, "Senator Caldwell's widow, Veronica Caldwell, is expected to make a major announcement today on the Quentin Hughes television show."

She concentrated on her paperwork until it was time for Hughes's program, removed glasses she wore for heavy reading and watched as Hughes's face filled the screen.

"You're about to spend a half hour with one of the most courageous women I've ever known. I'm Quentin Hughes. Stay tuned."

A public service message, then the camera zoomed in on Veronica Caldwell and stayed on her as Hughes said off-camera, "Just four days ago this nation lost one of its most able and important legislators, Senator Cale Caldwell. He was the victim of a demented, senseless act of murder." The camera dollied back to include both of them.

"Seated with me this morning is the widow of Senator Caldwell, Veronica Caldwell. She's been gracious and brave enough to face these cameras and the public, not only to answer questions about this tragedy but to make a statement of profound importance to all of us." He smiled at her. "Later this afternoon the governor of Virginia, the Honorable James P. Craighton, will announce that he intends to appoint Mrs. Caldwell to complete her late husband's term."

Lydia sat forward and her eyes opened wide. Veronica had, indeed, an important announcement to make. But she had to smile at the way the announcement had been made. It was so typically pompous of Hughes to have made it himself, rather than giving Veronica that privilege.

Hughes looked directly at his guest as he said, "I'd like to discuss with you your hopes and aspirations"—Lord, Lydia thought, didn't anyone *ever* have anything but that awful cliché, "hopes and aspirations" in the public sector?—"as a member of the United States Senate, Mrs.

Caldwell, but before we get to that, I know there's another very important announcement you'd like to make, one that holds a very special place in your heart."

A second camera caught Veronica in a three-quarter profile. She appeared composed, though her right eye displayed a minuscule tic, and the horror of the past few days was manifested in the drawn expression around her mouth, the ineradicable fatigue in her eyes.

"In honor of my late husband I'm establishing the Cale Caldwell Performing Arts Foundation. All donations will go toward fostering and supporting deserving young men and women who strive to develop and perfect their artistic contributions to our society."

"I think that's marvelous," Hughes said. "Your husband worked so hard in the Senate to see that the arts in America received their fair share of federal spending. I know he'd be a proud man today to see that his efforts will not go unfulfilled..."

The rest of the interview provided little news and few revelations. Veronica told Hughes that there had been no progress in the investigation of her husband's murder, although she was confident that it would be resolved within a reasonable period of time. Hughes asked about rumors that a special Senate committee would be formed to conduct its own investigation, and Veronica confirmed that this was in the works.

Hughes went on to tell his viewers that an interview taped with Cale Caldwell just before his death and scheduled to be aired that morning would be seen at a later date. He added, "It was my intention to cancel the program with the late Senator Caldwell out of deference to his family, but Mrs. Caldwell, after viewing the videotape of the interview with her husband, has urged me to reconsider, I—"

Veronica interrupted, "Cale would have wanted this interview shown. He spoke of legislation that was important to him, and I intend to try to bring with me into the United States Senate a continuation of his goals."

Hughes looked directly into the camera as it slowly moved in on him and production credits crawled up the screen. "I'm Quentin Hughes. Thanks for joining me." For once his show wasn't quite a one-man affair. He'd underestimated Veronica.

Clarence was uncharacteristically late for his brunch with Lydia at the Four Georges, in the Georgetown Inn. She'd made a reservation in her name and was given a comfortable corner table in the George II Room, which was decorated in a desert motif—sand-colored mesa brick walls, low tables and banquettes. A large party at a table across the room centered around Senator MacLoon.

Clarence arrived fifteen minutes later.

"You're late," she said.

"I know, I'm sorry, we'll have to find a new place."

"Why?"

He nodded toward MacLoon's table. "Certain politicians have a way of casting a pall over even the best restaurants." A waiter delivered a bottle of New York champagne in a bucket, opened it and poured some into each of their glasses. Clarence sniffed his, took a sip, and launched into a change of pace. "Lydia, my advice to you is never offer a cup of coffee to a policeman when he's questioning you about a murder, and especially when his nine-year-old daughter is taking piano lessons. When he found out about me he insisted on discussing music and whether his daughter's teacher is taking the right approach."

"Did he ever get around to asking you about the murder?"

"Eventually. Wanted to know whether I had any animosity toward Caldwell, whether we had had any business dealings, personal intrigues, mutual enemies, friends. As though I'd admit to any of that if I'd killed him."

"Did he tell you anything?"

"No, except that his daughter won't practice her scales. Well, what did you think of Hughes's interview with Veronica?"

"Mixed feelings. How about you?"

"I only saw bits of it because *he* wouldn't stop talking. From what I heard I'd say the lady isn't wasting much of her widowhood."

"Which, I think, is to be admired. You did hear about her appointment to fill out Cale's term in the Senate?"

"Yes, and about the foundation in his name. Let me ask you something, Lydia, and promise you won't have my head for it—"

"I promise nothing."

"Do you think it's at all possible that Veronica Caldwell could have privately envied her husband's power so much that she killed him, or had him killed, to get his Senate seat?"

Lydia looked around the dining room before leaning close to him and gently placed her hand on his arm. "See, no temper. The answer, of course, is *no*."

"Well, I don't think it's so far-out. After all, there were those who speculated that Lyndon Johnson might have had something to do with Kennedy's death in order to become President—"

"Some people—*I'm* not one of them."

"What are you having?" he asked, changing gears again.

"Eggs Benedict and a rasher of bacon. You?"

"Venison, fried egg on the side, over easy." He gave their order, then recounted for Lydia the details of his interrogation by the MPD detective. When he was finished and their food had been served, Lydia brought up Veronica's suggestion that she accept a post as special counsel to a Senate committee to investigate Cale Caldwell's murder. Clarence listened, commenting only by raising his salt-and-pepper eyebrows. Finally when she was done telling him about the offer and the circumstances surrounding it at the Caldwell house, he cleared his throat and said, "It depends entirely if you want to make a name for yourself. If so, by all means do it. If you value your sanity, for God's sake turn it down—and do it fast and mean it."

Lydia said nothing for a minute, then, "I have no interest in making a name for myself as special counsel to a committee to investigate the murder of a friend. But what do you do when his widow—who is also a friend—asks? Just walk away?"

"Exactly. Besides, what would you do with your private practice if you took it?"

"Leave it up to my associates, try to keep a handle on things from a distance. What's wrong with that?"

"Everything. As Louis Armstrong said when someone asked him what was wrong with a friend who'd suddenly died, 'When you're dead, everything's wrong.' Eat your eggs, they're getting cold."

"They already are." She placed her fork on her plate. "I love you dearly, Clarence, and have always had a big fat respect for your opinions, but there are times when I find you to be a trying ass."

He sat back, grinned. "And this obviously is one of those times. Sorry. It's my way of concealing unacceptable levels of anxiety about you. I can understand how you feel and why you're seriously considering Veronica's proposal. Personally I think it would be a mistake and that you'll end up regretting it. On the other hand if you don't do it you'll probably spend the rest of your days wondering if you should have. So take it if it's really offered."

"If I do, will you stand by me?"

He laughed. "Of course not. After all, I'm a prime suspect, and how would it look for the special counsel to be involved with such a person—"

"Oh, shut up..."

He did, but her mind wouldn't. Without quite meaning to, she was already beginning to think as though she'd taken the job.

Nine

The good weather of fall had given way to the harsher climate of early winter. It had rained heavily over the weekend. Now, at ten o'clock on Monday morning Lydia sat in a green vinyl armchair in the drab office of deputy chief of police of Washington's Metropolitan Police Department, Horace Jenkins. She'd been told to wait; Chief Jenkins had been called away from his desk for a few minutes.

"Hello, Lydia," he said as he came through the door. "Nature called." His voice startled her and she turned abruptly. He walked past her, fell heavily into his green vinyl chair behind the desk and grinned.

"How are you?" she asked.

"Terrific," he said, yawning. "I woke up alive this morning, still have my job according to the papers, and retirement is within striking distance. How are you?"

"Fair."

"Special counsel, huh?"

"Yes...I was flattered to be asked."

"Sure you were." He rubbed his baggy eyes, yawned again. Lydia had once commented to a friend that Jenkins looked like Walter Matthau *after* a bad night. Sitting across from him she realized how apt her descrip-

tion had been. He was in shirtsleeves, suit jacket a rumpled heap on top of a file cabinet. He had a full head of black hair that hadn't receded even in his latter stages of middle age. Flesh hung in folds from his jawbone, cheeks and neck. His eyes were large and watery, evoking all the pathos of a hound that hadn't been fed in days. He was a big man who tended to excessive weight, although his large frame carried poundage rather well.

"So tell me, Lydia, what's a nice girl like you doing in a place like the United States Senate."

"My duty, I hope. Besides, I'm not so nice, and you know it. I'm also no longer a girl."

"By me you're still a girl, and I won't forget how you stood up there in court and defended those bananas. And, damn it, you are nice, if not easy... anyway, how's the radio and TV business—?"

"Okay, Horace, let's cool the chitchat. Here I am as scheduled. I assume your invitation has something to do with the Caldwell murder."

"Yeah, well, I figured I'd spare you going through this routine with some of the idiots who work for me, or over me." He leaned forward, which caused his chair to let out a shrill squeak, leaned on his elbows. "I'm sure you realize this is awkward...here I am interrogating you about the senator's murder while you act as special counsel to a committee investigating that same murder—"

"Routine, I know. Besides I *was* at the party and so theoretically I could be a suspect—but you and I are going to have to work very closely, Horace. After all, we're after the same thing."

He grunted and answered his intercom. "No, damn it, that's not what I said I wanted." A pause. "Then do it over. Don't bother me, I'm wrapping up the Caldwell murder." There was a hint of mirth in his eyes as he looked across the desk at her. "You were saying?"

"That I assume we'll be working closely together on the Caldwell case."

"No, we won't. The last thing I need is to have a Senate committee getting in my way. Caldwell's murder, senator or not, is an MPD matter and it's going to stay that way."

"I didn't realize you controlled the Senate."

"I'm a cop, Lydia. Murder, however high-placed, is a cop's business. I don't know what the hell you people think you're going to accomplish over there with another damn committee at taxpayer expense. This case is simple. Caldwell has a party thrown for him by his wife. She invites a coupla hundred snowflakes and one of them gets carried away and sticks an ice pick into the guest of honor...Let me ask you a question."

"Go ahead."

"Did you kill him?"

"No."

"Right. Interrogation over. Take my advice, Lydia, go back to getting licenses for radio stations and tell your Senate chums to get back to the business of running the country, not running over it."

"I'll be sure to carry back your sentiments, especially to the committee that funds the District of Columbia. I'll also remind you, chief, that the committee is a fact of life. It exists, it's real, and it's been created to investigate Cale Caldwell's murder."

"Yeah, and it's about as necessary as a hind tit. Pardon me."

"You're pardoned. I'm no longer a little girl, like I told you...well, if you're through, I'll be going."

"Sure...look, Lydia, believe it or not, I wish you well with this. I always admired you when you were doing criminal work. I just hate to see you get messed up in a no-win situation—"

"I appreciate that." She stood and extended her hand over the desk. He took it, clicked his tongue against his cheek. "If I was younger, Lydia, I'd make a pass."

"Thank you, I'm woman enough to like to hear that, even from an old party like you."

"Yeah, old party, well, good seeing you. By the way, do you know how I figure it?"

She stopped at the door. "How?"

"That flake of a son, the religious fanatic."

"Have you interviewed him?"

"Sure. We told him to stay around town but he went back to his cult. I sent somebody down there to bring him up here and he starts screaming about freedom of religion and separation of church and state."

"And?"

"We left him there."

"You must have felt he wasn't that much of a suspect."

"As good as any, better than most. At this point, anyway. The way I figured it he's less likely to skip out on his fellow freaks than from the city."

"Can I see the transcripts of the people you've interviewed?"

Jenkins shook his head.

"We'll subpoena them, Horace."

"We'll play the game an inning at a time, Lydia...You *are* looking good. Like I said, if I was younger I'd—"

"Have a nice day, like they say."

"Yeah, you too."

She controlled any outward show of her irritation until reaching the street, then drew a series of deep breaths and began muttering to herself. Years ago, when she'd worked as a public defender, she'd enjoyed the daily battle with the MPD. The truth was she'd lost as often as she'd won, but the challenge was always a highly exhilarating one.

Now, instead of feeling challenged, she felt a deep, abrupt frustration. She'd been out of that arena for a long time, comfortable, secure behind her desk from which she navigated the tricky waters of the FCC on behalf of clients who paid handsome fees for her knowledge and expertise. Any infighting was accomplished with padded gloves. In criminal matters there were no gloves. She'd nearly forgotten that, and the realization sent a chill through her that a gusty north wind whipping up the street could not match. She pulled her coat collar tighter around her neck and walked briskly across town to her office, where she returned phone calls, dictated a brief to her secretary, then left for an appointment with Senator Wilfred MacLoon, who'd been chosen to chair the Caldwell committee.

The choice of MacLoon to chair the committee had disheartened Lydia, but she decided not to allow her feelings to interfere with her performance. She had, however, raised the question with Veronica Caldwell about whether it was a wise idea to have an avowed political enemy of her husband's heading up a committee to investigate his murder. Veronica's answer made sense. Because MacLoon and Caldwell were known to dislike each other, it could only add to the public's confidence in the committee's integrity. MacLoon would be under the gun to disprove any personal grudge, would be doubly aggressive in the investigation. At least that was the theory.

Lydia was kept waiting in MacLoon's outer office for fifteen minutes before an aide ushered her inside, where the senator was giving an interview to a young newspaper reporter. "With you in a minute," he told Lydia, waving his hand. He said to the reporter, "It will be the duty of the committee to assure the American public that the murder of Senator Caldwell was in no way connected with any government institution, nor did it have overtones or implications that in any way reflect on this nation's governing bodies or those of its allies. Got that?"

"Yes, I think so. Thank you, senator."

MacLoon grinned broadly, stood and shook the reporter's hand. "Anytime, my dear. The door is always open to you."

The reporter nodded at Lydia as she left the office.

"Sorry to keep you waiting," MacLoon said. "Sit down."

Lydia sat in an armchair next to his desk. "Isn't it a little premature to be giving interviews about the committee's work?" she asked.

"I don't think so. No sense in trying to play games with the press. I'd like to see this committee be an open one that the press and public can have faith in. No stonewalling. Doesn't that make sense to you?"

"Of course... within reason." She observed MacLoon as he swiveled his chair and began rummaging through a file drawer. She could hear his heavy breathing, the result of a lifetime of cigars and cigarettes and a paunch that threatened to burst through his belt. MacLoon was almost totally bald, and had a full face that was made to appear even more so because of a tight shirt collar that pressed into the flesh of his neck.

He found what he was looking for, turned back to his desk and suppressed a belch as he opened a file folder and thumbed through its pages.

"Senator MacLoon, I know you're busy but so am I. I wonder if we could discuss the committee and my role on it. I assumed that was your purpose in asking me here."

"Yes, sure. Just give me a minute." He frowned as he read a page from the folder, then called through the open door, "Margaret, in here." One of his aides, a buxom young woman wearing heavy makeup, entered and MacLoon handed the page to her. "Copy it and get it out to Markovich right away."

Lydia fought down her impatience, cleared her throat. "I'll come back when you have more time."

MacLoon looked up, appearing to be surprised. "Relax, we'll get to it in a moment. How about lunch? I'll have it sent up—"

"No, *thank* you. Senator MacLoon, I accepted this committee post at the request of Veronica Caldwell. I have mixed feelings about it. On the one hand I'm pleased to be able to contribute something to solving this tragedy. On the other, I have a pretty successful law practice that will suffer during my absence. I want to get on with my work on the committee. I want you to understand that."

He looked at her as though she were an errant daughter. "Miss James, let's not get off on the wrong foot. Frankly, when Veronica insisted on you as special counsel I opposed it. As far as I was concerned, what we needed was an attorney with a clean sheet who's used to working behind the scenes and fitting into a team that has a clear-cut game plan—"

"Why do men always use a sports metaphor? And in this case a mixed one." Before he could answer she added, "I just left Horace Jenkins at the MPD and he talked about playing an inning at a time. You talk about teams and game plans. I'm sorry, but I don't see this as a game."

He squinted through the heavy, mottled flesh of his face. "No need to get testy, Miss James. We're in this together, after all."

"Over your objections."

"That's right. After Veronica did some talking I decided that having you on the team might not be such a bad idea after all. Your reputation is solid, no obvious skeletons in your closet, you're close to the family and you understood Caldwell and all this arts nonsense he was involved with."

Lydia shifted in her chair. "You might as well know, senator, that I don't consider it nonsense. I've been involved myself, which is how I got to be friends with Veronica Caldwell."

"*Senator* Veronica Caldwell," he said.

"That's right. I also became friendly with *your* wife through the arts."

"The difference there, Miss James, is that my wife's dabbling never influenced my Senate duties."

"Are you saying that Veronica Caldwell's activities influenced her husband's?"

"You know it. You might also be interested to hear that Senator Caldwell was about to get in some hot water over it. The arts section of the last Interior bill upset a lot of people around here. The same thing happened when he worked behind the scenes to kill a committee bill to investigate these damn cults and the brainwashing they use. That was one of the things that drove Jimmye McNab out of the Caldwells' life."

Lydia wasn't sure whether to admit her ignorance of what he was saying or to pretend some knowledge of it in the hope that it would encourage him to say more. She decided to say nothing. It didn't work. MacLoon looked at his watch. "Tell you what, Miss James, I have some things to do. I'll have one of my people show you to the office we've found for you. It's not much but it'll have to do. We're cramped for space all over the building."

"I'm sure it will be fine. What about staffing?"

"It's in the budget. I'll have someone fill you in completely. I'd like to get started on this immediately so that we can get it over with."

"I'll do all I can to see that it's a thorough and efficient investigation. I'm concerned about leaks to the press of the committee's activities. I feel it's vital we be able to function quietly."

"We can talk about those things later." MacLoon unwrapped a cigar and chewed off its tip. "Hope you don't mind working with a cigar smoker."

"Not at all."

He held a lit match close to the cigar's blunt end and slowly, carefully inhaled. As his first exhalation of blue smoke curled easily toward the ceiling he said, without looking at her, "Let's understand one thing right from the top, Miss James. This investigation in the Senate has nothing to do with solving Cale Caldwell's murder."

"Pardon?"

He drew on the cigar again, stood and came to the edge of his desk, and leaned on it, his face close to hers. "Solving murders is for the MPD. This committee's function is to assure the American people that the murder had nothing to do with their government."

She leaned away from him as she said, "I gathered that was your position from what I heard you tell the reporter, although I assumed you viewed it as only one of the committee's functions. Now I take it you view public assurance as our only function."

"That's right." He perched on the edge of the desk.

"I'm afraid I don't agree."

"You will as it progresses."

She stood. "Thank you for your time, senator. I'd like to see my office."

He told a young man who'd been reading a newspaper in the outer office to escort Lydia and see that she had access to any supplies, furniture and staff help she needed. The young man, who introduced himself as Rick Petrone, and who told her he'd been working for Senator MacLoon for over a year, led her down a long corridor and up a flight of stairs to an office which, Lydia instantly decided, had once been a large storage closet that had recently been cleaned out. A battered metal desk occupied the center of the room. Rings of dirt on the buff walls outlined where a row of file cabinets had once stood. Two small windows were caked with dirt, and what light they did allow to pass through had a yellowish-gray cast to it.

"Just name it and it's yours," Petrone said. Lydia had taken an instant liking to him. He was tall and undeniably handsome, with a mop of brown hair that was appealingly unkempt. His smile was warm, genuine. He wore a brown plaid vested suit and tan knit tie.

"I can think of a lot of things," she said lightly, surprised and a little annoyed at her tone.

He took a note pad and pen from his pocket. "Let's make a list right now."

Twenty minutes later the list was completed. She thanked him for his courtesy and said she had to go back to her own offices for an appointment.

"Just call on me anytime, Miss James," he said. "I guess I'd be less than candid with you if I didn't admit that I'm hoping to be able to hang around during the investigation. I graduated from law school last year and took this job with Senator MacLoon as a way to get a look at how government works. Don't get me wrong. I've enjoyed it, and it's been interesting. But I'd like to get back to something that's a little closer to the law. I don't want to be a pest but—"

"Maybe I can have you assigned to me for the duration of the investigation. I'll suggest it to the senator, if you'd like."

"I'd really appreciate that, Miss James. I really would."

"All right, then consider it done."

They walked down the hall together. Lydia's gait was considerably faster than it had been earlier in the day, and Petrone had to move quickly to keep up with her. It had occurred to her as she stood in the small, temporary office that she deserved to be treated exactly as she had been since becoming involved with the Caldwell murder—like a small, helpless female child in awe of male authority. She'd been suffering from an unjustifiable fear of leaving the genteel comfort and security of her law practice to once again enter the more combative arena of Congress and criminal law, and was ashamed of how wishy-washy it had made her. Her dead father had had a favorite saying—"Drive it like you owned it," and the warm memory of him and his insistence that she work for excellence in every phase of life filled her, at once, with guilt, and with determination to jump into this new and challenging role with all the vigor and dedication she could manage.

"Remember what I said." Petrone shook her hand. "You can call on me for anything. I just want to help in any way I can."

"Thank you, I appreciate it." Very much, she added silently to herself.

Petrone went back to MacLoon's office, where he resumed reading his newspaper until the senator returned.

"She squared away?" MacLoon asked.

"I think so. We made a list of what she needs."

"What she really needs is a man," MacLoon said. "You up to it?"

Petrone smiled. "I'm always up for that. She intends to ask you to assign me to her for the duration of the investigation."

"I'll put up a good argument against it but she can have you. Just make sure you stay close to her and keep me filled in on whatever the hell she's up to."

"No problem there, senator. I just want to help in any way I can."

Ten

The next two weeks passed quickly for Lydia. Rick Petrone proved to be a most helpful and efficient young man, and Lydia's office was transformed into a workable, comfortable one. Besides providing all the necessary furniture and supplies, Petrone ordered extra touches—fresh flowers, prints on the walls, a radio and a love seat on which Lydia spent more and more time as she pored through a steady buildup of paperwork.

If she had had any illusions about being able to split her time between committee business and her own law practice, they were soon put down by the demands of her committee responsibilities. There was a daily meeting of the full committee—six senators, aides from their offices and the staff Lydia had brought together, five people in all including Rick Petrone, one of Lydia's associates from her law office and three people assigned by MacLoon, two secretaries and a researcher named Ginger Johnson.

Lydia's first reaction to Ginger had been less than enthusiastic. She seemed too young and flighty to provide the research Lydia was counting on. Short, tending to chubbiness, with long red hair that seemed always to be in search of a comb, Ginger had been introduced to Lydia by MacLoon as a former *Time* researcher, a graduate of the University of Missouri Journalism School and more recently employed by HUD in research. She didn't appear to be old enough to have gotten such experience and background, and Lydia took the time to question her during her first week. Ginger's answers, plus an informal background check, verified everything MacLoon and Ginger had claimed. And as the second week wound down and Ginger's efforts started to pile up, Lydia began to see her as a good tough questioner, at home with detail and not afraid to roll up her sleeves and make order out of the piles of material that soon took over nearly half the office.

The Friday meeting at the end of the second week ran until six in the evening. It dealt mostly with routine matters until Lydia told of her decision to examine all the circumstances surrounding the unsolved murder of TV journalist Jimmye McNab.

"Why?" she was asked.

"I think it's applicable," she answered. "And even if it proves not to be, we'd be derelict not to at least look at it and evaluate its potential relevance to the Caldwell murder..."

She didn't mention that her renewed interest in the McNab murder had been aroused by a long article in a national scandal newspaper, the *National Voyeur*. Ginger Johnson had routinely included the article in her research files and had mentioned it to Lydia, more as a joke, a light moment, than as a matter seriously to be considered. Lydia had laughed along with her researcher, but late the previous night she'd settled down on the love seat in her office and read it, along with other materials Ginger had marked for her attention. The writer of the piece had, of course, sensationalized every aspect of both the McNab and Caldwell murders to suit the style of the publication, but as Lydia made her way through the florid prose and shaky cause-and-effect scenario concocted by the writer between the McNab and Caldwell murders, she realized, in spite of herself, that it was a reasonable proposition... Two people had been murdered. Jimmye McNab, a TV journalist, had been raised by the other, Senator Caldwell, since infancy.

Lydia had honestly agonized over suggesting that the McNab murder be included in the scope of the committee's investigation...she didn't want to open old and very personal wounds in the Caldwell family. But after a sleepless night she'd come to the conclusion that at least a possible link between the deaths had to be acknowledged.

Her suggestion caused some of the senators around the oval table to shift in their seats and look to Wilfred MacLoon. As chairman his chair had a higher back, and was at the table's head. A cigar clenched between his teeth had gone out, and a heavy shadow of beard gave him a particularly dour look. He fixed Lydia in a hard stare. "I don't see any need to extend the scope of this committee *beyond* Senator Caldwell's death."

"I'm not suggesting that either," Lydia said. "Our charter charges us with investigating the circumstances surrounding Senator Caldwell's murder. If there's even a remote possibility that Jimmye McNab's murder might, in some way, put some light on that effort, I don't see how we can ignore it."

MacLoon leaned back and chewed on the wet cigar stub. "No, the McNab murder has nothing to do with us."

Lydia glanced at the others. Had MacLoon at least opened the issue for discussion, she wouldn't have been so upset. But his arbitrary dismissal of it...She pulled out of a file folder a copy of Public Law 66-107 under which the committee had been formed and funded. "I don't want to belabor this, but our charter says that we are to..." She read directly from the charter. "... *examine every detail and aspect of the death of Senator Cale G. Caldwell, using all available resources, agencies and individuals who might have bearing upon said death, and to prepare and deliver a full, impartial and accurate report to the Congress of the United States and to the American people.*"

MacLoon abruptly sat up and rolled his stubby fingers on the table. "We're all aware of what the charter says, Miss James. The fact is, which is not included in the charter, and as I told you, *solving* the murder is not Senate business. What you're suggesting is to open up a whole can of worms that represents nothing but a waste of taxpayer money and, I might add, of our time. You do that, and when we start calling witnesses to testify, we'll need the Kennedy Center to hold them. Forget about anything except what directly bears on the senator's death. Is that clear enough?"

Lydia looked at Senator Jack Markowski, the youngest on the committee and the one she felt the most rapport with. A trace of a grin appeared on his lips, and he narrowed his eyes as though to tell her that she should press ahead with her idea.

She looked at MacLoon. "As special counsel to this committee, Senator MacLoon, I can't in conscience ignore an area of investigation that might bear on the outcome of our work. Maybe I've prematurely introduced this line of inquiry. If so, I'll develop more compelling reasons for it and present them at a future time. When I do, a vote whether to include it in the full investigation would, it seems to me, be appropriate."

MacLoon looked as though he might explode. His face turned red and his breathing deepened, his massive stomach rising and falling as though steam were churning beneath it. "All right," he said, "come in next week with reasons for including McNab's murder and I'll listen to them. Anything *else?*" He surveyed those at the table. No one spoke, so he adjourned the meeting until three o'clock on Monday.

Ginger Johnson and Rick Petrone were in Lydia's office when she returned. Lydia sat on the love seat. "I'll be damned if I'll be railroaded into doing a half-baked job—"

"Hey," Petrone said, "what happened in there?"

Lydia told them. When she finished, Ginger said, "I kind of figured this would happen. I'll work on the McNab files over the weekend."

Lydia nodded. "Thanks, Ginger. Do you have much?"

"Quite a bit. I've picked up a lot of it from newspaper morgues and have a list of magazine pieces. I'll start Xeroxing tomorrow at the library."

"Is he giving you a hard time?" Petrone asked Lydia.

"Senator MacLoon? Yes, although I suppose he's only doing what he feels is right. I guess I should give him that. I realize this isn't the only committee in Congress, and the Caldwell murder isn't the only thing on his mind."

"What can I do?" Petrone asked.

"Go home and have a good weekend," Lydia said. "I think we all need a day or two to think about something else. *Anything* else."

"Thanks, troops," Ginger said. "While you two play I'll be grinding away."

"Let it go until Monday—"

"No, I'm too interested, and besides my man and I are on the outs. The weekend was a washout anyway...oh, Lydia, a Mr. Foster-Sims...very fancy!...called while you were in the meeting," Ginger said.

"Did he leave a message?"

"Yes. He said he's tired of hearing that you're busy and insists on taking you to dinner tonight."

Lydia laughed. "I'm so tired—"

"Go ahead," Ginger said. "It'll do you good."

"Well, we'll see. Why don't you two take off. I'll return his call and see you on Monday."

They left Lydia alone in the office. She made a mental note to ask someone on Monday to seal up the windows. A brisk, steady stream of cold air seemed to pass right through the glass and kept the office in a constant chill. She dialed out and reached Clarence.

"I won't take no for an answer," he said the moment he recognized her voice. "Dinner, and a little night music."

"I'm not up to it—"

"I'll do all I can to prop you up. Emlyn Edwards is performing Rachmaninoff at the Caldwell Center, including, I understand, the C-sharp minor prelude and two of the four concertos. And after that...I'm leering, can't you tell?"

"Clarence, I—"

"No arguments. At the rate you're going you'll be old and gray by the end of the year. I want you while there's still something left...I'll pick you up at seven. We'll go to the concert, have dinner afterward and..."

"All right," she said. "Maybe Rachmaninoff is what I need." Though she knew it was something considerably less lofty, and that he was offering that too.

They drove directly to the Caldwell Center. The audience was sparse as Lydia looked around for familiar faces, saw a few. Jason DeFlaunce elegented out from behind a screen near one of the stage entrances and had a heated dialogue with a stage manager, then disappeared as quickly as he'd appeared.

"So how are things in the halls of Congress?" Clarence asked after he'd examined the program.

"Hectic, also frustrating if interesting."

"You'll tell me about it over dinner."

The concert was short. When it was over they went to the lobby, put on their coats and prepared to leave the theater.

"Lydia!" She turned to see Jason crossing the lobby. "So glad you could come," he said. "Hello, Clarence. Lydia, could you and I find a quiet moment to talk?"

"I suppose so..."

"I mean now. It will only take a moment."

Clarence shrugged, nodded to her to go ahead and get it over with.

She followed Jason to a coatroom just off the lobby, and now empty. He looked back at the lobby.

"Yes, Jason?"

"I don't believe what I've heard," he said in a stage whisper, "and neither does Veronica."

"About what?" She too whispered, which struck her as silly.

"About wanting to drag poor Jimmye's death into the Senate investigation."

"Jason, I..." She paused as the realization of news having traveled so fast hit her. "Jason, how did you hear about it?"

"That's really not important," he said. "What's important is that you would even consider doing it."

Lydia looked through the wide opening of the coatroom. Clarence was leaning against the wall, his coat on his arm, his face showing impatience. "I don't want to be rude, Jason, but the committee's workings aren't your business—"

"What about Veronica? Are you going to tell me that she shouldn't be concerned? God, Lydia, the poor woman's gone through enough without having a trusted friend drag out old pain and suffering. Frankly I never would have thought you capable of that sort of—"

"Jason, Veronica asked me to take this job. I thought a lot about it before I agreed. Now that I've taken it on I've got to try to do it to the best of my ability, no matter what—"

"Even if it hurts Veronica?"

"I'm sure that Veronica knows that the last thing I'd ever want to do is hurt her. But if Jimmye's death has any bearing on Cale's death, then it *must* be included. I'm sorry, Jason, but if Veronica wants to discuss it with me, I'll certainly be available at any time. Well, good night."

As she started to leave the coatroom he said in a distinctly unpleasant voice, "Don't disappoint us, Lydia." It made her stop, turn and look hard at him. She started to say something, changed her mind and went on into the lobby, where she took Clarence's arm.

"What was that all about?" he asked once they were in his car.

"Nothing, really. Or more accurately, I'm not sure. Well, I've never liked Jason and I guess that colors my reaction to what he says or does."

"What did he say to you? You're obviously upset."

She shook her head and forced herself to brighten the mood. "Where are we eating?"

"Well, I originally was going to make a reservation

at Le Lion d'Or, but it'll be too noisy. I want to hear all about your first two weeks with the committee, so I made a reservation at Aux Beaux Champs. I'm in a beef mood."

"That'll be crowded too."

"Nothing like the other," he said as he turned down Pennsylvania Avenue toward the new Four Seasons Hotel in which the restaurant was located. "Besides, Doug McNeill will see to it that two fellow-Scotsmen are given a quiet table in a corner."

"Scots*men?*"

"Scots*people*, if you insist."

"I do, at least for the record."

For most of the meal—a fillet for Clarence that had been dry-hung to age for four weeks, according to the restaurant owner Douglas McNeill, and a terrine of baby coho salmon with truffles and pistachios for her—they avoided discussing Lydia's committee work. They talked about music, the season's concert activity in Washington and considered going to New York later in the year, if Lydia could free up the time, to catch some Broadway theater and just be together.

It was over dessert that Lydia finally brought up what had happened over the past two weeks. Clarence listened patiently, and noted that there was a firmness in her voice that had been conspicuously absent two weeks earlier. She'd been full of obvious doubt about her ability to handle the assignment. On the one hand Clarence had found her lack of confidence to be refreshing, this beautiful and bright forty-year-old woman demonstrating humility. It was a scarce commodity in the Washington thickets. But it had also worried him. Her performance on a special Senate committee called to investigate the murder of a powerful man would not be helped by taking a humble-pie, toe-in-the-sand position, any more than a concert performance would be. Two weeks into the job, the change in her was welcome. Fact was, he was damned proud of her.

She told him about her confrontations with Wilfred MacLoon, of the prevailing atmosphere on the committee that seemed to make it nothing more than a cursory public relations charade, and about Jason's comments to her in the coatroom and the implication that Veronica Caldwell was upset by her decision to go into the Jimmye McNab case.

"What a strange way to put it," Foster-Sims said after she'd repeated what Jason had said to her that evening. "'Don't disappoint *us*.' That's pretty damn presumptuous of him."

"I know this, Clarence, which may also be presumptuous, but if any real headway is going to be made by the committee it'll have to be me and the people assigned to me who'll bring it about. The senators see the committee as something to handle, not get too involved with. I suppose I can't blame them, they've got other things to worry about, but damn it, I've been given the responsibility to see that a full, fair investigation happens. That's what I understood Veronica to say she wanted when she pushed for a committee in the first place, and insisted that I be special counsel."

"Maybe she's changed her mind. Now that she's a senator, maybe her priorities have shifted—"

"I'd better have a talk with Veronica and see what her feelings are."

"That would make sense. What about your friends at the MPD?"

She sighed. "I'm afraid my so-called friends have been pretty uncooperative. They refuse to release anything about the murder. I have to draw subpoenas this week. Clarence, can we leave? I'm suddenly very damn tired."

"Sure, but you're stopping back at my apartment before you call it a night."

"Oh...I can't..." She gripped his forearm, hoping he'd understand.

"I brought you a special present, Lydia, in honor of your new responsibilities. It's at home—"

"Tomorrow?"

"No. I promise I won't keep you long." Well, he always had been a liar, he told himself.

This gift was a handsome, sleek, cassette tape deck

with two extension speakers. "For your office," he said. "And these go with it." The package he handed her had cassette tapes of many of her favorite jazz artists—Ellington, Bill Evans, the Modern Jazz Quartet. "I hope they help you cope with all that congressional jazz. Sorry...bad pun..."

"Clarence, thank you so much, not for the gifts, but for you..."

"Listen, you happen to be my favorite woman in the whole world, even though you did flunk as a piano student."

She wrapped her arms around him, and without another word they walked to the bedroom. "I want to stay with you tonight," she told him. The words confirmed the obvious, but somehow she felt good saying them.

The bed became a center of warmth and caring, their caresses tender and giving, the silence broken only by the sounds of their fulfillment.

There were, she told herself as she lingered on the edge of sleep, some things that were just too important to be interfered with, even by the Senate of the United States.

Outside, a heavyset man wearing a dark suit sat in a dirty, gunmetal gray sedan. He looked down at a steno pad on his lap on which he'd noted the time they'd arrived at the apartment and the time Lydia had said, *"I want to stay with you tonight."* He adjusted a knob on a powerful receiver slung beneath the automobile's dashboard that was tuned to an FM signal broadcast through a tiny microphone concealed in Foster-Sims's bedroom. Silence. The man stretched, scratched at his belly. He looked at his watch. It would be a long night, and he hoped they would wake up and say something else, anything else, before it ended, if only to break the monotony. That was what he disliked most about these assignments, the monotony, and the strain on his hemorrhoids from sitting all night.

Eleven

Quentin Hughes walked briskly through the terminal at Chicago's O'Hare Airport. His flight from Des Moines had been delayed, and he had only twenty minutes to make his connection to Washington.

He stopped at a wall phone, gave the operator his credit card number and waited for his call to go through. Christa, his producer, picked up the page at WCAP.

"I've only a minute, anything I should know about? Any calls?"

"Lots of them. A Ginger Johnson called...she's from the Senate committee investigating the Caldwell murder, says she's the special counsel's chief researcher. She'd like to talk to you."

"Anybody else?"

"Nothing that can't wait."

"I have to go. I'll probably be there just in time for the show."

He picked up a small leather overnight bag from the floor. An eight-by-eight-inch package wrapped in plain brown paper had never left its secure spot beneath his arm. He hugged it even closer as he headed for the departure gate.

"I can put that package in the overhead rack," a flight attendant said once they were aloft.

Hughes shook his head. "No, thanks, I'll keep it with me."

She looked at him more closely. "Are you Quentin Hughes?"

"Yup."

"I've seen you on TV."

"You live in Washington?"

"Uh-huh. I've heard you on the radio too."

"Ears and eyes check out. How about the rest of you?"

"Everything works." She didn't smile when she said it. "Excuse me, I have other passengers."

She provocatively ignored him throughout the flight, which had its desired effect. He liked her looks—medium height with dark brown hair and ultra-white, as the ads said, teeth that she frequently displayed, a little full in the hips but years away from that becoming a problem. As they prepared to land at National Airport she stood next to him. "Two whole days off. I think I'll celebrate."

"With anybody in particular?"

"Not yet."

"Discuss it at dinner?"

"A girl has to eat." Moments later she returned and handed him a slip of paper on which she'd written her address and phone number....

"I'll drive you home," he said. "Time's a problem for me, I'm afraid. I've got a show to do tonight."

He arrived at the studio at 11:45. He and the flight attendant...he still thought of her job as "stewardess" ...had ordered in Chinese food and had lingered in her small apartment until he'd had to leave. He told her he'd call the next day but knew he wouldn't.

He lingered for a few minutes after the show with the departing guest, a professor of geology at George Washington University. Out of the corner of his eye he saw Christa scooping up paraphernalia from the table, including the package he'd carried with him from Des

Moines, and that had sat next to the microphone throughout the program.

"Don't touch that," he said from across the studio.

"Pardon *me*. What's in it, a bomb?"

He excused himself from the professor, grabbed up the package and went to his office. Christa followed. "I was cleaning up, that's all," she said. "What's so important about that package, Quentin?"

"Nothing...something personal." He glanced down at a slip of paper on which Ginger Johnson's message had been recorded. "Am I supposed to call her back?"

"Yes, as soon as possible."

He put the paper in his jacket pocket. "What are you doing now?" he asked.

"Home to bed, like any good little girl about Washington."

"I'll come with you."

She felt a distinct twinge of displeasure...anger, even...at being so taken for granted, but a rush of expectation, willy-nilly, went with it. And in a way she was flattered. Obviously he wasn't in the mood for the mindless young woman he'd been living with....

She fixed him eggs the way he liked, loosely scrambled, no butter, while he took a shower. She noticed that the package wasn't in the bedroom. He came out of the bathroom wearing a robe he'd kept there for years, and carrying the package beneath his arm. He sprawled out on the bed and waited for her to bring the tray with his eggs. She did, then snuggled in beside him. "Why the hurry-up trip to Des Moines, Quentin?"

He talked between bites. "To see my mother, she hasn't been feeling so hot..."

"Oh? And she sounded so strong last week when she called—"

"Forget it, Christa...It was a good show tonight, huh?"

She punched him on the arm lightly. "It always is, and you know it."

"Yeah, right...Hey, I'm really beat, Christa, okay? Wake me at eleven. Big day tomorrow..."

She reached for him beneath the folds of his robe, but he turned his back. She could wait. She removed the tray and watched television in the living room until eleven, then woke him. He rubbed his eyes, yawned and pulled her down on top of him. Damn him, it was worth waiting for....

An hour later, Ginger Johnson received a call from Quentin Hughes. "Thanks for calling back," she said, then went on to tell him about her role with the committee and her need to talk with him about what he'd observed at the Caldwell party, and to see whether his long association with the family might provide some insight into the murder.

"I've been through all this with the MPD—"

"I know that, but Ms. James thought—"

"How is she?"

"Fine, just fine. Really, Mr. Hughes, I'd only need an hour of your time."

"All right. How about dinner?"

"I was thinking of—"

"That's the only time I'm free for the next six months."

"Well, if that's the case, I suppose I'll have to work overtime. Any preference in restaurants?"

"Is the committee buying?"

"I suppose."

"Good, make it Petitto's, on Connecticut, Northwest. See you there at seven."

Ginger reported her conversation with Hughes to Lydia. "Dinner? Protect your flanks, he's a dedicated womanizer."

"By me that's not all bad, Lydia. The way things are going...or not going...with Harold."

"Forewarned is...Did you ask him about getting the videotape of his last interview with Senator Caldwell?"

"I didn't have a chance but I'll bring it up at dinner. You said you wanted to discuss the Jimmye McNab murder before I interviewed Hughes."

Lydia nodded. "The rumor is that Jimmye and

Hughes had an affair. That wouldn't be so unusual, but some people say she represented one of the few real, two-way relationships he's ever had. I'll tell you what I know at lunch. Come on, my treat."

As Lydia and Ginger left the office to go to lunch, Quentin Hughes entered his apartment in the Watergate, placed the brown package in a fireproof, locked chest in the bottom of a closet and returned the key to its hiding place on a nail behind the refrigerator. He lay back on the couch, kicked off his shoes and thought about the last twenty-four hours. After a while he got up and called his mother in Des Moines.

"I was worried about you," she said. "You said you'd call when you got home safe. You know I hate airplanes."

"Yeah, I know, momma, but I got busy. It was good seeing you."

"You don't visit enough."

"Yeah, well, maybe I'll have more time in a couple of months. Thanks for keeping the package safe."

"I did just like you told me. I kept it under all the blankets in the closet and never told nobody it was here. I don't even ask any more what's in it. That's your business, I guess. Thanks for the money. It costs so much to heat the house these days. I called the furnace man but he said—"

"I have to run, momma. Thanks again. I'll call soon."

"You say that but you never do, son, except when you need somethin'."

"Goodbye, momma."

Now he slept until Christa called him at five. He showered, shaved and left for his dinner engagement with Ginger Johnson, wondering as he drove to the restaurant what she looked like. All right, so he was a rat...but at least he liked women, which was more than you could say about most of the men in Washington.

Twelve

Although Lydia had the power to issue subpoenas, she chose to make one final effort to obtain Horace Jenkins's voluntary cooperation at the Washington MPD. She called and asked to see him. Evidently she caught him in a good mood because he immediately invited her to visit his office at her convenience....

"What can I do for you, Lydia?" Jenkins asked after she'd settled in the green vinyl chair and was served coffee by a clerk. Good and hot. Jenkins and the MPD had their points.

"Tell me what sort of progress you're making in the Caldwell case." She sipped the coffee.

"Happy to oblige. Let's see, we've finally interviewed everybody who was at the party."

"And?"

"And we've ruled out about half."

"On what basis?"

"Instinct, connection or lack of it to the deceased, known attitudes about him, proximity to where he got it, witnesses who said somebody was with them when it happened, that sort of thing. How's the coffee?"

"Delicious."

"Well, we public servants aim to please...I suppose you want to know who's still on the list."

"I suppose."

He called out to a clerk to bring him the latest Caldwell file, looked across the desk and smiled. "That's a nice dress you're wearing. I wish my ever-loving wife had one like it..." He shrugged. "She's getting a little thick through the middle, if you know what I mean. Happens, I guess, to women."

"Men, too," Lydia said.

He glanced down at his waist and nodded. "Well, it's different too. I saw a play once where somebody says that men get better looking as they get older, and that women get to look more like the men."

"What was the name of the play?"

He shrugged. "I never can keep them straight."

The clerk brought in the file, and Jenkins handed Lydia six typewritten pages from it.

"Mind if I read it now?" she asked.

"When else? It's not leaving here."

She dropped the papers on the desk and leaned forward. "Why do we have to go through this all the time? I don't want to use the committee's subpoena powers, but you keep forcing the issue."

"Department policy, Lydia, and you know it."

"You won't make me a copy?"

He winced, placed his hand over his heart. "What do you want to do, Lydia, blow my pension?"

She said nothing, just sat there and stared.

He removed his hand from his chest. "All right, all right, I'll give you a copy." He opened the file folder and handed her a Xerox of the original she held in her hands. It was obvious that he'd intended all along to give it to her but was going to drag out the process. No easy victories with Jenkins.

"I'd still like to look at it here," she said.

"Be my guest."

She quickly scanned the list, and recognized many of the names, including both Caldwell sons; Veronica Caldwell; Jason DeFlaunce; Quentin Hughes; Caldwell's aide, Richard Marvis; Boris Slevokian; Charles, the assistant Senate restaurant manager; various members of the Caldwell Performing Arts Center's board of directors; Senator Wilfred MacLoon and his wife; the pianist who'd played the party and Clarence Foster-Sims.

"Some of these names are ridiculous," she said.

He puffed up one cheek and ran a finger around the perimeter of his ear. "Tell me why?"

"Clarence Foster-Sims, Boris Slevokian, the piano player?"

"What's the matter, Lydia, you got a thing for over-aged musicians?"

"I won't say what I'm thinking," she said. "Veronica Caldwell? Now, why would she kill her husband?"

"I didn't say everybody on that list necessarily had a reason to do him in. All I said was that this list narrows down the possibilities. Everybody on it was *un*accounted for at the time he was killed...Okay, so you've got the list. What next?"

"The transcripts of the interviews you did with everyone at the party."

"Why everybody? We already cut the list in half."

"That's right, *you* did. I haven't had a chance to make those same decisions."

"That's not my problem, Lydia. What you want is for the MPD to do your work. You want interviews? Then grow your own."

She sighed and pulled the hem of her dress down a little lower over her knees. He took his eyes from them and focused on something behind her. "Look, chief," she said, "I don't understand why you're viewing me and the committee as adversaries. It seems to me that a lot of money and time could be saved by sharing what we have. Doesn't that make sense?"

"Sure, if you had something to share. Have you?"

"I hope to soon. We're beginning to follow up leads and ideas. I have a small staff. We'll do all we can, but your help would make things much easier. Why won't you cooperate?"

"Because it's one-sided, Lydia. More than that, this department is under the gun from everybody and his brother. Somebody gets killed in D.C. and we're supposed to solve the crime. If we don't, people say we're bums. Nobody likes to be called a bum, never mind being one. Add on that the victim is a senator and everything gets magnified a hundred times. You remember the McNab case? Two years and nothing, not a damn lead. Did you read the column in the paper a couple of days ago? The hotshot who wrote it all of a sudden is Sherlock Holmes, and he claims there must be a connection between Caldwell and McNab."

She was glad he'd brought up the subject of Jimmye McNab. "Well, isn't there a possible connection?" she asked. "After all, Senator Caldwell raised Jimmye McNab from infancy—"

"Yeah, I know that, but that doesn't mean their murders had anything to do with each other."

"But maybe they did. Anyway, that's one line of inquiry we're following—"

"Lotsa luck, Lydia. From what I hear, Mrs. Caldwell...pardon me, Senator Caldwell...she's not what you'd call happy that the McNab and Caldwell murders are being linked. She wants the McNab thing put to rest as much as her husband did."

Lydia thought for a moment, then asked with genuine puzzlement, "Are you suggesting that Senator Caldwell wanted Jimmye McNab's murder investigation stopped?"

"I didn't say that, Lydia. All I meant was that neither of them, the senator or his wife, were happy about what developed. Can you blame them? It's bad enough your daughter gets killed by some nut in a park without having it dragged on and on, in the papers, on TV, all of that. It makes us look pretty foolish, huh?"

"Like bums."

"That's right. Hey, McNab was a popular TV reporter. Even though the family didn't push to have the murder solved, lots of other people did, and still do."

"There you go again, an inference that Senator and Mrs. Caldwell didn't cooperate in the investigation."

"Well, she wasn't really their daughter."

"I know that, but she might as well have been."

Jenkins checked a wall clock behind her. "Sorry, but I've got to move on. The commissioner wants to see me in a half hour."

"About the Caldwell case?"

"Who knows? Satisfied?"

"No."

"What'll make you happy?"

"The transcripts of the interviews you did, and a chance to look at the McNab file."

He shook his head.

"Back to square one, a subpoena."

"You want me to level with you, Lydia?"

"That would be refreshing."

"Come on, Lydia, I got a job to do, just like you, only for me the stakes are bigger. You and the committee will go through the motions and then announce that you didn't find anything that implicates the government or any government official in Caldwell's murder. Me, I'm still left with everybody looking over my shoulder and demanding that we solve the crime."

Lydia knew that much of what he said was true, and she felt some sympathy for him. She and the committee were dabbling in crime, dilettantes in a grimy game that he lived with every day and would continue to live with until he either retired or dropped dead.

Still, she knew she couldn't allow sympathy to get in the way of the job she'd taken on. She slipped her copy of the list into a slim leather briefcase. Jenkins saw the look of disappointment on her face and extended his hands across the desk, palms up, as though to say, Don't be mad at me.

"Thanks for your time," she said coolly.

"You want the transcripts?"

"I'll have them one way or the other."

"Just sit a minute." He swiveled in his noisy chair, opened a sliding door on a cabinet, leaned back so that

Lydia could see past him and said, "There's all the copies. They're too heavy for you to carry. Send somebody over for them."

She smiled. "Thanks, I really appreciate it."

His face hardened, and he pointed his index finger at her. "But I warn you, Lydia, that committee you're working for, like every other damn committee, has enough leaks to sink a destroyer. One leak on what I give you and you can go whistle for anything else. Now and forevermore."

"I'll remember that," she said, meaning it. His concerns were justified, and she determined to do everything in her power to keep the materials private and within the confines of the committee. "I'll have somebody over here this afternoon."

"Okay."

"What about the McNab files? Can I see them?"

"Yeah, but here. No copies."

"Fair enough. When?"

"Just call." He suddenly grimaced with pain. "Damn arthritis. I must have slept funny."

"Take an aspirin."

"Thanks, doc. Hey, do you know what I read in one of those flaky magazines my wife buys?"

"No, what?"

"That sex is the best medicine for arthritis."

"I wouldn't know about that."

"A pretty gal like you?"

"I don't have arthritis."

Lydia returned to her office in the Senate Building and arranged for a messenger to accompany her to MPD headquarters later that afternoon to transfer copies of the transcripts back to her apartment. She'd originally intended to ask Rick Petrone to handle the chore and bring the transcripts to the office, but Jenkins's warning about leaks weighed heavy on her mind. Until she'd personally had a chance to go through the transcripts there was no sense in having them in an office where staff members would have access to them.

She realized that Ginger had not been in all morning, and began to worry about her. At one o'clock the researcher called and said she'd been tied up at the library and would be in by three. Lydia asked about her dinner meeting with Quentin Hughes and was assured that she'd be given all the details when Ginger returned.

Lydia had lunch sent up from the Senate Dining Room. She'd been reluctant to do that but finally decided to take advantage of such services in the interest of saving time. She tipped the waiter, who delivered quiche Lorraine, a salad and black coffee. She wasn't sure whether tipping was proper in the Senate, but the quickness with which he accepted it settled the question.

Ginger arrived at four, just as Lydia was about to leave to meet the messenger service at Horace Jenkins's office. "Sorry I'm late," she said breathlessly, her red hair hanging in limp strands over her face. "I got engrossed in what I was doing and lost track of time. Where are you going?"

Lydia told her, then asked for a brief rundown on the Hughes meeting.

"I can't go over it that quickly," Ginger said. "I've got a zillion notes I made after I got home. But this is why I was late." She handed Lydia a copy of a newspaper article on which she'd circled in red a paragraph near the bottom.

Lydia skipped down to the circled portion.

> Chief Jenkins was asked whether an autopsy on the victim's body had been performed. He said that it hadn't, and went on to explain that the cause of death was so obvious that there was no MPD need for an autopsy.

"I don't believe it," Lydia muttered. "An autopsy is routine in murder cases."

"Not in the Jimmye McNab murder evidently," said Ginger. "It struck me as odd. That's why I circled it."

"I'm glad you did. I've got to go."

"Need any help?"

"No, thanks." The phone rang just as Rick Petrone entered the office. He picked it up, held it out for Lydia. "It's Senator Veronica Caldwell."

Lydia took the phone. "Hello, Veronica." She wasn't sure whether she should say "senator" despite their friendship, but her first name just naturally came out.

"Hello, Lydia, how are things going?"

"Getting there. How are you?"

"All right. I was wondering whether we could get together tonight?"

Lydia knew she had little choice but to agree, although she'd had her heart set on spending the evening in her apartment reading through the transcripts. "All right," she said.

"Would you come to the house?"

"Yes, of course. What time?"

"I won't be able to get away from here until six. Make it seven-thirty. We'll have dinner together."

"Fine, I'll see you then."

"Anything I can do for you tonight?" Rick asked after she'd hung up.

"No, thank you, Rick. I'm having dinner with Mrs. Caldwell."

"What happened today? I got caught up with Senator MacLoon's schedule and never got a chance to get over here."

"I thought you belonged to me."

"That's what I thought too, but he said you wouldn't mind losing me for a day. We had the vote on the Wyoming dam project and all hell broke loose. What did I miss?"

"Well, I think the MPD is about to start cooperating."

His face showed how impressed he was. "What did they give you?"

"Oh, not much, just enough to keep me reading for the next few nights." She started to leave. "You and Ginger will lock up?"

"Sure. Have a nice night."

It wasn't until she was in her Buick and about to join the flow of traffic that she realized she'd already told her staff members too much. She tried to remember whether she'd specifically mentioned that she'd been given the transcripts, then decided she hadn't and felt better about it. Besides, she had considerable faith in the people she was working with.

She headed directly for the MPD, where two young men from the messenger service were waiting. Forty-five minutes later they'd deposited the boxes of transcripts in her living room and left. She looked at the boxes, fought the urge to open one and headed for the shower.

At seven-thirty on the nose, dressed in a gray cashmere sweater and pleated green and blue tartan skirt, her face free of makeup, her hair pulled back, she arrived at the Caldwell house in Mount Vernon.

Thirteen

It wasn't until after dinner that Veronica drifted into a monologue about having taken Cale's place in the Senate. There was nothing maudlin about it, and she even spiced it with humorous asides about her Senate colleagues. "How about some more coffee in the den?" she asked.

"Love it," said Lydia.

The fire was almost out, and Veronica tossed two small logs into it, saying, "Cale made such wonderful fires. I suppose it was because he kept an eye on it, never allowed it to dwindle too low."

Lydia settled in a club chair and watched as Veronica arranged the coffee service on a rolling cart. It struck her then, as it had many times before, how smoothly and easily Veronica moved in a social situation. She had, of course, been born into a milieu in which social grace was expected. A good hostess never betrayed any hints of nervousness or lack of ease, and Veronica had learned the lesson well.

Aside from the pull of fatigue around her eyes, Veronica looked as lovely as ever. She wore a full plum skirt and frilly white blouse that buttoned high about her neck. Her auburn hair swooped softly over her temples and glistened in the flickering glow of the fire, like brandy picking up a candle's light. Her figure, always on the lean side, was still firm and supple, although a barely discernible thickening through the middle was evident if one bothered to look.

"Would you like something in your coffee?" Veronica asked.

"No, I don't think so."

"I think I will. Cale taught me the pleasure in that." She uncorked a bottle of cognac and added a few drops to her cup.

Veronica sat on the couch, sniffed the contents of her cup, then took a long, slow sip. "Well, where were we?"

"You were telling stories out of school," Lydia said.

"I suppose I was. Cale used to come home and we'd sit up late while he told me about what had happened during the day. God, Lydia, the Senate is an amazing mix of individuals, each with his own point of view. How anything ever gets done is a wonder of the world."

"I know what you mean. It's a maze."

Veronica sipped her coffee. "Exactly, a maze of conflicting needs and demands. Cale always said that negotiation was the key, negotiation and compromise. I used to argue with him sometimes for compromising his beliefs in order to get a bill through or to bring about harmony on a committee. I wish I hadn't..." For a moment, she thought her hostess might burst into tears. "Yes, compromise, Lydia, is the key to everything, including your work with the committee."

"Of course," said Lydia. "I'm well aware of that. I really haven't had to do much of it yet, but I'm certain my time will come—"

"Maybe it already has, Lydia."

"How so?"

"Suggesting that Jimmye's death be brought into Cale's investigation."

"Well...Jason mentioned to me that you were upset about that, Veronica. I'm glad you brought it up. I think we should discuss it."

Veronica placed her cup on the cart. "Lydia, I really

don't think there's too much to talk about when it comes to this matter. Frankly, personal feelings aside, I cannot for the life of me see anything of value to be gained by going into the old investigation of Jimmye's murder. It's a totally unrelated matter that coincidentally happened to a family that has just suffered a second tragedy. Jimmye was bludgeoned to death by a madman, probably a drug addict or former mental patient. At least that's what the police have decided. Cale was murdered by someone who obviously had some political or financial gain as a motive, or thought he had." Her laugh was forced. "I simply wouldn't have thought that someone with your usual clear view of things would even suggest lowering an entire Senate committee's role to something like this. This family is not a continuing soap opera, Lydia."

Lydia was taken aback at the tone of the comment. She said, rather reluctantly, "I'd hardly characterize my work with the committee as a soap opera, Veronica. I think that's unfair."

Veronica sat forward and held up her hands. "Please, Lydia, forgive me. I didn't mean it the way it sounded. It's been a long, hard day and my tongue evidently isn't connected to my brain at this point."

Lydia nodded. "We all suffer *that* malady now and then. Let's forget it was even said."

"Yes."

"But I would like to discuss Jimmye's death and how it might relate to the committee's investigation. I suggested to Senator MacLoon and to the full committee that we do it, and I still feel that way. Naturally, I'm willing to—"

"Compromise?"

"Well, to change my mind if there's some good reason that I've missed."

"Isn't the fact that her death is obviously not connected reason enough to drop it? The committee has a definite, narrow charter, Lydia—to investigate Cale's murder and to establish that it was in no way connected with government. Or, if it was, to identify that link, resolve it and allow the Senate to get on with its business with a satisfied American public behind it and not riddled with the sort of doubts that have plagued the Kennedy assassination for all these years."

"I understand that, Veronica, I really do. But what harm is there in at least looking at how Jimmye's death *might* shed some light on Cale's murder? I'm not suggesting a long drawn-out investigation, just a reasonable, limited examination of facts."

Veronica stiffened, although her voice did not reflect it. She said softly, "If you don't see the wisdom in what I say, Lydia, perhaps a more personal approach would be more acceptable. Frankly, I'm not sure I could stand up to another public hanging-out of Jimmye's wash. Can you understand that?"

"Yes, of course. You've been through far more than most people should ever be asked to take on. I recognize, I respond to that...perhaps more than you know. The thought of opening up Jimmye's case through the committee must be abhorrent to you. But I have to remind you, Veronica, that you were the one who pushed for a Senate committee in the first instance, and who asked me to serve as its special counsel."

"I'm aware of that. To be perfectly candid, one of the reasons for wanting you was the faith I had in your sense of decency and taste. I've always known you to be an extremely sensitive woman, Lydia, a compassionate one too. I'm asking for a demonstration of that now."

"Even if it means not doing my job?"

"We all bend at times, Lydia, in the name of decency, out of respect for our friends and their feelings."

Lydia was confused. What Veronica had said made sense, and yet something inside her rebelled against dropping the Jimmye McNab matter. "I'm having trouble sorting out how I feel, Veronica. I'm sorry, but that's the truth. If I promise to carefully reconsider introducing Jimmye into the investigation, will that do it, at least for this evening?"

"It will have to, won't it?" There was frost in her

voice. "Lydia...there's more to this than I've indicated."

"I wondered...I'd like to know."

"I'd hoped I wouldn't have to be this direct, but perhaps the direct approach is, as they say, the kindest. Senator MacLoon is extremely unhappy over you as special counsel. He feels that you haven't the experience in government to fully understand the meaning of such a committee and its role in Congress. As you know, he's dead set against expanding the investigation to include Jimmye's death. If you insist on going ahead, even though there isn't a shred of evidence to support it, I'm afraid your position with the committee might be in jeopardy."

"The committee job is not my life's work," Lydia said tightly. "I'm involved because I was asked to be by people for whom I care a great deal. I accepted the job because I think it's important. Also because it's a challenge. Naturally, I'd not like to be fired, but"—she shrugged and forced a smile—"if that's what comes from trying to do what I think is right, well, so be it..."

Veronica closed her eyes and slumped back into the cushions of the couch. "Of course, you're right," she said so softly that Lydia had to lean forward and ask her to repeat it. "I said 'you're right.' You must forgive me, Lydia, perhaps I've handled all this all wrong. That happens to people, I'm told, who try to act too brave in the face of personal tragedy and never allow the impact of it to be felt, to come out." She began to cry now. Lydia sat beside her and put her arm over her shoulder.

"I'm sorry," Veronica said.

"Don't be. You're right. There's a time to let down and perhaps this is it. Cry, cry until it's all out."

Which she did. Fifteen minutes later the two women stood together in the foyer.

"Thank you, Veronica...for a good evening."

"Thank you for being here when I needed you. I have to ask one thing, Lydia, about Jimmye."

"Yes?"

"Whatever you do, please do it gently, and discreetly."

"You can count on that."

"I knew I could...be careful driving."

"I will." She kissed her cheek and left.

She arrived back at her brownstone in Washington without any memory of the trip, her thoughts totally on what had happened with Veronica. She'd driven as though on automatic pilot, making her turns by rote, unaware of the automobiles she passed or of their occupants. Nor was she aware that a gunmetal gray sedan had followed her ever since she turned onto the highway outside the Caldwell estate.

Its driver parked a block away from the brownstone and waited until she had reached her bedroom and turned on the lights. He pushed a button on a cheap digital watch; its face lit up. He noted her time of arrival on a pad, lit a cigar and drummed his fingers on the steering wheel. He would be here for the rest of the night. An assignment was an assignment. As he often told his wife when she complained about his being out all night, "It's a living. You don't complain when you cash the checks."

Fourteen

It took Lydia two nights to read through the transcripts given to her by Chief Horace Jenkins, and she found little of overriding significance in them. Mark Adam Caldwell's statements were the most provocative. Although he'd said nothing overtly hostile toward his father, Lydia read between the lines a festering, unsettling animosity and wondered whether Jenkins had picked up the same thing. It occurred to her to check whether the interviews had been recorded. She assumed they had been. Certainly a great deal more could be found out by actually listening to the comments than from reading them on a typed page.

She called Clarence and asked whether his interrogator had used tape.

"Yes, he did. Why do you ask?"

"No reason, Clarence." She almost told him she had the transcripts but thought better of it. The fewer people who knew about it the better. As it stood, only she and Jenkins knew that they were in her possession. At some point, of course, she'd have to share them with the committee, but for now, there was something comforting about having sole possession.

She hadn't decided yet about whether to press the

McNab matter. She knew that if she did, she'd have to make a good case with the committee, and she couldn't even begin to build it until she'd had a chance to examine the McNab file at the MPD.

"Time," she muttered to herself as she sat behind her desk in the committee office and reviewed a preliminary list of potential witnesses to call before the committee once it shifted into that phase of the investigation. She had to do everything herself at this stage, though of course she'd created that situation by keeping the transcripts away from her office and staff, and by agreeing to personally review the McNab files.

She called Horace Jenkins at the MPD. He was grumpy, and when she said she'd like to spend Thursday reviewing the McNab files, he mumbled, "Just stay out of the way."

Ginger returned from lunch, hung up her pea jacket and closed the door. "Can I talk to you for a minute?"

"Sure."

The researcher, wearing beige corduroy pants tucked into tan cowboy boots, a heavy purple turtleneck sweater and a massive, noisy necklace made of random pieces of silver and copper, sat in a chair across from Lydia's desk and shook her head. "The older I get, the weirder people get."

Lydia couldn't help but laugh. "How old are you, Ginger, twenty-eight?"

"An old twenty-eight. Anyway, just before I went out to lunch I got a call from Quentin Hughes."

"What did he want?"

"Dinner."

"And...?"

"And this time he's invited me to his apartment at Watergate."

"Are you going?"

"Only because I'm a dedicated employee of the committee." Lydia smiled, but Ginger shook her finger. "I'm serious. Quentin Hughes is not my type. Well, I wasn't doing anything anyway. Harold still says he needs more space to get his act together about us. So,

(108)

I accepted. The point is I'd like to know just how important it is for you to know more about Hughes and his relationship with the late Jimmye McNab."

Lydia looked down at the mass of papers on her desk, sighed and said, "I don't know. You told me after your last dinner with Hughes that he wouldn't admit anything about a relationship with her. Right?"

"Right. But the way he avoided it makes me feel that there was something between them, maybe even more than the rumors indicated."

"The problem, Ginger, is that while it all might have some bearing on the Caldwell murder, I can't justify having you pursue it. To be honest, I'd have to say that at this point it doesn't seem to matter. If Hughes did have an affair with her, it can't tangibly be linked to what we're doing here. I wish I could encourage you because frankly I'm fascinated with it and have this nagging feeling that there *is* a connection between the two deaths. But I've been put on notice that to drag the McNab case into it might cost me my job and if I can't—"

"Well, maybe you're not so far wrong. This is what I really wanted to talk to you about. I had a date last night with an old friend, a nice guy who's recently divorced. He's really not my type, but what's a girl to do? I won't tell you his name because I wouldn't want to betray his trust. Understand?"

"I'm not sure...go on."

"Okay. Jack is an FBI man. I thought that was pretty heavy stuff until I got to know what he really does. He audits books, for God's sake, handles records, things like that. I mean, it was a real letdown when I realized he wasn't the one who shot Dillinger. Anyway, I told him that I was working on the Caldwell committee...I hope that's okay...I told him, and he asked me questions about it. I didn't answer all of them because I didn't want to be talking out of turn. But when I mentioned Jimmye McNab, he gave me one of those wry smiles and said, get this, that the rumor was that Senator Caldwell had had an affair with her—"

Lydia raised her hand to stop what was too offensive to hear.

"I'm not joking," Ginger said.

"How would this man know such a thing, even if it were true, which I'm sure it isn't."

"The pipeline."

"From the MPD to the FBI?"

She nodded. "He wasn't sure of the source and the circumstances, but he remembered talk about Senator Caldwell having been...how did he put it?...having been 'intimately involved' with Jimmye McNab."

"Nonsense. Caldwell was her father, or like her father. She was his wife's niece. They'd raised her like a daughter—"

"Not legally a daughter."

"It doesn't matter. I knew the man and his family. It's too farfetched even to speculate on such a thing." Or was it? she was forced to ask herself. She'd had a feeling about a connection. But *this*...?

Ginger fiddled with a broken fingernail and gave Lydia one of those "think what you want" looks. "All I'm doing is passing on what I was told. And he *is* with the FBI—"

"Did he say anything else that might substantiate it?"

"No."

"It's all too—"

"Too what?"

"Too soap opera." And Lydia immediately regretted saying it, remembering it was how Veronica had characterized her interest in the McNab murder.

"Some people say that's what Washington is, one long-running soap opera."

"Not to me, and not to you either. You're too young to be a cynic."

"Well, the point is that maybe there was a link between the murders...want my advice?"

"Of course."

"Follow it up. Ask around. Caldwell's sons, his wife. I think it's true."

"I don't." But of course she half did. It helped explain the feeling she'd had for so long that she couldn't express. "Let's go back to Quentin Hughes. You said he agreed to send over the videotape of the interview he did with Senator Caldwell."

"That's right. I'll ask him about it again tonight."

"Ginger, be careful tonight."

"Careful? Why?"

Lydia was sorry her motherly instincts had come out. She said in a deliberately light voice, "Well, you know, he's a lech."

"Old leches like him are never a problem."

Like hell, Lydia thought but didn't say. After Ginger left the office, she thought about their conversation, especially what Ginger had said about Cale Caldwell and Jimmye McNab. *"Absurd,"* she said to no one, not really believing her own disbelief.

Senator MacLoon's call broke in. He skipped the amenities. "Do we have a witness list yet?"

"I'm working on it, senator. It depends on decisions made by the committee this week. I wanted to bring it up at tomorrow's meeting."

"I'd like to have the list finalized by Friday and release it at a press conference."

"Press conference?"

"I think it's time to report on what progress we've made. Do you object?"

"I think it might be premature. The question of the McNab murder should be resolved first."

"You said you'd be presenting your reasons on that for the committee to consider. We're waiting."

"I'll try to do that on Friday. I think any press conference should be postponed until the middle of next week."

He made a show of patronizing indulgence. "All right, but let's wrap up things on Friday...a witness list, the McNab thing put to rest, all of it. Is *that* agreeable?"

"It will have to be, senator."

He hung up, and Lydia returned her attention to the

list of potential witnesses. It ran the gamut of Senate colleagues and employees, members of the Caldwell family, personal friends of the deceased and unspecified members of the Washington MPD.

She flipped through a Rolodex until coming to Cale Caldwell, Jr.'s office number, dialed it and told the woman who answered that she wanted to speak to Mr. Caldwell.

"Oh, hello, Miss James, this is Joanne Marshall. We met at Mrs. Caldwell's house. Hold on just a moment."

Cale came on the line. "Hello, Lydia, sorry to keep you waiting."

"That's all right. I was wondering whether we could get together today."

"Today's almost gone."

"I know, but there's been a shift in schedules that's pushed up my timetable. I'd really appreciate a chance to talk, even a half hour."

"Well, I can't get out of here this afternoon, but I could have a drink after work."

"That would be fine."

"How about Hogate's? Six?"

"Fine. Before you hang up, I was wondering whether you could put me in touch with your brother."

"Well, I...you could call him."

"I know, but I'd rather have you arrange a meeting between us, preferably before Friday."

"That might not be easy, Lydia. He's...you know how he is, very secluded down there with his friends, very much keeping to himself."

"Let me be honest with you, Cale. I'm making up the witness list for the committee. Naturally you and Mark will have to be on it. I thought it might be helpful for me at least to be able to preinterview your brother before he's subjected to the full committee's questions. I'm suggesting it for his sake, nothing else. I want to be helpful."

"I appreciate that, Lydia. Tell you what I'll do, I'll get ahold of him and suggest that he see you. I don't know what more I can do. I really don't have any control over my brother's life."

"I realize that, Cale. Anything you could do would be appreciated."

"I'll let you know when I see you how I made out. See you then."

An hour later she received a call from a man who introduced himself as Francis Jewel, executive director of the Center for Inner Faith, the cult Mark Adam Caldwell belonged to. "I understand you wish to speak with one of our brothers, Mark Adam."

"Yes, that's right. Did his brother call you?"

"Yes. It is our policy to shield our brothers and sisters from the secular life as much as possible. Naturally, since we are a law-abiding church, we are always willing to cooperate in legitimate matters..."

"That's to be admired, Mr. Jewel. Are you calling to arrange for the meeting I asked for?"

"Reluctantly. Obviously, our brother made a very unwise decision, attending a party. He was counseled against it but went against the wishes of his brothers and sisters, and his God. I recognize that there are certain obligations he now must meet regarding the investigation into his father's death. One must always pay for one's transgressions. His brother told me that you would be subpoenaing him to appear before your Senate committee but wished to speak informally with him first."

"That's right."

"You do realize that there is no binding reason for him to agree to this."

"Of course." His tone had begun to grate on her. "He's free, isn't he, to make his own decision in such a matter?"

"Apparently you're one of those who believe what you read about how we exert control over our members."

"I've heard things, Mr. Jewel. I don't prejudge. May I see Mark Adam Caldwell?"

"Under certain conditions. What happens to him reflects, of course, upon our entire church. I will agree to an interview with him, but I insist on being present. If that is acceptable to you, we can set a day and time."

"Why must you be there?"

"To protect his interests."

"His or *yours?"*

"Perhaps both. When would you like to see him?"

"Tomorrow morning?"

"Ten?"

"Fine."

"You know how to find us?"

"I'll manage."

Brother!

Cale Caldwell, Jr., was waiting at Hogate's bar when Lydia arrived. He was especially cordial as he greeted her, then placed their order with a busy bartender.

"Thank you for calling your brother's church for me."

"They got back to you?"

"Yes, a Mr. Jewel. I didn't like him, don't like anything about the arrangements that have been made, but I guess I have no choice. In order to see your brother, Mr. Jewel insists on being present during our conversation."

Cale smiled. "I agree with you, of course, but I suppose I've gotten used to it. Ever since Mark joined the Center for Inner Faith everyone in the family has been subjected to that sort of thing. I'm afraid there's nothing can be done about it. That's the way they work, and if you want something from them you play by their rules."

Lydia sipped her drink and stared at the highly polished bar. "It's bad, Cale. These cults and their hold over their followers. They're a real threat. There should be more investigations—"

"It's touchy," Cale said. "Start messing with religion, or what purports to be a religious group and you run the risk of being called intolerant, messing with constitutional rights...hey, you're a lawyer, you know all about it."

She nodded. "Still, after Jonestown...Anyway, what attracted your brother to it, do you know?"

He leaned on the bar and moved closer to her to allow a man behind him to reach for his drinks. "Mark is...well, Mark has always been different, Lydia. He has an intensity about him that, once upon a time, was appealing to mom and dad. He'd get into something and it became the only thing in the world. It didn't matter whether intellectually he knew it was dangerous. It was as though he went into a trance, all judgment was suspended. Still, it wasn't something that you could take serious exception to. After all, he excelled at whatever he did. He became the best wrestler in high school, the best weight lifter, the most knowledgeable astronomer. Nothing halfway with Mark. He could blot out the world once he dove into something. Frankly, I often envied him that single-minded dedication until, of course, it led him into something like this damn cult."

Lydia glanced around. The bar was filled with attractive people, animated in their conversations, eyes skirting the bar, appraising.

Someone recognized her and waved. She returned the greeting, then turned back to Cale. "Cale, do you think your brother was...capable of murdering his father? Do you think he had a reason to?"

For a moment she thought he might actually strike her. He gripped his empty glass, his mouth tensed. Then, abruptly, he seemed to relax. "Yes."

Now it was her turn to react. "You do understand that I'm not suggesting that he did."

"You said 'capable'...yes. My brother, as much as I love him, is a disturbed person. It's gotten worse over the years. Naturally, everyone in the family has denied it. After all, what's a family for?...Do I actually think Mark killed his father? Of course not..."

"Any ideas?" she asked, noting that his last words sounded more a demurrer than a denial.

"Your guess is as good as mine. I bet the police will never come up with a good answer, and the same goes for your committee. It will be another unsolved murder, more important than most because of dad's position, but unsolved...which of course will be the ultimate blow to mother, not having an answer to it. I hope it won't happen, but I bet it will."

"I'd like another drink, Cale."

"So would I."

After they were served Lydia decided to press him more on his brother as a good suspect.

He drew himself up straight, smiled pleasantly. "If you wouldn't mind, Lydia, I'd just as soon not talk about this any more."

"I'm sorry...well, how are things going with you?"

"Personally or professionally?"

"Either, both."

"Professionally, first-rate. Personally, up and down. Which makes me part of the human race, I guess."

"I suppose you're right. It seems easier to get professional things in line than personal ones."

"Ah, yes." He wiggled, Groucho Marx fashion, an imaginary cigar between his fingers. "Nothing is as unsolvable as the man-woman thing, right?"

"Right."

"Are you seeing Clarence?" he asked.

"We're old and good friends."

He shrugged, took a drink. "I thought there might have been more to it than that."

She said nothing. Then..."I had dinner with your mother."

"She told me, said it was a nice evening."

"Yes...she's an amazing woman, Cale, so strong, able to rise above the worst...I saw it when Jimmye died, and now again with your father."

The mention of Jimmye made him grimace. She decided to follow through on it. "Cale, can you think of anything that might link Jimmye's murder to your father's?"

He looked her in the eye, said very firmly, "No."

"Neither, it seems, can most people, including your

mother. She's quite upset that I've suggested it as an area of inquiry for the committee."

He nodded. "She told me."

"How do you feel about it?"

"The way she does. We'd all rather see Jimmye's death stay a thing of the past. It's too painful to bring it up, and it serves no useful purpose."

Lydia cocked her head. "Still, I'd think the family of a murdered daughter wouldn't... couldn't stop pressing until her killer was brought to justice—"

"Jimmye's a different matter—"

"Why?"

"Well, she wasn't, after all, a Caldwell—"

"Legally, no, in every other way, yes."

"Drop it, Lydia, for mother's sake. For *all* our sakes."

"I can't, not yet. I've promised to reconsider, but..." She thought about Ginger's news from her FBI friend, but of course made no mention of it..."Are you aware, by the way, that an autopsy was never performed on Jimmye?"

"I wouldn't know about that." He shifted position at the bar.

"Do you know why?"

He turned. "I said I wouldn't know about that."

"All right, Cale, I didn't mean to bring up a tender subject—"

"It's not a *tender* subject, it's just that..."

She waited for him to finish.

"Look, there were problems with Jimmye that no one outside the family knew about, and that's the way it should stay."

"I agree that family matters belong within a family, unless they have to do with a murder."

She waited for a response. He glanced at others at the bar, peered into his glass and ran a fingertip around its rim, then squinted at her. "Jimmye and my brother had a problem between them that damn near tore us all apart."

"What sort of problem?"

"A very personal one. It doesn't matter what it was.

The point is that to drag her life up now accomplishes nothing but opens all the sores. That's not fair, Lydia, it's not right."

"Cale, you have to believe me when I say that I have no interest in meddling in your family's affairs. Just the opposite. I hear what you say and I sympathize, I *do*...But I ask you again, is there *anything* to your knowledge that would support examining Jimmye's murder in light of your father's death? If there is, anything at all, it's not, to use your words, fair or right not to say so."

"No, nothing."

"This personal problem you mention between Jimmye and your brother. Are you inferring in any way that that might have had something to do with her death?"

"Of course not." He shook his head. "For God's sake, Lydia, how could you twist it around like that?"

"Cale, no matter what your feelings are, please at least take into account that I am special counsel, at your mother's suggestion, to a committee whose job it is to get to the bottom of—"

"I know, I *know*...one more for the road?"

"No, thank you. I appreciate your taking time to see me like this, and for arranging an interview with your brother. I'm sorry if I've upset you—"

"I want to help, Lydia. We all do. About Mark, just remember that you're dealing with a disturbed young man. Don't be shocked at anything he says or does. Don't take him too literally."

Lydia went to her brownstone, where she showered, slipped into a robe, made a sloppy grilled cheese and bacon sandwich and settled in again to review some of the transcripts, particularly those of Mark Adam Caldwell, Cale Caldwell, Jr., and Quentin Hughes. Perhaps it was the fact that Ginger Johnson was, at that moment, having dinner with Hughes that prompted her to dig his transcript out of the pile and read it again...

Later she put Mark Adam's transcript in her briefcase, took a map of Virginia from her desk and studied routes to her destination in the morning. The Center for Inner Faith. It was located on the Prince William County side of Occaquan Creek, a little over a mile from a small airstrip known as Woodbridge Airport. She couldn't deny her nervousness about making the trip and confronting Mark Adam within the grounds of the cult. She even considered calling in the morning and canceling the meeting. After all, nobody said she had to conduct private interviews with anyone of the suspects—just the opposite. MacLoon would be happy if she'd play the game, conduct a tidy, acceptable investigation leading to the desired conclusion that no one in official Washington had been responsible for or connected with the murder of the Senate Majority Leader. Get it over with, operate within the framework of MacLoon's dictates, enjoy the limelight and get back to private practice which would, undoubtedly, grow at an even faster rate because of the notoriety. A whole cadre of prospective clients had already approached her firm inquiring about representation. They'd read the articles about her in the papers and seen frequent mentions of her and of her role with the committee on the nightly news. *People* had called and wanted to do a feature about her. The advertising agency for a leading Scotch wondered whether she would be interested in being part of its ad campaign featuring bright, attractive and successful young women, for God's sake.

She'd become a celebrity in a town crawling with celebrities.

She forced the question from her mind, rolled a pillow beneath her head and virtually willed herself to sleep.

Ginger Johnson was using some willpower of her own at approximately the same time Lydia was searching for sleep. Quentin Hughes had turned nasty after she'd made it clear for the tenth—or was it fiftieth—time that she would not spend the night with him.

He'd started slow, had been a charming and entertaining host. He'd told her that the woman he'd been living with had recently taken off and that he was looking for a new "meaningful and permanent relationship." He'd actually said that. He'd served a pleasant white wine before dinner, then uncorked a bottle of red to serve with bacon-wrapped filet mignons he'd grilled on his Jenn-Air stove, complete with spinach salad, hot buttered French bread and for dessert, chilled slices of fresh pineapple.

Throughout dinner Ginger had asked questions about the Caldwell investigation. Hughes seemed disinterested in the subject. When she again brought up the videotape of his interview with Cale Caldwell, he told her that he'd changed his mind and that if anyone wanted to screen it they'd have to come to the studio. "I decided to cancel it at the last minute. Bad taste, showing an interview with a dead man."

Ginger knew Hughes had shown interviews with dead people before, and asked him why the Caldwell interview was different. He dismissed the question by coming around the table, putting his hands on her shoulders and kissing her on the neck. She squirmed free and they moved to the living room. From that point on the evening turned into an increasingly hectic seduction scene that ended with Ginger saying, "I don't really like men who come on too strong," and Hughes snapping, "And I don't like broads who tease."

There was no debate when the evening would end. Hughes had to leave to do his all-night show. Slumped in a chair, he asked Ginger to stay until he came back. She said she guessed not.

"You had your shot, you know," he said as she took her sweatercoat from the closet.

"At what?"

"At me."

"I'm sure I'll live to regret it, Mr. Hughes... Well, thanks for the dinner, and don't bother to get up. I can find the way."

She rode the elevator to the lobby, nodded to the doorman and went out to the street. She'd been lucky enough to find a parking space only two blocks away and started to walk to it, in the direction of the Potomac and the Kennedy Center for the Performing Arts...She sensed that someone was walking behind her, looked over her shoulder and saw the figure of a man shrouded in shadow moving quickly toward her. She increased her pace with each step until she was about to break into a run.

"Ginger."

The voice stopped her in her tracks. She turned... "Harold?"

"What were you doing in the Watergate?"

"I was...it's none of your damn business. What are you doing, following me?"

"Of course not. I just wanted to see what was so important that you couldn't see me."

"Me? You were the one who said you needed space to get your head together about us. I don't believe this. You were actually following me."

"You're crazy. I just happened to see your car and—"

"...and just knew that I was at the Watergate."

"I was around and—"

"Get lost, Harold."

"Please, Ginger, let's talk. There are things I want to say to you."

"Being followed, at my age."

"I told you I wasn't following you."

"Look, I don't want to see you again. Do you understand?"

He grabbed her arm, tried to pull her back in the direction they'd come from.

"Leave me alone, damn it."

"Just an hour. I've thought things out and—"

She wrenched free of his grip and stormed off toward where she'd parked her car.

"What were you doing up there?" he called after her. "Who'd you see?"

"The Washington Redskins, all of them," she said without looking back.

(121)

By the time she reached her car she'd softened some about Harold. Obviously he was jealous, which, after all, meant he cared a good deal. She'd think about that, and meanwhile decided she'd been too flip and mean with him about the Redskins. It was, though, a pretty good if nasty line...

She was half-smiling as she unlocked the car door, slid behind the wheel, started the engine and checked her mirror to see if it were clear for her to pull away from the curb. It was. She stepped on the accelerator and eased into the street. She hadn't gone ten feet when she realized that something was wrong. She got out and looked at the rear of the car. The tire on the driver's side was completely flat.

"Damn," she muttered, looking around for someone to help her. She went to the trunk and was about to open it when she noticed that the *other* rear tire was also flat.

This time her utterances were not as gentle. She realized she couldn't leave the car in the middle of the street but didn't want to drive on the flat tires. There was no choice. A few cars had already made wide circles around her, and one of the drivers had yelled something about women drivers who block traffic. Well, he knew what he could do.

She was about to get back into the car and go back to the space she'd just vacated when a man who'd been watching from the shadows of a building suddenly stepped out into the street, came up behind her and brought his fist down sharply across the back of her head. She fell to the pavement. He stepped over her, opened the car door, grabbed her oversized purse from the seat and ran up the street.

A woman who'd witnessed the attack ran to Ginger's side. "Are you all right?" she asked as Ginger struggled to sit up.

"My head," she said. "My God..."

"I saw it all," the woman said as she helped her to her feet.

"Who did it?" Ginger asked.

"I couldn't see his face, it all happened so fast."

Ginger suddenly swayed and grabbed the woman for support. "My head," she moaned.

The woman lowered her to the ground and told a small crowd that had gathered to call for an ambulance.

It arrived twenty minutes later.

Fifteen

The Center for Inner Faith consisted of a large main house and four outbuildings on sixteen acres of gently rolling farmland that sloped down to the banks of the Occaquan Creek. The land around the house was over-run with weeds and thickets. Bent, bare trees formed bizarre sculptures against a pewter sky.

A skinny yellow dog that had been asleep on the front porch raised its head and looked in the direction of Lydia's car as it moved slowly up a dirt road toward the house. The road was pitted and scarred, and she had to be careful to avoid some of the larger holes.

A young man with a shaved head, wearing a soiled, long white tunic, had been sitting by a front window. He too saw her car, sat up and shifted a .22 caliber rifle from his lap to a more ready position.

Lydia stopped twenty yards from the house, turned off the ignition and took in her immediate surroundings. She was overwhelmed by the bleakness and desolation of it all. If the Center for Inner Faith were, indeed, a church, it was not exactly advertising it. There were no signs, no crosses, no nothing but an old farm, its buildings weather-beaten, its land scarred by years of exposure and neglect.

As she got out of the car Lydia noticed the young

man in the window. She clutched her briefcase beneath her arm and went to the porch. The dog did not growl, nor did it get up to greet her. It stayed where it had been sleeping, its head raised. It had a sad face, or was that her imagination?

"Hello there," Lydia said as she climbed a decaying set of wooden steps. "Good boy." Calm down, she told herself. She needed it more than the dog...wrong, he needed it too.

A low, guttural growl made her stiffen. "Easy boy, easy...me Lydia, you friend—"

The front door suddenly opened and the young man who'd been observing her stood just inside, the rifle hanging loosely from one hand. "Miss James?" he asked in a high-pitched voice.

"Yes."

He stepped back to allow her to pass. She cast a quick, final glance at the dog and stepped inside. Immediately to the right was a large room furnished like an office. Logs burned brightly in a fireplace. A man sat behind an elaborately carved desk. He too had a clean-shaven head. He was considerably older than the one who'd let her in, and smaller. The massive desk dwarfed him even when he stood. "I'm Francis Jewel, Miss James. Please come in and warm yourself by the fire."

She entered the room. Jewel extended his hand and she took it. The touch of him was not pleasant. His hand was small and cold; it felt like wax.

"Thank you for allowing me to come."

"There seemed little choice," he replied, pointing to a ladderback chair next to the desk. "Would you care for coffee or tea? I'd recommend the tea. We make it with cinnamon, herbs and honey."

"The tea sounds fine." Jewel motioned to the young man at the door, then resumed his seat behind the desk. He leaned back, his tiny hands crossed on his chest, a weak smile on his lips. "Well, now, I suppose you'd like to see Mark Adam."

Lydia nodded.

"I'll have him summoned in a moment. Before I do

that, however, I must ask whether your interest in him is solely because of his father's death or because you have a parallel interest in our church."

Lydia wasn't sure what he meant and told him so.

"It's a reasonable question, Miss James. After all, when you've tried to serve God for years despite vicious attacks by those who do not share your faith and who feel threatened by it, you tend to become...how shall I say it, you become gun-shy."

Lydia crossed her legs. "I'm not threatened by your beliefs, Mr. Jewel. I'm here because of my work with a Senate committee charged with the investigation of Senator Caldwell's murder. Any personal interest in your church, if there were any, would be based on curiosity."

"You've read the untrue things said about us, I presume, heard them on television."

"Some, yes."

"And?"

"And how have I responded? Again, like most people. I do question some of the practices I've heard about, the means of raising funds, the alleged control exerted over church members." She almost said cult instead of church and was glad she hadn't. She was also disappointed in herself that she'd so quickly been drawn into a discussion about the cult in the first place. "I really would rather not discuss your church, if it's all right with you. That's not my purpose here."

"But you will take away with you certain impressions of us. I think it only fair that I have an opportunity as the executive director to present a more balanced picture...Oh, here's our tea." It was poured from an elegant silver teapot into antique china cups. Lydia tasted the tea, nodded her approval.

"I'm glad you like it, Miss James. That will be all, Richard." The young man left the room, closing a set of sliding doors behind him.

"Now, Miss James, while we enjoy our tea and the fire, allow me to tell you a little about the Center for

Inner Faith. *I* will tell you the truth. I hope you are ready to hear it."

"I'm not sure it matters whether I am or not."

Twenty minutes later he'd gone through what Lydia was certain was a canned speech, filled with positive images of The Center and its goals. He pointed out that cult members were in no way restricted in their movements. As long as they were faithful to the cult's beliefs, he told Lydia, they were free, actually encouraged to mingle with the outside world and to carry their faith to others.

Lydia realized that he was at least technically correct...members of the cult were often seen in town, handing out leaflets, stopping passers-by to tell their story and, of course, to solicit funds. Physically, at least some of them seemed free. The extent of mental control was another matter, which she was tempted to raise but didn't.

Jewel also said that he was only the administrative head of the church, and that its spiritual leader, the Reverend Sylvan Quarles, was the pivot point around which everything revolved.

Lydia knew about Quarles from what she'd read in the papers. He was in his late sixties, tall and charismatic, with a stentorian voice and flowery vocabulary, an impeccable dresser whose eyes, they said, blazed when he spoke. It was also said that he could mesmerize his audiences, although a psychiatrist friend had once explained to Lydia that the real power was within the listener. This psychiatrist used hypnosis in his practice for behavior modification, for smoking and obesity, and told Lydia that each person had an inborn capacity to enter a hypnotic trance. The ones with a high capacity were most easily persuaded. They tended to suspend critical judgment, surrender it, when confronted with an authority figure.

Throughout his lecture she nodded when appropriate, asked a few questions to clarify points even though she wasn't interested in having them clarified, and patiently waited for him to finish so that she could get to Mark Adam Caldwell.

"Any questions, Miss James?" Jewel asked as he finished his spiel.

"No."

"This administrative center is one of four sanctuaries in Virginia. We have centers in eleven other states, and have recently opened them in Germany and France."

"That's very impressive, and I might like to discuss it further with you at some later date, but I do have a time problem today. Could I please see Mark Adam Caldwell now?"

Jewel went to the door, said something to the young man, who'd kept a vigil in the hallway. Jewel returned to the desk and, moments later, Mark Adam entered the room. He wore the same sort of robe worn by the other young man, except that his was freshly laundered and ironed.

"Hello, Mark," Lydia said, standing.

His face was blank as he took two steps toward her, extended his hand and gave her a single nod of his head.

"Sit down, Mark," Jewel said. The boy took a chair on the opposite side of the desk and stared straight ahead, past Jewel and out a window.

"I told you that Miss James wanted to speak to you," Jewel said, "and I agreed that she could. I'll be here with you all the time."

It appeared to Lydia that Mark Adam was either drugged or in some unexplained state of altered consciousness. She felt as though she'd entered a mental institution and was visiting a patient. "How are you?" she asked Mark.

Slowly he turned his head and looked at her, as though to get a fix on her identity, then said in a near-monotone, "I'm very well, thank you. I'm very happy. How are you?"

"I'm fine, Mark. It's good to see you again."

He returned his attention to the window.

"Mark, are you feeling well?"

"Mark is doing wonderful work here at the center," Jewel said. "He's found an increasingly close relationship with God and serves him with all his spirit. Isn't that right, Mark?"

"Yes. God gives me the day and night, and I use them for his glory."

Lydia cleared her throat, opened her briefcase and pulled out a yellow ruled legal pad on which she'd written the questions she wanted to ask. "Mark, as you may know, I've been appointed special counsel to a Senate committee to investigate your father's murder. That's why I'm here. You'll be called to testify before the committee sometime in the near future, but I wanted to have a chance to talk with you first. You don't have to, you know. If you'd like, you can ask for a lawyer to be with you whenever you say anything about your father's death."

"I know that." He said it with more animation than before—a sullen-voiced animation.

"I discussed it with Mark," Jewel said, "and he realizes his rights. We have his best interests at heart here. We're all one large and loving family."

Lydia ignored Jewel. "Mark, do you know anyone who might have wanted to kill your father?"

He shook his head.

She hesitated, then asked matter-of-factly, "Did you want to see him dead?"

His face again took on a hint of animation. He looked directly at her. "No."

"You said things to the police, Mark, that might be construed as being . . . well, as being hostile toward your father. Would you agree that you felt anger toward him?"

"Of course he did," Jewel said. "Mark Adam's father was hardly what you would call a decent God-fearing man."

"Mr. Jewel, I'd appreciate it if you would allow Mark to answer the questions himself. Having you here is one thing, answering for him is another."

Jewel pursed his lips, which drew his small nose to an even finer line. One finger stroked his cheek as he prepared to speak. Lydia didn't wait. She went back to Mark and asked, "Do you understand why I'm asking these things, Mark? I've been a friend of your family for years and I want to help in any way I can. I also have a duty to attempt to get to the truth. I'd like to find that truth without hurting those people I care about, and you're one of them."

"No one cared about him until he came here," Jewel said.

Again she ignored him. "Mark, some people think that Jimmye's murder might, in some way, shed some light on your father's death. What do you think about that?"

Jewel raised up in his chair. "Really, Miss James, is it necessary for such cruelty? The boy has lost his father as well as a sister... to bring up that unfortunate incident is, to me, unconscionable."

"Mark, I ask you again, do you think that Jimmye's—"

"Jimmye was a harlot, a *Messalina hetaera*."

"What?"

"She sinned and was punished. It's as it should be."

"She was like a sister, Mark."

"She was a sister of the Devil," he said in his near-singsong voice. "She gave her body to the Devil." He shifted in his seat and placed his large hands flat on the desk. The thick, muscular body beneath the robe began to tremble. "Those who sin against the Father must be punished."

Or with the father? she couldn't help think to herself...

"I think this has gone far enough," Jewel said. He patted Mark's forearm. "I don't think Miss James has any further questions for you, my son. You can return to your duties."

"No, I'm not finished," Lydia said. "I'd like to know why he attended his father's party after so many years of estrangement. I'd like to know about Jimmye and his relationship with her. I'd—"

But Mark Adam had already stood up, turned and left the room.

"I resent the way this has been handled," Lydia told Jewel. "The boy seems in another world. What have you done to him?"

"We have given him peace and hope, something you probably wouldn't understand, Miss James. He came from a family of sinners, rich and powerful people who abused their position here on earth, who defied their God every day of their lives. Here Mark Adam is with those who shun the secular, the materialistic, the sins of society. Here, Miss James, he can fulfill his Father's wishes for him."

"His father is dead. His father has been murdered."

"Good day, Miss James."

She placed her materials in her briefcase, zippered it shut and left the house, her every movement under the scrutiny of the armed young cult member.

She drove back to Washington as quickly as possible, stopped in at her private offices, where she was filled in on developments during her absence, dictated a sheaf of letters into a recorder while she munched halfheartedly on a chicken salad sandwich delivered from a local luncheonette, called Clarence but didn't find him at home, then finally called her committee office in the Senate. Rick Petrone answered.

"How's everything?" she asked, her mouth half-filled with chicken salad.

"Where have you been?"

"I've spent the morning with crazies, I'm sorry to say."

"Looks like Ginger spent an evening with one."

"What do you mean?"

"She was mugged and robbed last night—"

"*What?* My God...is she all right?"

"A concussion. She's at Doctors Hospital. They say

she'll be okay. The guy hit her over the head and stole her purse. After he'd slashed both rear tires on her car."

"Good Lord, I'll be there in an hour. Will you be there?"

"I'll hang around."

"Any calls?"

"A dozen or so. Where were you this morning?"

She briefly told him of her trip to the cult headquarters.

"You ought to stay away from places like that."

"I'm sure you're right. See you."

Twenty minutes later Senator Wilfred MacLoon walked into Veronica Caldwell's Senate office, closed the door behind him. "This whole situation with Lydia James is getting out of hand. She thinks she's Sam Spade and Sherlock Holmes rolled into one."

"Why do you say that?"

MacLoon, briefed by Rick Petrone, told her about Lydia's trip to cult headquarters and her interview with Mark Adam.

Veronica's lips tightened. "All I can say, Will, is that if I've made a mistake in pushing for Lydia James to be special counsel, I meant well. I spoke with her recently and rather thought I'd gotten through to her that—"

"What did you tell her?"

"Oh...just that the committee has a limited function and that all other aspects of Cale's death are the business of the MPD."

"Evidently she doesn't listen too well."

"I'll speak with her again."

"Please do. I want this committee to be out of business within a month, and it never will be if I have to put up with her nonsense. By the way, did you hear about that researcher on her staff, Ginger Johnson?"

"No."

MacLoon told her what Rick Petrone had reported.

"Well...I certainly hope she's all right."

"Oh, they say she will be... I haven't had lunch yet. Today's Oregon Day. They flew in salmon steaks. Join me?"

"I'd love to. Thank you, Will."

Sixteen

Harold drove Ginger home from the hospital the following day. The doctors told her she'd suffered a concussion and was to spend a few days in bed. She protested but Harold insisted that she follow their orders. Reluctantly she crawled into bed while he went to the kitchen to heat up a can of tomato soup. When he came back to the tiny bedroom, she was on the phone with Lydia.

"You're not supposed to talk," he said in a loud voice.

She held up a finger to silence him, then said to Lydia, "I'm feeling okay, I guess. I just called to see what was going on."

"Nothing that can't wait. The important thing is for you to get some rest and come back to work fit as a fiddle. One thing, though, before I hang up. What about screening Quentin Hughes's videotape of the Cale Caldwell interview?"

"Oh, right. He says we can come to the studio to see it."

"Okay. I'll call him and set something up. Ginger, do what Harold says, and if you need anything, just yell."

"I will, Lydia, and thanks."

Lydia's call to WCAP-TV was taken by Hughes's producer, Christa. Lydia explained what she wanted and Christa told her she'd check with Hughes and get back to her. An hour later she did and suggested that Lydia come to the station at five that afternoon....

After waiting ten minutes in WCAP's reception area, Lydia was escorted by Christa to a small editing room in the building's basement. Waiting there were Quentin Hughes and a young woman who, although not introduced, was obviously a tape editor familiar with the room's dazzling array of electronic equipment.

Hughes barely acknowledged Lydia. "Ready?"

"Yes."

"Go ahead," he told the editor. She pressed some buttons and two TV monitors came to life.

A half hour later the videotape came to an end with Hughes saying goodbye to his viewers and thanking the Senate Majority Leader for being his guest.

"All right?" Hughes asked Lydia as the lights came on and the monitors went to black.

"Yes, thank you. It was so...sad seeing him there on the screen, so vibrant and alive—"

"Yeah, well he isn't that now."

"No, he's not. I may want to see it again. That will be possible, I assume."

"Yeah, I guess so, give a call."

She got up and Christa returned her to the reception area on the main floor.

"If there's anything else I can do to help you and the committee, Ms. James, please let me know," Christa said. "I mean that."

As they said goodbye Lydia asked, "Were you there during the taping?"

"Yes, of course. Why?"

"Oh, nothing. There were some things about Senator Caldwell's actions, his appearance, that seemed...well, seemed a little out of place, that's all."

"I don't recall anything unusual," Christa said.

"Probably just my imagination. Well, thanks again. I appreciate it."

"Anytime."

She drove directly to her Senate committee office, flicked on a tape machine and was about to dictate her thoughts about the interview she'd just seen when Veronica Caldwell knocked, opened the door and stepped inside. Lydia placed the microphone in its cradle. "Hello, Veronica. What a nice surprise."

"I was just getting ready to leave and thought I'd stop in and see how your researcher was doing. I heard about it and was shocked. How is she?"

"Doing well, I spoke with her today. She's home and resting."

"Thank God. And how are you?"

"Busy...I'm just back from WCAP. I saw the interview Cale did with Quentin Hughes."

"Oh? Why?"

"Curiosity, in part. But mostly to take every opportunity to try to better understand...This will sound foolish, I guess, but one thing that struck me...it was the first time I'd ever seen Cale less than impeccable...."

"What do you mean?"

"Well, he fiddled the whole interview at a nonexistent button on his shirt collar. Not like Cale to show up anywhere, let alone a TV show, like that..."

"Really?"

"Yes...for him to go to a TV taping with a button missing on a button-down shirt—"

"Oh, but he didn't."

"What?"

Veronica laughed. "Of course not. I remember that day very well. He'd just received a new shipment from Wendley in New York. He always ordered his shirts from them, they kept his measurements on file. He was so fond of their shirts, especially the button-down ones. He said he liked the slightly higher collar they had. Anyway, the day he went to tape Quentin's show he took out a fresh shirt from the shipment. I distinctly remember because he was showing it off to me. As they say, he had all his buttons."

Lydia laughed too. "Well, he lost one of them before the taping. So much for that..."

"I understand you paid Mark Adam a visit..."

"Yes."

"How was he?"

"Fine, he...oh, why am I saying 'fine'? I was shocked at what I saw. He seemed to be drugged, or under some other sort of control. Frankly, I was appalled."

Veronica's face hardened, she fidgeted with her purse. "I know it must be dreadful for you to know the situation he's put himself in. I'm so sorry..." She forced a smile. "You can never tell about children, Lydia. You bring them up, give them all you can and do your best. Then they become adults, and, well, you just don't matter anymore...They go their own way...Fortunately Cale, Jr., took a different direction. He made his father very proud."

"He must have...I'm hesitant to bring this up, Veronica, but I might as well take advantage of your being here—"

She held up a gloved hand. "From the way you said that, I think I'd rather not be here."

Lydia stifled an urge to ignore what was on her mind, but she pushed on..."I understand there was a personal problem of some sort between Jimmye and Mark Adam."

Veronica seemed to ignore her.

"What was the problem, Veronica?"

"Lydia, I have no idea what you're talking about."

"I can't believe that, not after what Mark himself said about her. Please, Veronica, it might put some light on what happened to Jimmye and to Cale. I'm *not* just prying, have never meant to..."

There was no masking Veronica's anger. She stood. "I've made a great mistake in trusting you, Lydia. I resent the inference in what you just asked me."

Lydia's early embarrassment was evaporated in her own rising anger, not just at Veronica but at the whole frustrating experience since she'd joined the committee. They gave her a responsibility, then the same people who'd given it seemed hell-bent on keeping her from carrying it out. Now, as Veronica got to the door and was about to open it, she decided to go all the way..."And what about *Cale* and Jimmye?"

Veronica stopped, turned slowly. "I've had enough, you've really gone too far. For reasons best known to yourself, you've twisted everything decent about my family to satisfy some extraordinary need that I never dreamed existed in you. You've taken a public trust and betrayed it, made a scandal sheet assignment of it. I assure you you will no longer be in a position to do that." She slammed the door behind her.

Lydia sat there, stunned. She dug her fingernails into the palm of her hand. *How could you?* Never before in her life had she acted so impetuously, spoken with such disregard for another person's feelings. She'd been totally out of line. Veronica's reaction was right and to be expected. She considered going after her to try to apologize but didn't. She'd wait a day, then call...

Sleep did not come easily that night, and she woke up the next morning feeling groggy and very out of sorts. She was due at the MPD to review the Jimmye McNab file and now was tempted to cancel the whole thing. After last night...

She wrapped a robe around herself, put on the tea-kettle and went to the front door, where the *Post* would be waiting. She tossed it on the kitchen table and took a shower, finishing off with very cold water to clear her head. She removed the whistling kettle from the stove and made a cup of black instant coffee.

As she sat at the table and opened the folded paper to its first page, her eyes focused on the top, heavy headlines. But then she noticed a small box at the bottom of the page, with a headline that read: BREAK REPORTED IN CALDWELL MURDER.

The article jumped to an interior page, but the paragraph and a half on page 1 gave the essence of the story.

A major break in the unresolved ice pick murder of Senate Majority Leader Cale Caldwell was reported last night by Deputy Chief of Police of the Washington Metropolitan Police Department, Horace Jenkins. Jenkins made the statement during an informal press conference in his office.

When pressed by reporters, Jenkins refused to elaborate, except to say, "The Caldwell murder has resulted in the most intensive investigation in this department's history, and it looks like it's about to pay off." Chief Jenkins went on to discuss certain elements.

cont. on page 22

The rest of the article simply recounted the events of Caldwell's murder and its aftermath.

Lydia dressed and drove to the MPD. Surrounding Jenkins's office were media people clamoring to talk with him. Lydia told one of the officers in the bullpen that Jenkins was expecting her. Moments later he came back to say, "He wonders whether you could come back this afternoon."

"No."

Some of the reporters came over to Lydia and asked her about the reported break in the case.

"I know what I read this morning in the paper, that's all," she said.

"Come on, Miss James, why are you here if you're not in on it?"

"Believe me, I was as surprised as..."

The young officer came out of Jenkins's office for a second time and motioned for Lydia to go in.

"Good morning," she said.

"Nothing good about this morning, kid."

"From what I read in the paper you should be celebrating."

"That'll happen when the time comes. You still want to see the McNab file?"

"You said I could."

"Things change, you're wasting your time."

(140)

Lydia sighed and sat up straight. "You know, chief, I'm really getting very tired of people telling me that I'm wasting my time."

"In a few days it won't matter anyway."

"Why?"

"Nothing. Look, this Caldwell thing is going to be over very soon. You can make book on that. There's not going to be a need for any Senate committee because there won't be anything left to investigate."

"What is this so-called major break in the case?"

"I wouldn't tell you if my life depended on it. In fact, my life does depend on it." He leaned across his desk, said conspiratorially, "Do you really think I'd tell you, or anybody else, what we've got? Hey, Lydia, I may not be a genius but that dumb I'm not. This is the biggest case I've ever had, and sharing credit for breaking it doesn't hit me as very intelligent."

"You know who did it?"

"No comment."

"I'm not with the media, I'm—"

"Got to go, Lydia."

"When do you expect an arrest?"

"Soon, have a nice life."

"I'm not leaving until I can see the McNab files."

"I told you to forget it."

"If you want, I'll go outside and tell the press how the MPD has refused to cooperate with the Senate. I'll tell them—"

"Don't threaten me. I prefer to remember you as you were. Sorry, but that's all the time I have."

Lydia picked up her purse and briefcase, and went downstairs and left the building.

As she reached the end of the street, a car carrying four men turned the corner, just missing her. She stood at the curb and watched two of the men get out and waited for a third to exit through an open rear door. A couple of reporters who'd been hanging around the side entrance to the MPD approached the car. The driver jumped out and intercepted them.

Moments later, the fourth man in the car slowly

came through the door. He was handcuffed. The other two men grabbed his arms and led him toward the entrance. He turned and looked down the street to where Lydia stood, then looked up at the sky. The flesh at the rear of his shaved head and neck folded over the loose collar of his white robe.

Before Lydia had time to mutter the name Mark Adam, he was whisked away from advancing newsmen and shoved through the door.

Seventeen

Lydia and Clarence, sitting on a couch in his apartment, stared at the television screen as the anchorman came on and said, "The top story tonight is a confession in the Senator Caldwell murder. Back with details after this."

Rousing, dissonant march music, the newcast's title and subtitle, commercials, for antifreeze and a feminine deodorant. Then:

"Good evening, I'm Richard Bourne. A confession today in the ice pick murder of Senate Majority Leader Cale Caldwell. In an announcement at MPD headquarters this morning, Deputy Chief of Police Horace Jenkins had this to say..."

Jenkins was seen seated behind his desk, surrounded by reporters, reading from a piece of paper in front of him: "Mark Adam Caldwell, the older son of slain Senate Majority Leader Cale Caldwell, has confessed to his father's murder. He is in custody here..."

A rush of questions. Jenkins held up his hand. "There's nothing more I can say at this moment, ladies and gentlemen. The resolution of this murder has resulted from a painstaking and thorough investigation by this department. It's a sensitive case, and everyone concerned with it is determined to protect the integrity of the investigation and the rights of the accused."

The anchorman took over. "Sources close to the investigation have informed us that the younger Caldwell's confession was detailed and complete, and that the motive for having murdered his father derived from a long-standing personal problem within the Caldwell family."

Followed by a commercial.

"Clarence, it just can't be—"

"Why not?"

"It's too...it's just too simple, too pat. And if Mark Adam did kill his father, why confess to it? Or why wait until now? No, I can't buy it."

"Well, I do. Murder will out, it's over, and now you can go back to making more time for me...for us. As you know, I'm a very selfish person."

She managed a smile, put her arms around him—and the phone rang.

Clarence answered, shrugged and held out the receiver for Lydia.

"Hello," she said.

"What about Jimmye McNab?" A female voice.

"Who *is* this?"

"Don't believe what you hear."

The line went dead.

Lydia told Clarence of the call.

"You didn't recognize her voice?"

"No. But it sounded like she was trying to disguise it, make it sound deeper."

Clarence gave her a sidewise look and put on a recording of harpsichordist Wanda Landowska playing Bach's dance suites. "Landowska to the rescue. Stop thinking and listen."

Lydia sighed, leaned back and closed her eyes as the slightly twangy, mandolin quality of the harpsichord filled her ears and touched down to her soul.

After a while she said, "Clarence, I'm exhausted, drained, like somebody pulled a plug. I want to go home, hit the old sack. I'm sorry..."

She didn't immediately move to leave the comfort of the couch, and he reached over and stroked her hair, her forehead. "Such deep, dark thoughts," he said softly. "Your forehead is a mess of furrows."

"I suspect it will be for quite a long time." She turned to face him. "Remember the night of Cale's murder, Clarence, when we talked about crime in terms of the cycle of fifths?"

"Sure. Like a piece of music, murder has resolved itself too. It started in the key of C and has returned there, to the tonic chord."

She smiled and stood up. "Unless we've reached a C-seventh."

"Don't get smart."

"A C-seventh, instead of just C. Once you add the seventh to a chord, it stays up in the air, suspended, looking for its own tonic."

He stood up too and put his hands on her shoulders. "If it *is* a C-seventh instead of the tonic C, that means it goes into another key."

"Exactly. It could resolve to F and the piece will be over. Then again the C-seventh might only be the second chord in a new key we're playing in."

"And if that's true, the 'Caldwell Sonata' could have a long way to go before it's over."

"That's what frightens me, Clarence. I was listening to one of the cassettes you bought me. The tune was 'Mack the Knife,' and the group took twelve choruses on it, playing each one in a different key. They started in C, went up a half step each time until they eventually returned to C."

"And?"

"And *I* think Mark Adam's confession is only one half step toward a long series of key changes."

"I won't argue with you," he said as he helped her on with her coat. "I'd rather make love, but you do look exhausted. Sure you don't want to stay?"

"Thanks, yes...but also no. I'll call you in the morning."

All the way home she thought of the phone call and

the unidentified woman's reference to Jimmye McNab. The thoughts stayed with her as she sat in the tub and enjoyed the warm, sensuous feeling of muscles relaxing. She dried herself vigorously, slipped into a chocolate brown monk's robe that reached the floor and turned on the television. She fell asleep, waking as the eleven o'clock news came on. She rubbed her eyes and tried to focus on the screen. The first words out of the anchorman's mouth jolted her upright and to the edge of the couch.

"Extraordinary developments this day, ladies and gentlemen, in the Cale Caldwell ice pick murder. Not only has the deceased senator's elder son, Mark Adam Caldwell, confessed to his father's death, but we have just been informed that he has also confessed to the murder of journalist Jimmye McNab. McNab, you might recall, was not only one of Washington's most respected television reporters, she had also been brought up by the Caldwell family from infancy. I'll be back with more details in a moment."

The phone rang. It was Rick Petrone, aide to Senator Wilfred MacLoon.

"You've heard?"

"Yes. I'm shocked."

"Everybody is, I guess. Anyway, Senator MacLoon would like a meeting of the Caldwell committee at nine. Can you make it?"

"Yes, of course. By the way, have you heard from Ginger?"

"She called, says she's feeling fine. She'll be in in the morning."

"I think she should take more time to rest."

"There'll be plenty of time for that now."

"What do you mean?"

"The Caldwell murder has been solved by the MPD, there's no need for a committee."

"I'm not so sure..."

"Okay, Lady Hawkshaw, have it your way. See you at nine."

* * *

The meeting was held in a large committee room a few doors down from Wilfred MacLoon's offices. Lydia was surprised that in addition to the regular members of the committee and selected staff members, Veronica Caldwell and Deputy Chief of Police Horace Jenkins were there. She told Veronica that she hadn't expected to see her.

"Why not, Lydia? You should be very pleased with yourself. It seems you were right, that there was a connection between Cale's and Jimmye's..." And then she turned away, to hide her upset, Lydia assumed, at this awful news about her first-born son.

Lydia hesitated, then caught up with her just inside the committee room door. "Look, Veronica, I apologize for some of the things I've said and thought, but I'd like to say something else that you may welcome hearing—"

"Then for God's sake say it. Say it and go back to your comfortable little law practice and leave me and my family alone."

"I don't believe Mark Adam did what he's confessed to."

"I wish it were true—"

"I know you do." She touched Veronica's arm. "Don't just accept this, Veronica, for your sake and for your son's. You demanded a committee to get to the bottom of things. Don't let that committee dissolve because Mark Adam has said things that might not be true. He's not a well person, Veronica, not responsible. At least you could..."

"*That's* enough, Lydia. On top of everything I don't need your amateur analysis of my son." She turned and walked off to where some committee members stood, leaving Lydia feeling very much alone.

When she returned to the site of the meeting, Wilfred MacLoon had just arrived and had taken his place at the head of the conference table. Others settled into chairs. Lydia sat at the far end of the table, between Senator Jack Markowski and Horace Jenkins.

MacLoon lit a fresh cigar, opened a file folder,

glanced around the table. "Glad everyone could make it this morning. I'd especially like to welcome Senator Caldwell and Deputy Chief Jenkins. I'm sure we all share the grief our colleague, Senator Caldwell, has suffered. The only bright spot is that finally the pain of all this will be alleviated by putting to rest the public speculation that has turned this tragedy into a media circus." He looked down the length of the table at Lydia. "Now, let's get down to business and do what we all agree must be done. Because the MPD has done its job, two murders have been solved. I congratulate the MPD and you personally, Chief Jenkins, for an exemplary piece of law enforcement."

"Thank you," Jenkins said.

Nuts to you, Lydia thought.

MacLoon continued. "Chief Jenkins and I conferred last night, and the upshot is we're convinced—I know how this must pain you, Veronica—that the confessions will hold up. Is that correct, chief?"

Jenkins cleared his throat, rubbed his eyes. "That's correct, senator." He looked unhappily at Veronica Caldwell. "I hate to even talk about this thing with Mrs. Caldwell sitting here, but I suppose the fact that she is here shows what kind of woman carries the Caldwell name. You've got more guts than any ten other women I know," he said, his voice faltering as he wondered whether he was putting it in the right words.

"Thank you," Veronica said. "You are right, this *is* very painful and distasteful, but I've assured Senator MacLoon that it is my job not to let personal feelings interfere with...justice. I'll overcome the personal impact of it in the interest of seeing that I do my job...I love my son very deeply and I tell you now I will do all I can to help him, defend him...He's a troubled young man, and regardless of what he has done...my love for him remains. I'm sure you understand that."

Jenkins cleared his throat. "Like I said, this woman is incredible." He turned to MacLoon. "The young man's confession is complete for both homicides, and his rights were protected every inch of the way, so there's no chance of—"

"Does he have an attorney?" Lydia asked.

Her question caused everyone to turn and to look at her. Jenkins answered her question in a voice that unmistakably reflected his annoyance. "Of course," he said.

"Who?"

"His brother."

"Cale, Jr.?"

"That's right. He plans to retain other counsel for his brother in due time, but he was there the minute we went down to the cult and picked up his brother. Like I said, the accused's rights were protected every inch of the way, not only by a qualified attorney but by his own brother."

Jenkins concluded his statement with an assurance that not only had Mark Adam confessed, he'd given every detail of both murders that had not, in any way, conflicted with known facts. Rather, they'd confirmed them.

MacLoon said, "It's my suggestion that we immediately conclude this committee's business and issue a public statement to that effect."

Silence, until Senator Markowski put in, "Isn't that a little premature, Will? After all, the suspect hasn't even been indicted yet, let alone tried and convicted." He looked at Chief Jenkins. "With all due respect, chief, simply having someone from the MPD proclaim that the murder we've been charged with investigating is solved isn't, it seems to me, sufficient reason for a Senate committee to fold up and go home."

"I disagree, this isn't a court of law—"

"Senator MacLoon," Markowski pressed on, "the Dallas police *solved* the murder of Jack Kennedy, didn't they? But that hasn't precluded Congress from conducting continuing investigations into it."

MacLoon chewed on his cigar, glared at his younger colleague. "If somebody else wants to come along later and make up another committee, that's their business.

As far as I'm concerned, this committee's business is finished."

"As special counsel to this committee I must agree with Senator Markowski," Lydia said. "It seems to me that the least we can do for the American people we're supposed to represent is to continue our work until there is a conviction. At that time, after listening to the complete report of the MPD and examining the trial record, we can determine that no branch of government was involved, nor any member of government."

"Miss James, it should make you feel better to know that your insistence that there was a connection between Senator Caldwell's murder and Jimmye McNab's has been proven right. With that victory in your portfolio, perhaps we can all get on with more pressing matters."

"I resent that, senator. Not your manner, which is irrelevant, but your implication that I've been after victories, personal vindication. That is inaccurate and I think you know it. So, as you say, let's get on with more pressing matters than sarcasm and cheap shots."

"A pretty speech, Miss James. Too bad there's no jury." He shifted his attention from her to others at the table. "The advice of counsel aside, I advise that we begin to close down this committee's activities. Naturally, a report must be written to satisfy the charter under which we've been operating. That report can be written in conjunction with Chief Jenkins and his people."

"I do think," Jack Markowski said, "that we at least should move slowly enough to keep pace with the MPD's and the court's prosecution of the case. I agree with you that there seems little value in having the entire committee continue to function, but the staff, under Lydia's direction, should stay in place for a while."

Another senator who'd remained impartial throughout the countless internal debates within the committee said, "I think Jack is right. I'm all for folding up, but if we do it too quickly we'll end up with the same second-guessing and sniping as happened with the Kennedy assassination. Let Miss James and her staff begin to prepare a report based on progress in the case. I'm sure Chief Jenkins will cooperate with her."

His comment took Jenkins by surprise. He looked around, checked Lydia for a reaction, then said, "That's right. Always happy to cooperate with the Congress." Lydia raised her eyebrows and slipped her notes into her briefcase.

Jenkins intercepted her outside the conference room and offered to buy her a cuppa.

"Thanks, no," she said, looking at her watch.

"Come on, I've got something I want to talk to you about."

He drove to a nearby coffee shop and they settled into a booth.

"All right, chief, what?"

"I meant what I said in the meeting."

"Okay. And...?"

Jenkins shrugged, drank his coffee and said into the cup, "I just wanted you to know, Lydia, that there are no hard feelings. Now that I've cleaned this thing up, you're free to do the job you were supposed to be doing in the first place. I mean, come up with a report to the American people."

A tinge of sarcasm in his voice? "Which is what I intend to do."

Jenkins finished the contents of his cup, sat back. "There's going to be things come out of the indictment that probably should stay between friends, if you get my drift. I'm talking about personal things, family matters. The point is that you'll hear about some of them and be tempted to put them in your report."

"And you're telling me that I shouldn't?"

"Suggesting it. I don't think anything is to be gained by dragging out family dirt, even for the American people."

Lydia dabbed at her mouth with a paper napkin and grabbed the handle of her briefcase.

"Calm down," Jenkins said as she slid to the edge

of the booth, reached across the table and took her wrist. "What are you so sore at? You act as though you expected a different ending to all of this and are mad at the world it didn't come out like you wanted..." He glanced around the coffee shop, then leaned over the table. "If you want some juicy gossip, Lydia, I'll give it to you. Frankly, I didn't figure you got off on that kind of thing."

Don't, she told herself, rise to the bait. Stay in the game. She took a breath, affected a smile and returned to the center of her seat. "All right, I've calmed down." She expanded the smile, which brought one from him.

"This," he said, "has nothing to do with your report, although I suppose it wouldn't hurt anybody to add it. Caldwell was going to die anyway."

She cocked her head. "What do you mean?"

"Well, you know that the autopsy on him was sealed at the family's request. He had cancer."

"How bad?"

"Terminal. The doc who did it figured he had maybe six months."

"Did Senator Caldwell know he had cancer?" she asked, not so much of Jenkins but of herself.

He shrugged. "Could be. It really doesn't matter, does it?"

"I suppose not." She spent a few moments lost in her own thoughts. Finally, she said, "It's interesting how the Caldwell family tends to pull strings where autopsies are concerned."

"Why say that? I don't blame the family for not wanting details played out in the scandal sheets."

"I wasn't referring to the senator's autopsy, Horace. I was talking about the Jimmye McNab autopsy that never was." She glanced up. He didn't respond, so she pushed further. "Why wasn't an autopsy done on Jimmye?"

Jenkins motioned for a waitress to bring their check.

"Why did Cale Caldwell prevent an autopsy on Jimmye McNab?"

"Who says he did?" Jenkins asked as the waitress handed him the bill.

"I do, and so do some other people. Why?"

He shook his head. "Yeah, Caldwell brought some pressure on the department to skip an autopsy. Why, you ask? The way the story goes, the esteemed Senator Caldwell was, as they say, having his way with Miss McNab for quite a while. Who knows, maybe he even made her pregnant. But so what? They're both dead. If which elected officials were cheating on the side was important after he died or left office, there wouldn't be space in the newspapers for much of anything else...."

He dropped her off in front of the Senate Building. "Forget the McNab thing, Lydia. That's really over now. Do your report nice and neat, take the bows and get back to making money. If there's anything I can do, give me a call. As I said, I'm always happy to cooperate with the U.S. Congress."

Eighteen

It was the early morning hours and the Quentin Hughes show was in progress. Christa Jones noted that her boss was edgier than usual in his interview with his guest.

It had been a trying day, although no worse than many other days of the recent past. She'd been staying with Hughes in his Watergate apartment for a week, returning home during the day only to feed her cats and to get a change of clothing. The beginning of the week with Hughes had started smoothly enough; in fact, the first few days found Hughes in as good a mood as she could remember. Of course, in the early phase of their relationship he was often relaxed and pleasant to be with. Those early days in Des Moines provided Christa with one of the most pleasant memories of her life...

Her father had deserted the family when Christa was an infant. Her mother, an industrious, uneducated woman, had done what she could to provide a home for Christa and her two younger sisters, but the woman eventually buckled under the pressure. After six months in a state institution, she'd returned home, packed a few belongings and left Des Moines with a truck driver she'd met only days earlier. Because there were no relatives, the three Jones girls were placed in a state home.

Memory of life in that home could reduce Christa to immediate tears and terror. She'd found a job and taken courses at night at a local community college; she'd always been an avid reader and found herself immersed in her classes, particularly those dealing with communications.

Hughes, who'd become the most successful and well-known broadcaster in Des Moines, lectured one evening at the college. It was, as they say, love at first sight for the orphaned Christa. She was enthralled with his sureness, his ability to spellbind anyone within listening distance, his tall good looks. When they'd talked after class, his slate gray eyes seemed to burn right through her. He was power and authority.

Until Quentin Hughes, Christa had never been particularly interested in how she looked or in what she wore. But after that night at the college she found herself making a conscious effort to look better. She knew even then that she was attractive, tall and fair-skinned, with a figure full enough to encourage appreciative stares from men on the street. Now she did what she could to enhance her attributes, then went to the radio station where Hughes was employed, asked to see him, and to her surprise was immediately ushered into his office.

He hired her on the spot to replace a young woman who'd been his producer and was leaving to marry someone from another city. The pay wasn't much, but that didn't matter to Christa. The job created many perks for her, to say nothing of the pride she felt at being inside the exciting world of radio and television. And, of course, there was the fringe benefit of being close to Quentin Hughes on a daily basis.

She was a virgin when she took the job with Hughes in Des Moines. That lasted two days. Soon they were living together, although Hughes insisted that she maintain a separate apartment for, what he termed, "appearances' sake." She hadn't argued, simply looked forward to when they would be together in a house he rented on the outskirts of the city, six blocks from the home in which he was born and where his mother still lived.

Christa had assumed—presumed, Hughes would say—that one day they would be married. Hughes had been married before meeting her, and had gotten his divorce during the time they were together. Christa understood that to push him would be a mistake, and so she said little, dropping only occasional hints and hoping that he would respond to them. He didn't. He also occasionally saw other women and, to Christa's shock, one day announced that he was marrying one of them. That time she stayed away from the station for a week, mostly in bed in her apartment. Eventually Hughes came to visit her, and told her he needed a producer and if she was quitting he'd have to find somebody else.

It wasn't easy, but she went back to the station. Hughes treated her well, gave her substantial raises and seemed understanding of her occasional flip-outs that made her stay away from the job for a few days at a time. Of course, she was paying her dues to him for such minor indulgences.

And so it had gone for all these years, Christa always there even as he went through his succession of women, marrying some of them, only sleeping with most of them, all during his rise in the broadcasting business to his present position in Washington. Not that Christa was monastic when he wasn't available. She dated a variety of men, but always found something lacking in them—or in her...She knew it was a failing, but. .the only close female friend she'd ever had told her that she was throwing away her life by staying with Hughes, dancing attendance on him. Christa had to agree, but divorcing her emotions from her intelligence was another matter. Somehow, and for no good reason, she had the notion that one day Quentin Hughes would realize the mistake he'd made in not committing himself to her and would do something about it. She was too much like too many women—even in the so-called age of liberation....

She snapped out of her reverie and glanced at her reflection in the glass separating the studio from the control room. She knew she'd been reverting back to her younger years when she'd done so little to improve her appearance. Especially over the past year. At the moment her hair was disheveled. Her powder blue turtleneck sweater had a coffee stain over one breast. A black felt skirt was rumpled and covered with cat hair. She wore no makeup and noticed that a streak of black ink from a Flair pen was still on her hand after she'd inadvertently picked up the pen by the wrong end almost two days ago. My God, Christa, you're a mess...She considered taking a Valium from her purse but fought the urge. She knew that pills had become too much a part of her life. They were so easy to get. Always on hand were amphetamines and the depressants, Desoxyn and Plexonal, always something to pick her up from the depths or to bring her down from the heights. There had been other drugs, too, that Hughes occasionally enjoyed using recreationally, particularly to enhance his sexual pleasure. They'd done nothing to Christa, although she never argued with him when he insisted that she share his use of them.

And there was alcohol. As much as she knew how dangerous it was to combine drugs and alcohol, she'd been drinking more heavily than ever. In fact, she'd gotten quite drunk two days ago and had gone through a shaky, painful day-after.

A recorded commercial, then Hughes's voice through the intercom: "How about some coffee?" Christa went to a small room, drew two cups and delivered them to the studio.

"Thanks, babe," Hughes said.

She nodded, returned to the control room and remained there for the rest of the show.

"I have to feed my cats," she told him as they stood together in the office and prepared to leave the station.

"They'll live."

"Just drop me off. It will take ten minutes and I'll feel better."

"All right," he said, tossing letters as fast as he could open them into an already overflowing wastebasket.

They arrived at the Watergate, parked his car in the underground garage and rode the elevator to his floor.

"Can I get you something?" she asked after they were in the apartment.

"No, thanks," he said, kicking off his shoes and sprawling on the couch.

"I think I'll make myself a drink," she said.

"You drink too damn much," he said.

"No, I don't." (Yes, I do.) "Sure you don't want one?"

He didn't answer. She went to the kitchen and poured herself a gin over ice, returned to the living room and sat next to him on the couch, drawing her feet up beneath her as she did. Hughes looked straight ahead across the large room.

"What are you thinking about?"

"About you."

His comment pleased her. She touched his arm. "That's nice to hear. Good thoughts, I hope."

He continued to stare straight ahead. Then: "I think it's time for you to move on, Christa."

For a moment his words didn't penetrate. He turned, looked into her eyes. "Did you *hear* me? I said, it's time for you to move on."

Her laugh was purely nervous. She quickly took another drink of the gin. "Move on?... what do you mean? From my apartment?... From here?..." She knew damn well what he meant, was too terrified to acknowledge it.

He continued to focus on her eyes, and as hard as she tried to avoid his look she found herself drawn back to them like metal shavings to a magnet. "I mean *really* move on," he said. "We've been together too long, Christa. I think you ought to get out of the station, out of Washington. You'll have no trouble getting another job in the business. I can arrange that with a phone call."

Her stomach knotted, she had difficulty swallowing the remaining gin in her glass. Often when they would fight she would be overcome with the same grip of inertia, nerve ends all activated at once and trying to propel her in a dozen different directions. She wanted to cry, to scream, to physically hurt him, to wrap her arms around his neck. She could do none of them.

She went to the kitchen, where she filled her glass to the brim. She gripped the edge of the Formica counter and tried to stop herself from trembling. She drank, grabbed her purse and popped a Valium in her mouth.

"What are you doing?" Hughes called from the living room.

She came around behind him as he sat on the couch and used the back of it as a brace for her trembling hands.

"Sit down, damn it," he said, turning so that he could look up at her.

She took a chair across a coffee table from him.

He squinted. "We've had a good long run, Christa. Everybody moves on at some point in their lives." He moved to the edge of the couch and reached for her hand. She pulled it away. She knew what she looked like at that moment. She remembered her mother looking that way...

"Calm down," Hughes said. "I'll see that you're set up with one hell of a good job. I'll also make sure that you leave here with plenty of money in your pocket—"

"You are a terrible person," she said softly.

"What did you say?"

"I also love you. God, don't you know that?"

He placed his arm on the back of the couch, crossed his legs and jiggled his stockinged foot. "Love. That's for kids, Christa. Grow up."

"I *was* a kid when I fell in love with you." A large, immovable lump was in her throat. "I've stayed all these years because of that love—"

"That's your problem. I never told you to do it. I never promised you anything. It was your choice. I say it again, grow up, Christa."

She stood up and threw the contents of her glass in his face.

"All right, damn you, I just have."

It took him a moment to recover from the shock. He shook his head, quickly got to his feet, pulled a handkerchief from his pocket and wiped his face. He was across the room in a moment, took her by the throat with one hand, crossed his right arm over his body and brought the back of his hand sharply against the side of her face. He stood over her, forced her face up so that she was looking directly at him. "You're sick, Christa. I've been telling you that for a long time. You're sick and need help. Do you want help from me, Christa? Do you want me to see that you're put someplace where they can help you?" He, of course, knew all about what had happened to her mother.

Nothing in her now except terror. She broke down, begged him to forgive her, not to tell her she was sick. He finally let go of her hair. She fell back on the carpet and stayed there, motionless, while he disappeared into the bedroom.

He came back wearing fresh clothes. "I'll be out for a while. I want you gone when I come back. Go home, get drunk, pop some of your damn pills and sleep it off for a couple of days. When you come back to the station I'll have it all worked out for you, a new job, a new city, a new life. That's the trouble with people like you, Christa, you can't tell the black hats from the white hats. I'm doing this in *your* best interests, but you're either too stupid or too sick to understand that." He left the apartment, slamming the door behind him....

Fifteen minutes later Christa Jones stood at the wide expanse of window overlooking the city of Washington, D.C. She'd been standing there all that time, her mind a jumble, her breath coming in short spasms, her chest filled with the ache that had been there for so many years.

She left the window and entered the bedroom, where she went directly to one of the closets that held Hughes's extensive wardrobe. She got down on her knees and found what she was looking for on the floor of the closet, his fireproof storage vault. Quickly she went to the kitchen and felt around behind the refrigerator, removed a key from a nail, returned to the bedroom and opened the vault with the key. It was filled with papers, some cash, jewelry. None was of interest to her. She removed a package wrapped in brown paper, closed the lid, locked the box and returned the key to its hiding place behind the refrigerator. She put on her coat, looked about the apartment, then left.

She hailed a cab outside and rode in it to her own small apartment, the package cradled on her lap as though it might have been a living thing. She locked the door behind her, took off her coat and flipped on the overhead lights. She was terrified. She drew a glass of water from the kitchen tap and used it to wash down another tranquilizer. An empty gin bottle stood in the sink along with dirty dishes. She found an almost empty bottle of cognac in a kitchen cupboard and poured what was left of it into a glass, then returned to the living room where the brown package sat next to her telephone. She found a slip of paper on which a phone number was written, picked up the phone and dialed the number. She let it ring fifteen times before hanging up.

Lydia James had just left her apartment on her way to an appointment with Cale Caldwell, Jr. She heard her phone ringing and debated going back to answer it. She didn't. "They'll call back if it's important," she muttered to herself as she continued toward where she'd parked her car.

Christa Jones hung up the telephone. One of her two cats jumped up on her lap and meowed. The animal pressed against her and rubbed back and forth. From its throat came rumblings of contentment.

Christa looked down and smiled. "There, there, babe," she said as she petted the cat's head. "There, there, now. Mommy loves you. Love..."

Nineteen

Cale Caldwell, Jr., had called Lydia earlier that morning and asked her to come to his office to discuss an important matter. She hadn't spoken with him since the night they'd had drinks together at Hogate's.

Joanne Marshall, Cale's secretary, was behind a receptionist's desk when Lydia now entered the outer office. She stood. "Cale will be free in a moment, Miss James. Please take a seat."

Lydia sat on an antique church pew that was covered with red corduroy cushions. She took in the office and realized what an influence Veronica Caldwell had on her son's tastes. The reception area had the look of an old schoolhouse. The wood on the walls was dark, and the floor was covered in a green carpeting in which scenes of early America were woven. There was a genteel calm to the room.

Moments later Cale came through a door, smiled. "Come in, Lydia. I'm glad you could make it."

Cale's office looked much the same as the outside area, except that it was four times as large. There was a wall of framed photos, built-in bookcases, a small round conference table with four ladder-back chairs. Cale's desk was massive and old. Burns along its edge testified to a previous owner's habit of leaving lit cigarettes or cigars on it.

Cole went to a window and looked outside. He turned, propped himself against the sill. "Lydia, I know you're busy. I've debated asking you to meet with me for quite a while now. What I want to talk to you about isn't pleasant, at least for me, but the more I thought about it, the more I realized that you were entitled to know what's on my mind."

"That's a turn of events, Cale. I was getting the feeling that the one thing I was not to have was information. From anyone."

"I can understand why you feel that way. It must have been rough." He pushed away from the window and leaned against his desk.

"It isn't all past tense," Lydia said as she adjusted herself in a bentwood rocking chair. "I'm still involved. I suppose you know I'm to write a report based on what the MPD comes up with."

"Yes. I'm still his official counsel. I expect to have another attorney brought in within a few days. It's a decision the family must make, Mark Adam's defense. Some of the best legal minds in the nation would probably prove counterproductive. I think of the Patty Hearst case. F. Lee Bailey, brilliant as he is, was wrong for her, I feel. I think when an attorney becomes famous, juries often want to see him lose even before the trial begins."

Lydia agreed. His defense would apparently be based on legal insanity, and there were certain attorneys who could better present that plea to a jury than others.

An awkward silence, broken by Caldwell. "One of the things I insist on with any counsel chosen for Mark Adam is that the entire matter of Jimmye's murder be excluded from the proceedings. In fact, and you're one of the few people I'll talk to about this, part of the arrangement made with the MPD had to do with that issue. It was the only consideration given us, but it was an important one. Mark Adam confessed to both murders in exchange for an understanding that Jimmye's case would be closed without further examination. Actually it wasn't much of a concession from the police. Mark Adam is being charged with and tried for the murder of my father only. Solving Jimmye's murder provides a bonus to the MPD. Lord knows, they solve few enough cases, and when they can close the door on one this easily, they're damn pleased."

Lydia took a moment to digest what he'd said. True, there was nothing so unusual about the arrangement. In multiple murders the accused was usually brought to trial for only one of them. Why then, she wondered, was she reacting with skepticism, even anger? Perhaps because they'd tried to dissuade her so many times from following up leads on Jimmye's murder.

Caldwell continued: "I've heard through the grapevine that you're still interested in looking into Jimmye's case. I honestly don't know why you would want to do that, Lydia. It doesn't make much sense. From what I can understand, the committee formed to investigate dad's death is virtually out of business. The only thing left is for you to prepare a report. If you had any questions before about whether Jimmye's death links up with my father's, they should be truly a thing of the past now that Mark Adam has come forward."

She decided to be direct. "Cale, I can't come up with concrete evidence, but I simply can't accept Mark Adam's confession."

Cale shook his head. "You're an amazing person, Lydia. You won't let go of some notions, no matter what facts stare you in the face. Look, we're family. Yes, we all wish that Mark Adam had not done what he's done. We all wish that he was a normal, rational human being. But that's not the case. He's seriously disturbed. It doesn't take a psychiatric genius to come to that conclusion. The fact is, he killed our father out of a long-standing hatred for him. A lot of young men dislike their fathers. A lot go through life coping with it one way or another. Mark Adam, sad to say, wasn't able to do that. When he came to dad's party and again had a chance to see the man he'd built such a dislike

(165)

for from his early teens, well...it was just too damn much for him."

Lydia started to say something, but he cut her off.

"Lydia, think of how mother and I feel about forcing Mark Adam to attend the party. It had been a long time since dad and my brother had had any contact. We *should* have known better. But that's Monday-morning quarterbacking, isn't it?...You asked me when we had drinks together if I knew why an autopsy had not been performed on Jimmye."

Lydia looked intently at him. "Yes, I remember that...Why do you bring it up again?"

"Because I know you will, Lydia, unless I give you enough reason not to. The only thing I feel will accomplish that is the truth. Fact is, I admire people who demand the truth, even if they are annoying." He picked up a pencil and doodled on a fresh, clean lined yellow legal pad. "It's true that the family brought pressure on the MPD to avoid an autopsy on Jimmye. Dad, because of his position in the Senate, was successful in that effort."

"Why? What were you trying to hide?"

He pressed down hard on the pencil and drew a long slash across the page. The pencil's point broke when it went off the edge of the pad and hit the desk. "Because...she was pregnant, Lydia. Jimmye was pregnant when she was killed—"

"My God...how awful—"

"For whom?" He looked up at her. "She was carrying my brother's child."

Mark Adam's child? Yes...not as Chief Jenkins had sordidly implied—but there was a Caldwell in Jimmye's picture. She'd concocted scenarios based on the few facts that had surfaced during the investigation, but mostly on hints and rumors. Never once, though, had she sexually linked Mark Adam Caldwell to Jimmye McNab. "But...he was in the cult long before Jimmye was killed," she said. "How?..."

There was a pause as he played with the broken pencil, slapped it down on the desk, took out his pocket watch and looked at it, not as someone checking the time but almost as though it were an object in which he could hide. The watch still in his hand, he said, "I've told you this much, Lydia, I might as well go all the way. You'll remember when we had drinks that I mentioned there had been a problem in the family that developed from my brother's relationship with Jimmye. I suppose 'relationship' is the appropriate word. Jimmye and Mark Adam had become involved long before he joined the cult. It was the sort of thing any family would try to sweep under the rug. Imagine the reaction inside a family like ours. Here's a United States senator, and a wife who is one of the leading patrons of the arts in America. They take in an infant girl who's related to the wife and bring her up as a daughter, giving her every advantage, treating her as an equal to their two natural sons. What does she end up doing? She ends up climbing into one of the sons' beds, not just once but on a regular basis."

Lydia felt very sorry for Cale at that moment. His eyes asked for understanding, not only of the story he was telling but of the difficulty he was having in putting it into words.

He then moved into a long monologue, a sort of stream-of-consciousness recall of the events in the Caldwell household that centered around the discovery that Jimmye and Mark Adam had been intimate. "You've got to understand that Mark Adam is a very intense person. Sure, especially a young woman, might feel this was a dynamic quality, be drawn to it. And, sad to say, along with the pleasure of it, our Jimmye's ambitions were not unreasonably keyed to the older, first-born Caldwell...

"...I'll never forget for the rest of my days that moment when mother walked into Jimmye's room and saw them together in bed. God, Lydia, it was the beginning of a nightmare in our family—"

"What did your parents do? Surely they must have tried to put an end to it."

"Of course. They counseled, pleaded, threatened—

(167)

the works. There would be long stretches where it appeared it was over. During those times the family almost seemed to return to the normalcy it once had. But then it would surface again and all hell would break loose."

Lydia slumped in the chair. She couldn't escape the mental images of the stocky, brooding Mark Adam Caldwell with Jimmye McNab...She'd really not known Jimmye very well, though the occasions when they had been together had been pleasant, and Lydia recalled that each time she was quite impressed with the young journalist. No question, Jimmye had been an extremely beautiful girl—tall, slender and lithe. Her hair was more a mane, and she wore it loose, which gave her a hedonistic quality to men.

Lydia also recalled that Jimmye's ambitions were nearly as different as her appearance—not necessarily a bad quality; in fact, it made her seem sort of disarmingly frank, honest. Veronica had wryly observed on occasion that Jimmye would undoubtedly become *whatever* it was she wanted—the top network anchorwoman in America, or the world's leading brain surgeon. The girl was bright, talented and, above all, goal-directed...

"It must have been an awful thing to live with," Lydia said, and meant it.

"It tore us apart," Cale said. "I suppose every family is tested. Well, this was our supreme test. In a way, it showed that the Caldwell stock is a strong one. Lots of people I know would have folded under the pressure."

"What happened when Mark Adam joined the cult? One would think that would have put an end to it."

"No. It *seemed* to have ended before that. Jimmye had left the house and was involved with other men. We still suspected that Mark Adam was seeing her on occasion, but nothing was ever said about it. Usually, brothers are close enough to share those kinds of secrets, but there was never any of that between Mark Adam and me. It was as though we were from two different worlds. Two very different people. We may share some genes, but they sure worked in wondrously different ways in us...Of course, we could only speculate that the experience with Jimmye had, in some way, helped provoke the psychic break that led my brother to go for a life in a religious cult. Who knows what guilt he carried with him? Whatever it was, it was enough to drive him to kill Jimmye—who I guess he came to see as some evil force he had to exorcise, or whatever their damn jargon is."

"What about Jimmye?" Lydia asked. "Didn't she feel guilty about what had happened? It would seem to me that a young woman in her position, having been taken into a loving family and treated as an equal to that family's natural children, would have *some* sense of honor, some commitment to that family."

"I'm afraid Jimmye wasn't bothered by such restraints. We all loved her very much, and in her own way I suppose she loved us. But...well, we've all known ambitious people, but Jimmye's ambition had crossed the line into ruthlessness. I don't know whether you were aware of that."

"No, I wasn't. Not to that extent. I knew that she was hard-driving and determined to succeed, but... frankly, Cale, all of this comes as a shock. I'm not sure I'm able to absorb it all at this moment, put it into perspective."

"You may never be able to, Lydia. I haven't."

As Lydia prepared to leave his office, she asked him why he had decided to take her into his confidence this way.

"As I said when you first came in, Lydia, the Caldwell family has been embarrassed and hurt enough by Jimmye's actions. Mark Adam did obviously manage to see her again after joining the cult—or *she* managed it. He's also told me that Jimmye threatened to go to our mother and father and demand cooperation—"

"'Cooperation'?"

"Money. I told you, Jimmye had crossed over the line to ruthlessness. Of course, my brother...not exactly stable...tragically overreacted. We'd dealt with so many problems with Jimmye that this would not have been as monumentally important as he felt. I've no doubt that that cult and its mysticism helped push him to the act too. Who knows, he may have seen himself not as the family savior but some kind of avenging angel. That cult helps them think in those terms, it seems...The point is, Jimmye is dead and my brother, God help him, killed her. There are very few people I'd have shared all this with...I know it will stay with you." His expression made the point that to violate his faith would not be taken lightly.

She asked. "Does your mother know you planned to tell me this?"

He hesitated, then said, "Yes. And she approved."

"What about the rumors that...well, that your father had had an intimate relationship with Jimmye too? I'm sorry to ask but since we're getting everything out—"

He threw his hands up into the air. "It's nonsense, Lydia. It's cruel gossip. I'm not going to protest too much, because that will only add to it. No, the only Caldwell—and one is too many—who got involved was my brother."

Lydia stood, picked up her briefcase and took a few steps toward the door. She stopped, turned. "Thank you, Cale. I'm pleased that you think enough of me to trust me with this."

He came around the desk and shook her hand. "Mother and I both felt that you *deserved* to know. And we have the ulterior motive of hoping, by this full disclosure, that you'll agree there's no need for any of this to become part of any further investigation or any report by your committee."

Lydia nodded. Under the circumstances, it was the least she could do. But she also did no more, quickly departing.

After Lydia had left, Cale Caldwell picked up a private telephone and dialed his mother's office number.

"How did it go?"

"Just fine, mother. I think Lydia *finally* understands that there's no need to expose our family secrets. She's a friend, mother, and I believe a good one."

"Yes, I've always known that," Veronica Caldwell said. "I would never have considered her for the special counsel's spot unless I at least had been confident of that. Well, thank you, Cale. I feel a little better. Maybe all of this will *finally* be over."

"It will, mother. You know, as I talked to Lydia, I felt a renewed pride in being a Caldwell. Something I caught. You..."

His mother sighed. "That is, at bottom, all *anyone* has, Cale, pride in one's family..."

It was not until late that night, after Lydia had returned to her apartment, taken a long, leisurely hot bath and finally settled in to watch the late news on television, that she was able even to begin to sort out her reactions to what Cale Caldwell had told her. She did feel a sympathy for everyone involved, with the exception of Jimmye McNab. But now there was another reaction. She was about to give it equal time when the phone rang.

"How are you?" Clarence asked.

"Confused. You?"

"Okay. I hope I didn't wake you."

"No, I was just thinking, which isn't recommended recreational exercise."

"Right. Well, I spent the afternoon at the health club."

"Sounds a lot better than the way I spent mine."

"Join up, Lydia? Yoga, exercise, dance classes...tones up the muscles where they count, and so forth."

Lydia couldn't stop her mind from racing. When she didn't say anything Clarence asked, "Hey, are you there?"

"Yes, I'm sorry. I was just thinking of what you said about your club having dance classes...you know, I think it's possible I've been dancing all day."

He laughed, and she cut him off.

"I mean it, Clarence. It just penetrated that I just might have been choreographed into a Caldwell ballet. Then again, all this unaccustomed life-and-death action may be making me into a paranoid. Maybe I should get me to a cult too..."

"You do, sweetheart, and I'll kill you. With love, of course."

"Good night, Clarence. I think you've finally given me something to dream on."

Twenty

"Get up," John Conegli's wife thundered from another room in their small tract house in Rockville, Maryland.

He got up in stages, knowing he needed to be on time for his client this morning.

Marie was in the kitchen.

"Good morning," John said through a long yawn.

"Out all night again—"

"Don't start now, Marie. It was no different when I was on the force."

"When you were on the force you had days off. When you were on the force we got a steady check. So you had to get yourself kicked off the force and be a bigshot private detective."

He started to argue with her, then thought better of it.

When he'd finished dressing he asked, "How do I look?"

She turned from the sink where she'd been scrubbing the baked-on remains of lasagne from a pan, narrowed her eyes and took him in. "You look tired."

"I am. If I didn't have this client meeting I wouldn't get up this morning."

She wiped her hands, came up to him and kissed him on the cheek. "You'll kill yourself with no sleep."

"Yeah, I know, but it's a living, huh?" He returned the kiss and felt much better now that he knew he would leave the house on a pleasant note.

He had a lot of time to think during the long ride from Rockville to his destination in Virginia. He'd only met the client once, and that was when he'd initially been hired. At first Conegli had debated turning down the assignment. Ever since starting his own detective agency he'd tried to operate under a set of principles. In fact, he'd turned down the first case ever offered him—a wife who wanted him to bulldog her errant husband. "No matrimonials," Conegli had told her. He took the next case that came through his door, however, a husband who wanted his wife followed. Somehow that was different, Conegli told himself. A guy had a right to a little on the side, but not a married woman. Besides, the rent was due on his tiny office, he needed the money. Soon he took most anything that came through the door, including matrimonials, never mind who was doing what to whom.

This case was different. He'd wanted to turn it down, but again money talked. He'd asked for a fee far in excess of what he usually charged per day, and the client hadn't batted an eye.

He thought about his client and what he represented, and some of his initial misgivings returned as he continued south. As a cop, he'd followed the basic rules: it was okay to take from prostitution, gambling and other pursuits that did nothing more than prey on man's natural need for diversion. Who gets hurt? was the way it was always put. Drugs were another matter, however. Every cop had kids of his own, and Conegli was proud that he'd never taken a cent from a pusher. That's why he considered his dismissal from the Washington MPD to have been so unfair. He'd taken "clean" graft, which was more than some of those judging him could claim.

But that was long ago. No sense crying over spilled milk. His wife did enough of that for both of them...

He followed a narrow road through gently rolling farmland, then proceeded along Occaquan Creek until reaching a narrow entrance to the Center for Inner Faith. Some of the bald, white-robed members stood in front of the main house. "Bunch of weirdos," Conegli mumbled to himself as he stopped his gun-metal gray sedan in front of the house. He struggled from behind the wheel, slammed the door and lumbered toward the house. He was intercepted by two young men who asked the purpose of his visit.

"I'm supposed to meet Mr. Jewel," Conegli said, angry that he had to explain himself. He felt the heft of the .38 caliber police special he carried on his right hip and wished, for a moment, that he could use it.

He was kept waiting in the foyer for ten minutes. Finally, a young man came through the doors immediately to Conegli's right, quickly closed the doors behind him and said, "Come with me, please. Mr. Jewel will be detained for a few minutes."

He was led to a small, sparsely furnished office at the rear of the house, with one metal desk, three folding metal chairs and a row of battered file cabinets. The young man closed the door, leaving Conegli alone to take in his new surroundings. He went to the window. One pane was cracked and held in place with Scotch tape. An elaborate spiderweb spanned a set of dirty drapes. Conegli looked outside. There was considerable property in the rear. He saw members of the cult performing chores around the outbuildings.

After some fifteen minutes, he angrily placed one of the chairs in front of the window and plumped himself down on it. He patted his suit jacket pocket, reached inside and pulled out a cigar, lit it, put his feet up on the desk and wished he were back home in bed, even with Marie.

While Conegli waited in the rear office, Francis Jewel, executive director of the center, was in the midst of a difficult conversation with the cult's founder and spiritual leader, the Reverend Sylvan Quarles. Quarles had arrived the previous evening and had stayed overnight. The discussion had begun immediately after the guru's arrival and had lasted into the early hours until Jewel, exhausted, suggested they get some sleep and pick it up in the morning, which is what they did.

"...he's here now," Jewel said to Quarles.

"And I ask you again, Mr. Jewel, what he has accomplished besides taking our money?"

Jewel squirmed in his chair. The reverend stood larger than life in the center of the study. "We're doing all we can, sir," he said. "It's imperative that we proceed slowly and carefully so as not to arouse suspicion—"

"Perhaps you've been too careful and slow, Mr. Jewel," Quarles said. "I sometimes wonder whether you truly understand the importance of this matter. You do understand, do you not, that if someone were to gain possession of the tape it would have severe and lasting consequences for our mission."

"Reverend Quarles, we're investigating *every* avenue to recover the tape. I've even gone so far as to send people to Iowa, where Quentin Hughes's family lives. I expect a report within a day or two. We've kept close tabs on everyone leaving or entering Hughes's apartment. And, of course, we've maintained a constant contact within the Caldwell family, as well as within Congress itself. You know that we have friends in high places, thanks, if I may say so, to my efforts. That, of course, was one of the reasons I encouraged the young Caldwell boy to join us in the first place."

"And look where that has gotten us," Quarles said. He crossed the study, reached up to the top shelf of a bookcase and pulled down a copy of Jimmye McNab's book on brainwashing and mind control. He returned to the desk, slammed the book down. "This is what it got us, Mr. Jewel. You should have anticipated the problems the Caldwell boy would bring with him, having a sister or whatever she was who is a journalist, having a father who is a member of the Senate."

"But that was the point, wasn't it? You told each of us years ago that for the church to survive in a hostile America we were to do everything possible to bring to our midst those men and women who were in a position to help advance our goals. Certainly the Caldwell boy fit that criteria, didn't he?"

"It doesn't matter now, does it, Mr. Jewel? What you thought fit the criteria proved to be wrong."

Jewel winced. "Actually, we've made strides toward solving this problem, have we not? The boy is gone from here and has confessed to two murders, including the sister you spoke of who caused us so much grief. I've no doubt that he will be found...insane...and spend the rest of his days in an institution. No matter what he might say in the future, no one would give credence to it."

Quarles shook his head. "I'm disappointed in you, Francis. You seem to spend your life making mistakes and then trying to find a bright side for them. It certainly has not helped our image to have one of our members confess to murdering his sister and his own father, who also happened to be Majority Leader of the United States Senate." His voice, which had lowered, now rose.

"Please, Reverend Quarles, I didn't mean that—"

"I am tired of having my mission on earth thwarted by incompetence. I must leave now to attend to other matters, Mr. Jewel. I will leave you with a message that I trust will not be misunderstood. I suggest you listen very closely to me." He came to the desk, leaned on it and thrust his face close to Jewel. "I wish this matter resolved immediately. I don't know whether you understand that word, Mr. Jewel, but I understand it, and so does our God. Our God is a forgiving one, but he does not suffer incompetence easily. I assure you that if the tape is not found and in our possession by the time I return, you will be subject to the divine punishment you will have earned."

Jewel watched the self-chosen divine take up his cashmere overcoat from a coat tree, pick up his briefcase. He turned and asked, "Any questions?"

"No, sir."

"Mr. Jewel. Good day."

It took Francis Jewel several minutes to recover. Finally he summoned one of the cult members and told him to bring Mr. Conegli to the study.

After a proper blasting of Conegli, Jewel demanded: "Well, Mr. Conegli, *where* is the tape?"

Conegli crossed his legs, exposing a large expanse of white calf between where his pants leg ended and the top of an ankle-length black silk sock began. "Rome wasn't built in a day. I've been doing everything I could, have followed up every lead you've given me. I've kept tabs on who comes and goes at Hughes's apartment. You told me that you figured that redhead who works for the committee might have been given the tape so I took a shot with her, but that didn't work out—"

"And I was very displeased that you used violence with her, Mr. Conegli. You were told no violence unless absolutely necessary."

"Violence? That wasn't violence. So I tapped her on the head, so what? The kid is all right from what I hear, back to work and feelin' fine. The point is that I've followed up every lead you've given me. I had the bug put in the piano teacher's place like you said so we could get a handle on the James woman, but that hasn't turned up anything yet. I might bug her place, too, but it'll be tougher to do. If you have any better ideas, just let me know."

"Have you searched Hughes's apartment?"

"That's on my list. I figured I'd take a look where the girl who works for him lives, and maybe even bug into James's place. But I can only do so much. I'm one man. If you want things to move faster, well, you'd better up the budget so I can hire some help."

Jewel nodded grimly. "Yes, do what you must, spend what you must, but get the job done fast." He thought of what Quarles had said. *"Immediately."*

"Okay, Mr. Jewel, but I'm not about to lay extra money out of my own pocket. Besides, you owe me for last week."

Jewel wearily left the study, returning minutes later with an envelope containing two thousand dollars in cash. Conegli counted it, nodded his approval and put it in his inside jacket pocket.

Conegli went to the door, paused. "Just what's on this tape that's so damned important?"

"Mr. Conegli, I told you when you first asked that question that—"

Conegli held up his hands. "Okay, you don't have to explain again. It's just that in my business, you've got to have ethics. I don't like working on a case where I don't know what the case is all about, if you follow what I mean."

"I follow, Mr. Conegli. And spare me your ethics. I want a call from you at least twice a day from this point forward."

"Sure thing, Mr. Jewel."

Conegli spent much of the drive back to Rockville speculating on what could possibly be on the videotape. As he pulled into his driveway it occurred to him that the tape might be pornographic, scenes of cult people frolicking in the buff. It brought a smile to his face as he pictured Francis Jewel with a porn star.

"How did your meeting go?" Marie asked as he entered the house.

"Okay." He remembered the envelope. "I got a bonus."

She opened the envelope he gave her and counted the cash. "We can use it."

"Not so fast. I need some of that to operate on."

"And we need a new refrigerator. How come the bonus?"

"Because I do such a good job."

"Who's this client?"

"Makes no difference, Marie...now I want another bonus," and he slapped her rear playfully.

True love had its way.

Francis Jewel dictated into a tape machine on his desk his recollection of what had occurred that day and the previous evening. He tried to recall in some detail the conversation with Sylvan Quarles, and also made comments into the microphone about what he had told Conegli.

He flicked off the switch on the microphone. One name stuck in his mind. It was the name he'd scribbled during the meeting with Conegli. He wasn't sure what to do, whether to call the person now or to let it go until he'd had further time to think.

He picked up the phone and dialed. After three rings a voice answered, "Caldwell Performing Arts Center. May I help you?"

"Mr. Jason DeFlaunce, please."

Later that day, Jewel received a call from one of two young cult members he'd dispatched to Des Moines, Iowa.

"It wasn't there."

"You're sure?"

"Yes. We went to the old lady's house like you told us. No tape."

Jewel took off his glasses, rubbed his eyes. Then into the phone: "Come back immediately."

He placed the phone in its cradle, opened the bottom left drawer of his desk, reached beneath some papers and withdrew a Colt .32 caliber automatic pistol. He looked at it, hefted it, checked that it was loaded. He went to where his topcoat hung near the door and slipped the weapon into a pocket.

Twenty-one

It felt good to be running again. The morning had dawned bright and clear, the temperature having moderated overnight, which caused Lydia to wonder whether spring was within striking distance. She considered the day to be a good omen for her return to a jogging regimen that had been important to her but that had slipped on her priority list since she joined the Caldwell committee.

She wasn't the only person who'd headed for the Reflecting Pool that morning. There were at least twenty other joggers, men and women, old and young, their outfits a contrast in style and personal preference. Some wore garish shiny jogging suits. Others were dressed in drab sweat pants and sweaters. Lydia wore one of two jogging suits she owned, this one a royal blue outfit with a hood on the jacket, which she wore up that morning.

She'd finished four laps around the pool, decided to do an extra. She was halfway through it when another runner came up beside her. "Hi, Lydia, where have you been?"

She turned without breaking stride and recognized Sanford Bain, a psychiatrist she'd been friendly with for some years. In fact, they'd dated for a short time until he went the vocational route to matrimony and fell in love with a psychiatric resident.

"What's new in the shrink world?" Lydia asked as they settled into a comfortable pace.

"Nothing that Freud would approve of," Sandy said. "Couches are being thrown out by the hundreds. Short-term is *in*. And you? Don't tell me, I read the papers. You're a regular celeb." They ran in silence for a quarter of a lap before he asked, "Do you really think the boy did it?"

"Not sure," she said. "You?"

He shrugged. *"Seems* unlikely, though I hear he had his strong motives. Still, to take seriously a confession from an acknowledged cultist..."

They completed the lap and Sandy asked if he could give her a lift.

"No, thanks, I have my car...Sandy, you said something before about not putting much faith in a confession from someone like Mark Adam Caldwell. Could you develop that a bit for me?"

"I'll try...We've been doing research for years now at Georgetown on mind control and brainwashing. Naturally the cults and the hold they seem to have over certain people have been a part of that research. In fact Jimmye McNab spent time with us when she was researching her book on the subject. There's been a lot written about it ever since Korea but no one really has an answer yet. We've been trying to correlate all the available research into one data center but it's been a long, tough job. All the leading thinkers in the field have different ideas about what causes one person to fall easily under another person's control while the next person is capable of resisting it. London and Spiegel in New York have one theory, Borne in Pennsylvania another. Researchers at Stanford have been looking at it for years. Anyway, no matter whose theory you take, the bottom line is that there are individuals who by virtue of their genes or upbringing or psychological set, or maybe all three, have a frighteningly enhanced capacity to be brainwashed."

"Do you think that Mark Adam Caldwell is one of those people?"

"The fact that he could so thoroughly commit himself to something as questionable as that cult would naturally lead me to believe that he's a highly suggestible individual. Someone in a trance, an altered state, might confess to anything... You look skeptical."

"I guess I am, a little," she said. "I can understand someone being suggestible and doing another's bidding in certain situations, but to confess to a murder he hasn't committed... God, that's pretty extreme, isn't it?"

Sandy shrugged. "Do you remember the Reilly case in Connecticut?"

She shook her head.

"He was a young man accused of murdering his mother. In fact, he was convicted of the crime. He'd made a full confession, which was the basis for his conviction. Arthur Miller, the playwright, got interested in the case and started a campaign to reopen it. He brought in psychiatric experts. After examining the kid and the circumstances of the confession, they came to the conclusion that he'd literally been brainwashed, in this instance by the police. I'm not suggesting that it was done deliberately, nor were they. The point is that if you take a highly suggestible person, and I'm talking about someone who is at the extreme end of the scale, and place him in a pressure situation in which he's faced with very imposing authority figures, he's capable of slipping into a trance state as a defense against the pressure. Once he's done that, he's likely to go along with almost anything, including a suggestion that he did, in fact, murder someone. By the way, Reilly had a new trial and was acquitted."

"Do you think that's the case with Mark Adam Caldwell?"

"Who knows? All I'm saying is that I wouldn't be too quick to jump on the MPD bandwagon just because someone with the Caldwell boy's known capacity to be controlled has admitted to a double crime."

"Would the psychiatrists brought in to examine him come to the same conclusion?"

He smiled. "Probably not. It's nearly a dice roll. There are many psychiatrists who still hang onto the old analytic model, which doesn't leave much room for this kind of testing and theorizing. They're more apt to come up with a psychiatric evaluation based on Freudian principles, unresolved Oepidal conflicts, sibling rivalry, thwarted drives, id and superego clashes. Like I always say, Lydia, anybody looking for a therapist is involved in a real crap shoot. You can't tell the therapies without a scorecard...."

Home again, Lydia felt annoyingly confused as she sat in the kitchen and gazed out the window. Mark Adam Caldwell seemed to fit closely the profile Sandy had been talking about. She'd have liked to see Mark Adam examined by someone like Sandy, but she knew she didn't have the authority or influence for that. The family, the police, the public seemed to accept it—not to mention the congressional committee.

She moved to the living room. If it were *true* that Mark Adam had been brainwashed to confess to the murder of his father and Jimmye McNab, the question was, who'd done it? The MPD? Horace Jenkins had certainly been under the gun to solve the murders. It wouldn't be the first time that a high-ranking police officer had forced a confession. No matter how she explored it, there was still the nagging fact that a young man, disturbed as he might be, was sitting in a jail and was about to be tried for two murders that he maybe didn't commit.

Twenty-two

The local politician on whose behalf Senator Wilfred MacLoon had flown to Utah was sincerely appreciative of the senator's support in his campaign for reelection. It had been touch-and-go since the request had been made through MacLoon's office whether he would make the trip and deliver a speech. The decision had been made at the last minute, which sent the local campaign staff into a flurry of activity to get the word out that MacLoon himself would make an appearance.

"It means a great deal to me, senator, that you came back here to help me out," the local man told MacLoon following the fund-raising dinner held in his honor.

MacLoon slapped him on the back. "Hell, if we don't help each other there won't be any of us left pretty soon." Which brought a laugh from people who'd gathered around him at the rear of the catering-house dining room.

"Another drink, senator?" someone asked.

"Don't mind if I do." He'd had a great deal to drink on his flight from Washington, and had continued imbibing throughout the dinner and a succession of preliminary speeches. The food, he'd decided after a stab at it, was inedible.

"The missus and I would love to have you back to the house for a nightcap, Will," the local politician said.

"Thanks, but I have some meetings scheduled at the hotel."

"Don't know *how* you do it, senator," an overly sincere middle-aged woman said.

"I try," MacLoon replied as he inched toward the door. He held up his hands to silence those still left in the dining room and took the opportunity to say in a loud voice, "One thing I promise every citizen of Utah—the missile system *will* be in this state."

Cheers trailed him as he left the room and went to where a driver stood outside a rented car. He got into the rear seat with some difficulty and drove off toward the comfort of his suite at the Little America Hotel on South Main Street. As he settled back and took in the passing sights of Salt Lake City he couldn't help but think how two-faced some of his Mormon constituents were when it came to alcoholic beverages. The Mormon Church controlled the state of Utah, which meant that all public restaurants and bars were prohibited from serving anything stronger than 3.2 beer. Things had loosened up recently, and certain restaurants were allowed to serve two-ounce mini-bottles of cocktails, but only if the patron also ordered food. The fact was that there were probably as many heavy drinkers in Utah as in any other single state in the union. Only difference was that the drinking was done in private clubs and, like this evening, at political dinners held in such clubs. MacLoon also knew that there would be an ample stock of his favorite whiskey in his suite at the hotel. Ah, it paid to represent, no question...

One of MacLoon's Senate aides who had accompanied him to Utah had stayed at the Little America. He greeted his boss and immediately asked whether he could pour him a drink.

"I need some food," MacLoon said gruffly as he went to the suite's bedroom to strip off his jacket and shirt and change into a freshly laundered dress shirt and a rust-colored cardigan sweater that barely managed to button over the girth of the waist it had to span.

"I'll have something sent up, senator," his aide said. "What's your pleasure?"

"Whatever you can get fast at this hour," MacLoon said. "Have you heard from Morgan and his people?"

"Yes, sir," the aide said as he went to call in the order. "They called an hour ago and said they'd be a half hour late."

"Figures," MacLoon said as he settled in a chair and picked up a newspaper. "When they get here you'll have to disappear."

The aide's face reflected his disappointment in not being invited into the meeting. He'd often been dismissed from rooms when the senator conferred with important people. He and another aide, Rick Petrone, frequently joked about what went on in meetings they were forbidden to attend, and they'd come to the conclusion that once they were gone, the pros—call girls— came through a back door to attend to the distinguished lawmakers.

MacLoon ate heartily and was almost finished when the desk called to announce his visitors.

"Anything else you need before I leave?" his aide asked.

"Nope, but check in with me in a couple of hours."

"Yes, sir." The aide had been trying to think of something to do with his time during the meeting and couldn't come up with anything especially exciting. He decided to simply go to the bar, nurse a 3.2 beer and hope that some appropriate action came along....

The two men who arrived at MacLoon's suite were a study in physical contrast. The first through the door, Jedediah Smith, was tall and handsome. In his early sixties, although he could easily have passed for fifty, he had steel gray hair close-cropped to a square head, face rugged, tanned and lined, like a veteran pilot who's spent too many hours squinting into the sun. His shoulders were broad and thick, and only the slight swell of a middle-aged belly testified to his age. He was dressed in expensive western clothing, including a highly polished pair of alligator boots and the largest Stetson available from any shop. His belt buckle was massive and made of solid silver. An eagle dominated the buckle, and the initials J.S. flanked the metallic bird.

Jedediah Smith was one of the richest industrialists in Utah. He was given his name because his mother claimed to be a direct descendant of the legendary mountain man, Jedediah Smith, who in 1826 explored what would become the state of Utah from north to south. No one had ever proved the genealogical link between the industrialist and the mountain man, but no one had ever disputed it either.

Smith warmly shook MacLoon's hand, then went immediately to a bar that had been set up by the senator's aide and poured himself a stacked tumbler of bourbon. The other man, Ted Proust, was considerably shorter and thinner than Smith. He wore an expensive gray three-piece suit that seemed to have been made for someone with a larger frame. Although not yet forty, he'd lost much of his black hair and what was left was pasted along his temples and over a bald spot. He had a pinched face, a large aquiline nose and dark eyes that were in constant motion, like ball bearings.

"Hello, Ted," MacLoon said to Proust. "Put your bag down and have a drink."

The three men sat in a tight circle and exchanged pleasantries until Smith shifted in his chair, which allowed his jacket to fall open and reveal a .45 caliber semiautomatic revolver on his hip. "How did the speech go?" he asked MacLoon.

"You're not interested in that, Jed. You told me on the phone when you encouraged me to come out here that you were getting nervous about where the missile system debate was going. I told you not to worry, but you never did listen to me."

Smith laughed, exposing a remarkably even and white set of teeth. "Whoever said anybody should listen to a politician, Will?"

All laughed.

"The point is, Will, myself and some of the other people have been reading troublesome reports about the missile system. I'm not talking about where in hell it's put, I'm talking about whether the damn thing will ever get built in the first place."

"It will if I have something to say about it," MacLoon said. He wished he hadn't. It was a weak comment, which he chalked up to having had too much to drink. He told himself to forgo what was in his glass, which he placed on the carpeted floor.

Smith's face reflected his displeasure at what MacLoon had said. He looked at Ted Proust, then back at the senator. "It's our feeling that we've got too much invested in this thing now to sit back and let it take its own sweet way. The way we figure it, Will, is that it needs a final push to get it over the hump and make sure it ends up right smack in the middle of Utah. What the hell... its biggest opposition died when the late, beloved Senator Caldwell checked out."

MacLoon was growing increasingly uncomfortable with the conversation. He wished he'd stayed in Washington to work on the missile project without interference by Smith.

But he also knew that it was an unreasonable wish. Smith had spearheaded an anonymous, private committee of leading citizens to insure that the missile system would be placed in Utah. The group had attacked the problem on many levels and from many directions. A sophisticated propaganda campaign had been launched directed at lawmakers who held the decision in their hands. Committees were formed in Utah to sell its citizens on the virtues of having the system located there. There were a significant number of Utah residents who were firmly opposed to it on many grounds, including ecological, but their efforts had paled in the face of the massive amount of money pumped into the other side's campaign.

"What's the problem, Jed?" MacLoon asked. He'd begun to perspire.

"The problem, Will, is that things don't seem to be working as they should. To repeat myself, we all assumed, as you'll recall, that once Caldwell was out of the way the opposition to the system itself, and to having it put in Utah, would fade away. In fact, you told us that right after Caldwell was...well, anyway, it doesn't look as though it's really moving in that direction. At least not quickly enough."

MacLoon ignored his previous private pledge, picked up his glass and took a hefty swig of the whiskey. "Well," he said, "the opposition did seem to splinter once Caldwell was dead. That was a reasonable assumption, and it happened like we expected. The *problem* is that out of the woodwork have come a couple of others who've picked up where Caldwell left off. I'm not particularly worried about them. I think when the chips are down they'll come around. There's other legislation that means a lot to them and to their home states, and I pull strings where those bills are concerned." He drank again, shook his head. "No, Jed, I still say that things are going pretty much the way we wanted them to."

Smith took a long, thin black cigar from his pocket and lit it with deliberate flourish, then asked MacLoon, "Want one, Will?"

"No, thanks."

"Your problem," Smith said, tilting back his head and enjoying the feel of smoke slowly being exhaled through his nostrils. "Cuban." He took another satisfying drag on the cigar, flicked an ash into an ashtray, leaned forward and said to MacLoon, "I think you said before, Will, that things were going *pretty much* the way we want them. That's not good enough. There's no sense in building seven-eighths of a house and then not moving in because you don't want to pay to put doors on it. Get what I mean, Will? We've invested more than seven million dollars to make sure the system comes home to roost, and I'm not about to lose it for the sake of another million or so."

MacLoon looked at Proust and extended his hands

in a helpless gesture. "What good would a couple of million more do?" he asked. Proust looked away from him, forcing MacLoon to return his attention to Smith. "We've distributed the money to those people who count, at least those we knew would take it and be appreciative. Giving them more won't help. They're already in line."

Smith fiddled with the turquoise clasp on his string tie, pursed his lips. "What about these newcomers you mentioned?"

MacLoon shook his head. "It would be a mistake to even approach them."

"Why?"

"I just don't think they'd be receptive. After all, I've been in the Senate for a long time, Jed. I can size up a man pretty good in that situation."

"Who are they?" Smith asked.

"Markowski, for one. Jennings is another, so is Hannigan."

"What about other considerations?" Smith asked. "Who's got what on them?"

MacLoon laughed nervously. "I don't really know."

"They're not virgins, are they?" Smith said.

Ted Proust laughed appreciatively.

MacLoon hesitated. "I can do some checking with the MPD, but I wouldn't count on it turning up very much. This new breed we've been getting in Congress is pretty straight-arrow. They'll trade for things they believe in, but—"

"Bull," Smith said. "Like they say, every man has his price. Even a distinguished senior senator from the great state of Utah."

MacLoon stiffened against the back of his chair. He tried to ignore the comment and assured Smith that he would do whatever he could to push things along.

Smith said to MacLoon, "Ted brought some candy." Which all knew meant money. "I want you to go back to Washington and come up with some more people who like candy, Will. Look outside Congress, as we've done before. This decision involves every agency in government, and most people have a sweet tooth. I do. So do you."

MacLoon wanted them to leave, wanted the evening to be over. "Don't worry, Jed, I'll go back and make a final push that will make sure this thing is wrapped up. You can count on me, and you can tell the others that."

Smith stubbed out the cigar, stood and placed a hand on each of MacLoon's arms. "Will, it's a pleasure and a privilege having you represent the state of Utah in the United States Senate. Believe me, when this matter is satisfactorily resolved, the people of Utah will be behind you as they never have been before."

"I appreciate that, Jed. Shall I call you tomorrow?"

"No, call Ted in a few days. He'll fly to Washington and distribute the candy to the kids you think deserve it. By the way, Will, we arranged for an old friend of yours to be here tonight."

"Who's that?"

"Come see," Smith said.

The three men left the suite and went down the hall to a room two doors away. Smith knocked. The door was opened by a tall, statuesque girl in a transparent negligee. "Hello, senator."

"I'll be damned," MacLoon said, stepping through the door. "Kitty..."

"I wouldn't be surprised, senator," Smith said as he and Proust walked up the hall.

Twenty-three

Lydia had wanted to contact Senator Caldwell's physician ever since Horace Jenkins told her that Caldwell had cancer at the time of his murder. Obviously the doctor, whose name was George Clemow, would be bound by the restrictions of the doctor-patient relationship. Still, the notion stuck in Lydia's mind and, after arriving early at her Senate office, she placed the call.

Clemow's receptionist told Lydia that the doctor was with a patient but would get back to her. Thirty minutes later he did.

Lydia had met George Clemow some years before. He'd been Cale Caldwell's personal physician for years and had been present at social gatherings in the Caldwell home. Clemow was a New Zealander who despite many years in the United States had not lost his native accent.

"I'm hoping you remember me, Dr. Clemow," she said.

"Oh, yes, I certainly do. And if I didn't, Miss James, I certainly know you *now*. You've gotten quite a bit of attention from the media...How are you?"

"Just fine...I appreciate your returning my call, doctor. Naturally, I'm calling about Senator Caldwell."

A moment of silence. Then: "A terrible thing. Bad enough that the man was murdered, but to have his own son guilty...well, it's mind-boggling—"

"Yes...Dr. Clemow, I realize you can't talk in detail about Senator Caldwell's health, that certain matters are confidential, like they are between a lawyer and client, but I was told by what I consider a very reliable source that Senator Caldwell's autopsy revealed cancer—"

"Miss James, as you said, I'm still not able to discuss that—"

"Yes, I understand, doctor, but perhaps you could tell me *something* that wouldn't compromise your situation. *Anything*..." She realized she sounded almost desperate, but what was there to lose? She was fishing, of course, but in the face of the situation, with Mark Adam now indicted and facing trial and the committee preparing a report...well, anything went. Besides, how do you catch a fish if you never go fishing?...

"It sounds as though you're not particularly pleased with matters—"

"Doctor, I'll be indiscreet and tell you. I'm having trouble accepting Mark Adam's confession. You said it was mind-boggling yourself. So if there's anything at all that might help to—"

"Well...there is one thing that I might mention, and I don't think it violates the confidentiality of my relationship with the senator—"

"What's that, doctor?"

"Senator Caldwell was...distraught over the results of some tests. He told me he thought he should tie up some loose ends in his life. He didn't tell me what they were...and I'm not telling you what the tests showed..."

Lydia allowed herself to feel a tingle of excitement...were the fish finally biting?..."Of course not, doctor. Anything else?"

"Well, the senator told me that he was writing a

(194)

letter in which he would set some things straight, and that the letter was to be opened on his death."

Lydia, holding her breath, said, "I've heard of no such letter—"

"Well, he told me that he intended to give the letter to me to hold until he died. He never did."

"Maybe he never finished it, doctor? He died sooner than he'd anticipated—"

"No, Miss James, he did finish the letter. At least he told me he had...he was angry at himself for forgetting to bring it to me and said he would on the next visit. I'm afraid there never was a next visit."

"Who has the letter, do you suppose?"

"I don't know...his family, I think...In any case, it distresses me that his wishes weren't carried out. I'd suggested that he leave the letter with his attorney or with Veronica, but he said neither was possible. Strange..."

Lydia forced herself to make a few moments of small talk about the senator, then thanked the doctor for his time and hung up.

Ginger Johnson came through the door, red hair hanging down in her face, breathing heavily, as though she'd been running. "I'm really not late, Lydia," she said, taking off her coat and tossing it on a chair. "I was here at seven."

"Why?"

"I couldn't sleep. What a night. Harold and I sat up all night and talked about us. He's so crazy, Lydia, but so nice. He wants to marry me—"

"That's wonderful—"

"No, it really isn't. He told me he wants an old-fashioned woman who'll be a mother to his children and run a nice, neat house from which he can go forth to build his career and so forth. Imagine me housebound, wearing an apron, doing dishes, washing diapers."

Lydia smiled. "Nobody washes diapers any more, Ginger. They're disposable."

Ginger rummaged through a large pocketbook she'd purchased to replace the one that had been stolen the night of her attack, pulled out a tissue and blew her nose. "I don't know what to do, Lydia. On the one hand, Harold is square enough to be a good husband. I mean, I wouldn't worry about his running around. But is that enough? What I mean is, there are lots of men out there who are fun to be with. Harold is ... well, face it, Harold is dull, in a nice sort of way." She directed a stream of air from her lips up to the hair on her forehead. "What's a girl to do? I'm exhausted from being up all night, which is how come I came in here early ... Did you get the message?"

"What message?"

"A call from Christa Jones. Right after I arrived this morning. There, it's on your desk." She pointed to a mass of paper that virtually covered the desk's surface.

Lydia shuffled the papers until she saw one on which Christa Jones's name had been scrawled. "What did she want?"

"She wouldn't say. She sounded off-the-wall, though. Panicky. When I told her you weren't here, she said she would call you again when she could."

"I'll try her now," Lydia said, picking up the phone and dialing the number for WCAP. She asked the operator to be connected with Christa Jones's office.

"I'm sorry, but Miss Jones is no longer with the station."

"Oh ... where can I reach her?"

"I have no idea. Sorry, ma'am."

"Did you know Christa Jones isn't working for Quentin Hughes any more?" Lydia asked Ginger after she'd hung up.

"No."

"Do you have a home phone number for her?"

"It's unlisted."

"I hope she calls back. There was something about her that stayed with me."

"What do you mean?" Ginger asked.

"I'm not sure ... I had the feeling she wanted to tell me something but couldn't bring herself to do it."

As Ginger left the office Lydia called Cale Caldwell, Jr., and was put through to him by Joanne Marshall.

"I'm glad you called, Lydia. Frankly, after all the things I told you the other day, I worried about how you might have taken it. I hope you know it wasn't so easy to tell you those things about Mark and Jimmye. But mother and I respect you. We trust you. End of speech."

"Cale, I appreciate it...But here I am, the investigator again...sorry...Cale, do you know anything about a letter your father wrote that was to be opened on his death?"

"A letter? No...I've never heard of one..."

"Do you think your mother might have?"

"I really don't, Lydia. I mean, if she had, she'd certainly have told me about it."

"Well, I'm sure you're right, Cale—"

"Why do you ask? Did someone tell you there was such a letter?"

"It's just part of the morass of facts, half-truths and gossip I've been awash in ever since getting my committee assignment. Believe me, I've an idea of what you all have been going through. I've said it before, but I'll say it again. You come from a...a remarkable family."

It was a warm, appreciative laugh. "Yes, I do, Lydia. I damn well do. No matter what's happened, I'll always be grateful for that..."

Her next call was to Quentin Hughes's apartment in the Watergate. The line was busy. She tried again five minutes later and again the annoying busy signal buzz. She'd wanted to ask Hughes how she might reach his former producer, Christa Jones. When her third try brought the same busy signal, she gave up. Probably Christa had left because of her problems with Hughes, and it was unlikely he'd give a damn whether anybody contacted her or not. She'd just have to wait for her to call again.

Quentin Hughes listened as his mother told him on the phone about what had happened to her in Des

Moines. Two men had forced their way into her house, ransacked it and terrified her. She was still shaken, and a family physician had come to the house and sedated her. The police had been called, but when it became evident that nothing had been taken from the house, they seemed to have lost interest in going after the two young men who'd forced their way inside.

"...and you have no idea what they were looking for, momma?" Hughes asked.

"No, I don't. It was so terrible, Quentin. I wish you had been here."

"I do too. Did they go through the closet?"

"They went through everything, Quentin. The house was left a mess."

"What did they look like?"

"Oh, I can't remember, except one of them was bald, and so young too...that struck me..."

"Look, momma, I'm glad you're safe and sound. Do what the doctor says and get some rest. They were probably just a couple of nuts looking for drugs."

"Drugs? Why would they look for drugs in my house. I don't use drugs."

"I know, I know, momma. Look, I have to go. I'll make plans to fly out there as soon as I can."

"You always say that but you never come."

"I was there just a little while ago—"

"Yes, I know, but you only stayed for a little while. You only came to get that package." She groaned.

"Are you all right?"

"Do you think they were looking for that package you had here?"

"Don't be silly. I told you what they were, a couple of nuts. Rest and take care of yourself. Have the locks changed on the door. I'll pay for it."

"I don't like being here alone."

"We'll talk about it soon. Goodbye, momma."

He hung up and quickly went to the kitchen, took the key from the nail behind the refrigerator and went to his bedroom. He pulled the fireproof chest out into the middle of the room and nervously opened it. The brown package was missing.

He went to the living room, took a violent swipe at a lamp on the desk, sending it flying across the room. He clenched his fists. Christa...damn her soul...*damn her*...

Twenty-four

They missed each other by only minutes.

John Conegli pulled up in front of Christa Jones's apartment building just as she was turning the corner in search of a cab.

He circled the block twice before he found a parking spot. He walked to the front of her building, looked up and down the street, entered the foyer. He removed a set of master keys from his pocket and tried several before one worked. He opened the locked door separating the foyer from the interior of the building, closed it behind him, listened for sounds. The mailbox said that Christa's apartment was number 4. He looked for an elevator. There wasn't any. He cursed silently as he began the long trek up four flights of stairs. By the time he reached the top he was breathing heavily, and his right leg that had been treated for phlebitis two years before had started to ache.

He stood in front of Christa's apartment door and again listened for sounds. This time the first key on the ring opened the door.

One of Christa's cats looked at him from where it had been asleep on a windowsill, yawned, then put its head back on its paws. The other cat came from the kitchen and rubbed against Conegli's leg. He gently brought his shoe up under its belly and pushed it away. "Get lost, cat." He'd never liked cats. Sneaky creatures.

He looked in the bathroom, the kitchen. A large bag of dry cat food had been emptied onto a succession of paper plates. Next to the plates were two animal feeding bowls that were filled to the brim with water. An eight-quart pot had also been filled with water and sat on the floor. "Looks like she took off for a while," he mumbled to himself. "Looks like she's planning to come back, too."

He systematically searched every corner of the apartment. He could have worked faster, but he didn't want to leave evidence that someone had been there, which meant carefully replacing each thing he moved.

Two hours later, his search completed, he sat on the couch, put his feet up on a coffee table and closed his eyes. Five minutes later he left the apartment, returned to his car and drove off in the direction of Clarence Foster-Sims's apartment. He'd listened in on a conversation the other night between Foster-Sims and Lydia James. Because it had taken place on the phone, he'd only heard Foster-Sims's side of the conversation, but it was enough to learn that they were having dinner that night at Foster-Sims's apartment. He stopped at a tobacco shop and stocked up on cigars. Chances were, it would be a long night.

The phone started ringing as Lydia fumbled in her purse for the key to her brownstone. She hurried opening the door, ran into the living room and grabbed up the phone. "Hello."

A pause. "Miss James?"

"Yes. Who is this?"

Silence. Then, "This is Christa Jones, Quentin Hughes's producer..."

"Oh, yes?"

Lydia cradled the phone to her ear with her shoulder as she quickly sorted through the mail. Along with bills and junk mail was a brown envelope just slightly larger than a standard number 10. It was addressed to her by hand, and the upper left-hand corner read: "C. Jones."

"It's nice to hear from you," Lydia said. "I was just looking at my mail and see that I have something from you—"

"Miss James, I—" She started to cry.

"Miss Jones, are you all right?"

"Yes...no, I'm not all right. I hate to bother you, and I know this isn't your problem, but I have to talk to someone..."

"I'm happy to talk to you. What's wrong? Has it anything to do with the envelope I just received from you?"

"Yes, that and more. Could we meet tonight?"

Lydia was due at Clarence's apartment in an hour. She'd been very much looking forward to it. Still, how to ignore the urgency in Christa's voice...she'd call Clarence, tell him she'd be an hour late...She asked Christa whether what she had to say had anything to do with the Caldwell case.

A hesitation, no immediate response. Only background noise that indicated a public booth. When Christa still didn't answer, Lydia repeated the question.

"Yes...in a way it does."

"Where are you?"

"In the bus station, downtown."

"All right, it will have to be quick, though. Can I meet you now?"

"Yes, *please*. I'm leaving very shortly."

Lydia placed a quick call to Clarence, calmed him as best she could, slipped into her shoes, ran a brush through her hair and headed into the center of Washington.

The bus depot was teeming, complete with the usual assortment of derelicts and prostitutes mingling with a wide variety of citizens about to catch buses. She walked through the terminal, trying to spot Christa Jones. After one complete tour of the place proved unsuccessful, she went to the main door. Should she try again, she wondered? Which was when she did spot Christa coming out of a rest room, carrying a piece of molded Samsonite luggage. She was wearing a long, quilted, apricot down coat. Her hair was in disarray, her face reflected the upset that had been in her voice over the phone.

"I was about to give up," Lydia said as Christa came up to her.

"I'm sorry. I was in there." She half turned and pointed toward the rest room.

"Well, here we are. Where can we talk?"

They surveyed the main passenger area. Most seats were taken, and those that weren't were singles or next to other people.

"How was the ladies' room?" Lydia asked.

"Almost empty."

"Let's go," Lydia said.

Two women were in the rest room but soon left. Lydia and Christa were alone.

Lydia pulled an envelope from her bag. It had been inside the larger envelope Christa had sent her. The flap had been sealed and covered with Scotch tape. Written on the front was "To be opened 3 days from receipt."

"What's this?" Lydia asked.

"Something I want you to have in case anything happens to me."

Lydia frowned and ran her fingertips over the envelope. There appeared to be papers in it, and a hard object...maybe a key? "Christa, why do you think something might happen to you?"

"I can't go into it now." She looked at her watch. "I have to catch my bus soon. Please don't open it for three days. I need time. I hope I'll be back by then. If I am, we'll open it together. If not...well, open it, and the rest is up to you..."

"Why me, Christa?"

"Because I have no one else, Miss James."

Two women came in, and Lydia and Christa put their conversation on hold. Other women arrived, and Lydia suggested they leave the room and continue the conversation outside.

They stood next to a row of vending machines. When Lydia was certain no one was within earshot she asked again, "Why do you think something might happen to you? Who would want to hurt you?"

Christa, who'd appeared to have calmed down in the rest room, was now visibly anxious. She fiddled with the buttons on her coat, pushed a discarded cigarette butt around the floor with her foot and glanced nervously at everything except Lydia.

"Christa," Lydia said, placing her hand on her arm, "you've chosen to include me in whatever is happening to you. It isn't fair, it doesn't make sense to drop hints and then cut me off."

"I know, I know. I didn't mean to include you...Let me have the envelope back...I'm sorry, I've been very upset and I'm not thinking too clearly—"

"Christa, I'm not suggesting that I don't want to be involved. What I'm saying is that if I am I'd like you to be honest with me. I asked you when you called whether this had to do with the Caldwell murder. You said it did. What?"

Christa slumped against the side of one of the machines. "Oh, my God, why did this have to happen?"

"Why did *what* happen?"

"The whole thing...Jimmye McNab, Quentin...it was all so unnecessary. I told him that he was making a terrible mistake, that she was no good for him—"

"Quentin Hughes and Jimmye McNab?"

"Yes." Her face hardened now. "Yes, *them*. He said he loved her more than any other woman...he did that to me, talked about other women...God, how it hurt..."

"And yet you loved him, didn't you?"

She closed her eyes. "Yes, and the disgusting thing is, I still do." She opened her eyes. There was fear in them. "She was the worst, Miss James."

"Who?"

"Jimmye McNab. She was so cruel, but he couldn't

see it, or didn't care. Or maybe he liked it...She used people like nobody I've ever met, and I've met some in my day, believe me. Ironic, Quentin is a user too. Maybe it's like what they say about salesmen...They're the easiest to sell. Anyway, *I* knew what she was up to, what she was doing to him."

Lydia knew she was running out of time, Christa had said she was catching a bus. How much stock to put in what she'd been told...Christa Jones was obviously a very disturbed woman. No time for subtleties..."Christa...did Quentin Hughes kill Senator Caldwell? Or Jimmye—?"

It was as though her question had covered Christa in a sheet of ice. She seemed to freeze, her mouth set.

"Is that what you want to tell me?" Lydia pressed. "Are you telling me that Quentin Hughes killed out of jealousy—?"

"No."

"Then what?"

"She deserved to die, Miss James. I hated her with every cell in my body—"

"You?"

Christa seemed confused.

"Did you...kill Jimmye McNab?"

"I would have loved to."

Before Lydia could ask any more questions, Christa said she had to go to her bus.

"I'll come with you," Lydia said. She really wanted to escape the bus terminal, escape to the quiet and comfort of Foster-Sims's apartment. But she was also afraid to lose Christa, to lose the lead she represented...disturbed or not, Christa was also convincing. Her fear and anger seemed increasingly genuine as she talked.

"No, I want to go alone. I'll be back in three days. If I'm not, open the envelope. Please, Miss James, not before then. I need these three days to think, to figure out whether I'm doing the right thing. I have a good friend I can stay with."

She squeezed Lydia's hand and was suddenly swallowed by a crowd.

Lydia pushed through that same crowd and watched the back of the apricot coat go up to a waiting bus that said *New York*. Christa never looked back, simply handed her ticket to the driver standing at the open door and disappeared inside.

In her car Lydia tried to sort out her jumbled thoughts. She was annoyed to have been enticed by Christa to the bus terminal on the promise of learning something of importance to the Caldwell case. That hadn't, so far as she could tell, happened. Of course she was sorry for Christa Jones, a rejected woman afraid for her life. But damn it, the frustrations were getting to her.

She started the engine, about to head for Clarence's apartment, when she happened to look down at the seat next to her and saw Christa's envelope. She touched it, felt the hard object inside, shut off the ignition, tore open the envelope and removed a locker key. There was a long letter she didn't read all of because what seemed to matter most were the words: *"You'll find a videotape in a locker at the bus station. The key is to that locker. It explains so much..."*

Well, she'd gone this far...She went back to the terminal, found and opened the locker. Inside was a package wrapped in brown paper that she removed, tucked under her coat, then went to her car and drove too fast to Clarence's apartment.

"What do you make of it," Clarence said as they sat at the dining room table, about to dig into his dinner of rock Cornish hens, baked potatoes, string beans and a tomato-and-onion salad with Italian dressing. Clarence, Lydia thought—and warmly—the complete man.

"She seemed to want to tell me that she or Hughes killed Jimmye McNab. When she called me she said she had something to say about the Caldwell murder, but then she never mentioned Caldwell...Well, she's obviously been crazy—and I use the term advisedly—in love with Quentin Hughes for years, apparently since she first met him. I know it's hard to understand,

Clarence, especially for a man—but there are women, unfortunately, who fall in love with a man and stay with him no matter what happens, no matter how much abuse he heaps on them. That's even part of the attraction, I'm afraid. Think of the battered wives who keep coming back for more. And I couldn't help but think of the Jean Harris case in New York. The doctor she killed was a Quentin Hughes of sorts, a womanizer who for fourteen years shoved his affairs under her nose. Still, she hung in with him. I hate to admit it but it seems a female failing at times, this need to love a man no matter what he is or what he does."

"Could be . . . by the way, do you know where Christa was going?"

"Yes, to New York, to stay with some friends."

"And she claims the videotape has the answers to this mess . . . or some of them . . . Let's see the letter again . . . All right, so she accuses Quentin Hughes of murdering Jimmye McNab and Senator Caldwell, with no evidence."

"She says the tape will explain things, although like you I'm not sure exactly what." She hesitated, knowing what he was thinking and not wanting to face the next step . . . "Clarence, I felt I had to betray a confidence to the extent of opening the letter, but the tape . . . ?"

"Well, look, you can't do anything about it tonight. And to see the tape you'd need special equipment. Let's leave it alone for now."

It was, of course, what she wanted to hear.

"You know, Lydia, I can accept the fact that she stayed with Hughes despite, or even because of, the s.o.b. he is. But it's also logical to assume that Christa Jones killed Jimmye McNab out of jealousy—"

"But what about Hughes?"

"Why, if he was so crazy about her?"

"Remember, Christa also said that Jimmye was as bad as Hughes, a user . . . she could have provoked him to murder . . . except how does all this relate to Senator Caldwell's murder?"

"Eat before it gets cold. We'll solve this over coffee and dessert." He smiled when he said it.

But when they were finished he had a better idea. "You know, murder will out but it can also wait... how about coffee in bed?"

Lydia looked up at him. "Best offer I've had all day."

John Conegli sat in his car outside Clarence's apartment building and leaned close to the speaker that picked up some of the dialogue between Lydia and Clarence. He'd heard Lydia say that Christa had gone to New York, and he'd picked up the reference to the tape. From what he heard he assumed Christa had taken the tape with her, but of course he couldn't be sure. He also heard that Lydia had opened some letter from Christa, and wasn't feeling too good about it...

The sound of the television set and the rustle of the bedclothes now took center stage. He sat back and bit his lip. He wanted to stay and keep listening, but knew he had a much more pressing obligation. He got out of the car and went to a phone booth on the corner, pulled out a little black book from his pocket and thumbed through it until finding the name he was looking for. He dialed the New York City area code, then a number. To his relief, it was answered by the person he wanted to reach.

"Johnny, how the hell are you?" the voice from New York said.

"Not so good, Hal. Look, I don't have much time. I'm working on a big case down here and I need your help."

"I'm busy."

"Just tonight, Hal. There's a woman arriving on a bus from Washington any minute now. I don't know exactly how long it takes buses to get up there but I figure it should be pulling in about now. Her name is Christa Jones. She's kind of a wacky-looking broad, tall, lots of gray streaks in black hair, doesn't wear makeup, as I remember. The point is she's getting off the bus and visiting a friend. All I want you to do is meet the bus, if it's not too late, follow her and find out where she's going to be for the next three days."

"Hey, Johnny, I got a date and—"

"This client of mine pays good, Hal. I'll take care of you. Besides, you owe me a couple."

Hal yawned. "All right, all right, I'll do it. I wish I had a better description."

"Just do your best and let me know."

Conegli went back to his car and took up his listening again. He heard sounds, which he matched to his fantasies.

Eventually, no sound from the bedroom. The television set was turned off. Conegli looked at his pad, reviewed what he'd written. Obviously the most important piece of information was the mention of an envelope that Lydia James had been given, and that she was to open if this Christa Jones didn't come back to Washington.

Home and a few hours sleep, but first he needed to stop at a luncheonette in Maryland, where he met with a young man with long black hair, who wore a fringed suede jacket over a red-and-blue cowboy shirt, dungarees and cowboy boots. "I got a job for you, Billy," Conegli told him as they had coffee at the counter.

"Can use some work."

"This one's important."

"They all are, ain't they? Lay it on me."

Twenty-five

Boris Slevokian, noted violinist, had spent the afternoon at Foster-Sims's rehearsing pieces he'd perform on a tour of the Far East. It had taken considerable arm-twisting to convince Clarence to work with him, and Clarence was even more surprised than Boris that he'd agreed to do it.

It had been the first time he'd touched a piano in so many years, the Steinway seemed a formidable enemy.

He interrupted the rehearsal with Boris—less painful than he'd thought—to phone Lydia and tell her he'd gone back to the ol' debbil piano. She'd like that.

"Lydia?"

"Hi," she said as she continued stripping off her clothes for a calisthenics session she felt she needed to pick her up.

"I've been worried all day about you."

"Why?"

"Because of the letter Christa Jones gave you. You must realize that certain people might do just about anything to get it away from you—"

"Clarence, no one knows about the letter or the tape except you, me and Christa. I sealed the letter in a committee envelope and gave it to Ginger to put in the office safe, along with lots of other documents. I didn't tell her what it was, and she didn't ask. I'm always giving her bundles of documents to secure—"

"You gave it to Ginger? Do you think that was smart?"

"Smart, safe—pardon the pun—and sound. Ginger may talk like a flake but she's far from it. I also put the videotape in the safe, me myself. I checked with the Senate television studio and they told me it can only handle three-quarter-inch tape, the kind used in electronic news operations. The tape I took from the locker is two inches. I guess the only place to see it is at a television studio that has two-inch equipment."

"I have a friend who has his own recorder at home—"

"No good. Those are too small too. Willy-nilly, it looks like I'll come close to honoring Christa's request. Which, matter of fact, I'm kind of thankful for.

"And now I'm off for dinner with the fair Ginger. I like her a lot. She's full of beans..."

"Not my style, lady, but...Hey, guess what...I've been playing the old piano all afternoon."

"That's terrific. What brought it on?"

"The people's choice...Boris Slevokian. I've been working on a new piece he's going to incorporate in his next tour. The fingers are pretty stiff, Lydia."

She smiled, allowing herself a prurient thought without a single redeeming social value. "Clarence, darling, I've got to go...I'll call you if I don't get home too late..."

"Please *do*, I'll be up late."

John Conegli, who'd arrived in front of Foster-Sims's apartment an hour earlier, had heard Clarence's side of the telephone conversation with Lydia, heard him echo Lydia saying that Ginger Johnson had been given the envelope, which meant that Conegli needed to change some plans he'd made for the evening. He pulled quickly away from the curb and drove to Ginger's address, checked the mailboxes to note that she lived in

14-F, then left the building and went to a phone booth. His call was answered on the first ring by a woman.

"Let me speak to Billy."

"He ain't here."

"Who's this?"

"His mother. Who's this?"

"A friend. Did he say where he was going?"

"He said he had some work to do."

Conegli hung up and stepped outside the booth. He considered trying to head Billy off himself but was reluctant to leave. Given what Foster-Sims had said, the best shot he had at the envelope was Ginger Johnson. Besides, he reasoned, nothing would really be lost by having Billy go through with the job he'd assigned him to. Sort of an insurance job.

Lydia sat in a booth in Martin's Tavern on Wisconsin Avenue in Georgetown. Martin's had been a landmark since it opened in 1933. To Lydia it somehow represented the quintessential Georgetown hangout—dark wooden booths, veteran waiters in green jackets, a long oak bar behind which an extensive collection of steins stood proudly on shelves. Martin's attracted the athletic set, which was not surprising considering the fact that it had been opened by a former baseball player with the Boston Braves, Bill Martin. A small back room was known as the Dugout.

Lydia was not worried by Ginger's lateness. She was never on time. As she sat alone and sipped a kir, she thought on her theory about people who were chronically late. It was a way to insure attention...people were either waiting for their entrance or helping them make an exit for an appointment.

It didn't really matter, she decided, unless it was deliberate. She took another sip and waited for Ginger to come through the front door in her usual state of high energy, plus a little high anxiety.

When another twenty minutes had passed, Lydia put aside philosophy and began to worry. She was sure this was the night they'd planned to meet...she considered calling Ginger's home, told herself she's probably on her way right now...

Fifteen minutes later Lydia made the call to Ginger's apartment. Harold answered.

"This is Lydia James, Harold. I was supposed to meet Ginger for dinner but she hasn't shown up yet. I was getting worried—"

"You were right..." He sounded out of breath and in a hurry. "I just got a call from the police. Somebody attacked her again."

"*What?* My God...is she all right?"

"I think so. They were taking her to the hospital when they called. I heard her yelling in the background that she didn't want to go to any hospital, I'm glad they insisted..."

Lydia told the waiter that her plans had been changed, paid for the kir and left Martin's. She was annoyed at herself that she'd been so upset she hadn't asked what hospital Ginger had been taken to. She'd go home, wait for a call.

She pulled her Buick into a tiny alley to the rear of her brownstone, got out and walked quickly around the side of the building and toward the front door. In the darkness she stumbled over a loose red brick in the narrow sidewalk. She'd noticed it before and had meant to fix it. She continued along the path—

"Don't move."

A man stepped out from behind bushes that lined the side of the house, brought his left forearm around her neck and pushed the point of a knife into her back.

Lydia felt paralyzed.

"Walk nice and easy to the front door."

She did. When they got to the front door she said, "I don't have any money in the house, it's in my purse, take it and please leave me alone—"

"Shut up and open the door."

Her only thought was that she was about to be raped. If he didn't want money, what else? As she fumbled for her keys, she actually tried to remember what she'd

(214)

read or seen on television about how to handle a rapist. It had all seemed so clear and sensible before. Now, faced with the reality, it was anything but...was it better to put up a struggle, or go along and try to talk him out of it? She opened the door and they stumbled inside, his arm still around her neck. He kicked the door closed, loosened his grip and pushed her. Her face hit the wall and she felt a dull ache in her cheekbone.

"Don't turn around, lady."

She didn't, but caught her first sight of him in a mirror—young, long black hair. She was surprised to have enough composure to take stock of him. She also noticed he wore a buff, fringed suede jacket over a dark shirt.

He looked around the entrance hallway. She saw the knife for the first time. It looked like what she thought of as a hunting knife, and large.

"Come on, let's go in," he said motioning his head toward the living room.

Lydia turned to face him. "Who are you?" Not, she told herself, a particularly sensible question under the circumstances. Come on, Lydia...

He smiled. "Don't be silly, lady. Now take it easy, I ain't going to hurt you unless I have to."

He was going to rape her. Well, she'd damn well put up a fight, he'd have to use his knife to—

He grabbed her arm and whirled her into the living room. "You can save me a lot of time, lady. Just give me the envelope that's so important." (Conegli, a real sweetheart, hadn't bothered to call off his dogs.)

His demand shocked her. Why would he want Christa Jones's envelope? How did he even know about it? Did he know its contents, or, more likely, was he acting on someone else's orders?

"I don't know what you're talking about—"

"Lady, I don't mind tying you up and tearing this place apart if I have to. Be a smart lady and give me the envelope and save us both time and trouble."

She decided to tell the truth, which as any lawyer could tell you, was often the least convincing in a court

y

(215)

of law. Well, this was no court of law. This was, for God's sake, the real thing...She said, "I don't have the envelope you're looking for. I gave it to someone on my staff, it's in my office..."

Of course, he didn't believe her..."It could be so easy, lady, but you don't seem to care." He stepped closer. The knife in his right hand was pointed at her stomach. He grabbed her right shoulder and spun her around. She stumbled across the room, fell onto the couch. He was on her, twisting her left arm behind her back and forcing it up with increasing pressure toward her shoulders. She called out in pain, furious to give him that much satisfaction. "Shut up and tell me where that envelope is or I'll break your arm off—"

"I don't *have* it...let go of me and I'll tell you how we can get it."

He slowly released her wrist, stood, propped one scuffed cowboy boot on the edge of the coffee table. Slowly Lydia pulled herself up, turned and sat on the arm of the couch.

"Okay, lady. I'm all ears."

She closed her eyes against the pain in her arm, tried to collect her thoughts. "I told you the letter is in my office. We can go there now and get it, I promise you I'll give it to you there—"

"How far is your office?"

"Senate Building—"

"You a Senator. A woman?"

"I work there, for a committee." More truth, which she gambled he'd never believe.

He seemed to think for a moment, and as he did she felt a rising, pulsating anger. No question now, if she'd had a gun she'd have used it on him, would have taken *pleasure* in doing it. She'd stood in court many times and defended people like the man threatening her right now. She'd *pleaded* for their rights, pointed to their sad "socioeconomic" disadvantages, used everything the law allowed to combat the prosecution and, often as not, was successful. She'd believed in what she was doing, genuinely felt for most of her clients.

Not now. What attorney...possibly herself?...had set this man free so he could put a knife to her...

He'd made up his mind. "Get up."

"What are you going to do?" He slapped her. She was surprised how little it hurt. "Where's your bedroom?"

She stood and slowly led him from the living room to the bedroom. He flicked on an overhead light. "Nice," he said. "Nice big bed."

She said nothing, just stood there and waited for his next move. He was directly behind her, she felt the knife was poised for action.

"Let's see, where would a classy lady like you hide an important letter? Hard to say. Have you got a safe here?"

"No."

"You sure?"

"Yes, I'm *sure,* just as I'm sure the letter you want is"—and then she glanced at the night table next to her bed on which a lamp, a clock and a small box of Kleenex sat. The table had one drawer. She drew a deep breath. "All *right,* I *do* have the letter here. If I give it to you will you promise to leave me alone?"

"Now that you got smart and stopped lying, I'll take it into consideration."

"I'll get it for you." She went to the night table. She couldn't see him but knew he was following closely behind. In the drawer were envelopes containing legal documents from her law practice, to be reviewed at home before returning to the office.

She paused, then bent over and slowly opened the drawer. Her left hand reached inside and found a long, white envelope stuffed with legal carbons. She quickly turned and thrust the envelope at him, saying as she did, "Here's your envelope." In the moment it took him to receive the envelope her left hand fell back into the drawer, her fingers clutched a four-inch black cylinder of CS tear gas—more commonly known in its packaged state as Mace. She'd been given it a year ago by an attorney friend, who'd told her she needed it, given the city she lived in and the people she represented. He'd actually wanted her to apply for a gun permit, but she'd always been against keeping firearms in a house. More to appease him than anything else, she'd accepted the Mace, had put it in the night table drawer and pretty well forgotten about it. She had no real idea what effect it had on a person.

Her thumb went to a white trigger on top of the cylinder. Her friend had showed her that all that was necessary to activate the cylinder was to swing a white trigger a quarter-turn, which took it from a lock position. She did it, and as the man pulled pages from the envelope and asked if she was sure this was the letter, she brought her left hand up so that it was less than a foot from his face and squeezed down with all her might on the trigger. The orthochlorobenzalmalononitrile gushed from the cylinder with a hiss. It covered his face. His mouth opened; Lydia directed the stream of gas into it.

He fell to the floor, writhing. The knife dropped to his side, and the envelope and its contents went out of his hands. Lydia couldn't stop herself, leaned over and went on pressing the trigger until the twenty-two grams of Mace had been fully discharged, directly into his eyes and mouth.

Now, a kind of revulsion set in. She was appalled at what she saw. He clawed at his eyes, and a long, agonizing cry came from him.

She ran to the kitchen, grabbed the receiver from a wall phone and dialed the MPD. An officer answered on the first ring. "This is Lydia James." She gave her address and said that an intruder was in the house. He asked why she was able to get to a phone. "It doesn't *matter,* send someone immediately."

She dropped the phone, leaving it dangling on its cord, and ran out of the house and across the street, where she leaned against a lamppost, put her cheek against its cool metal and waited for the police to arrive...

The first officer out of the car was Horace Jenkins,

deputy chief of police. He saw Lydia and ran across the street to her. "What happened?"

She tried to speak and couldn't. And then she buried her face in her hands and, like any other human being, broke down into deep, heaving sobs.

Ten minutes later a police ambulance arrived and Lydia's attacker was taken away.

She was taken back to the house and now was in a small study, where she sat on a window bench and stared out the window. Jenkins came in. "Okay, it's over, Lydia. The kid is a punk named Billy Baulkis. He's got a long sheet on him. What did he try...rape?"

Lydia shook her head.

"Money?"

"No," she said so softly that it was barely audible. "It doesn't matter, does it."

"We'll go into that later. Probably not...no harm, no foul, is the way these damn things work out...By the way, where did you get the Mace?"

"It was a gift. If you want to arrest me for possession, feel free."

Jenkins patted the pocket of his raincoat. "No, I'll toss it when I get back to headquarters. Good thing you had it, but don't quote me. Will you be all right now?"

"Yes, I will, thank you."

"Maybe you shouldn't stay alone here tonight."

She assured him she would leave immediately to spend the night with a friend. "And thank you, Horace, for coming. I'll be all right."

"Glad I came on the call myself," he said. "Well, good night, Lydia. Don't let it get to you. Punks like him are all over this city these days."

After he was gone Lydia called Clarence. She quickly told him what had happened and said flat-out she wanted to spend the night. He told her not to drive. Ten minutes later he was at her front door and had a cab waiting at the curb.

Much later that night Clarence provided the medicine she most needed. Only then did she manage to sleep....

When she awoke in the early morning it occurred to her that her attack had coincided with the one on Ginger. She called Ginger's apartment.

"How are you?" Lydia asked.

"Disgusted. I'm sorry I stood you up last night, but it was due to circumstances beyond my control."

"Well, kiddo, even though we weren't together we shared an evening."

"How so?"

"I'll tell you when I see you. How are you feeling?"

"Not so bad, actually. At least I got a look at the guy and his car. I ended up with a bump on the head again and one more lost purse, but, like they say, it could be worse. I'll be in this afternoon."

"So will I," Lydia said. "I think we have some debriefing to do."

Twenty-six

Senator Wilfred MacLoon was nearing the end of his press briefing. He'd set a routine of weekly meetings with selected members of the press a number of years before, and had found it to be a useful way to help keep his name in front of the public and help deflect press and other criticism before it could develop to a serious degree.

He'd covered a variety of weighty-sounding subjects in the briefing, including whether or not the new missile system would get through the Congress. He told the reporters he was confident it would, and added, for rather obvious home consumption, that every strategic study made it increasingly clear that Utah provided the best possible site for its deployment.

His final item had to do with a proposed Senate investigation into the practices of religious cults. He'd been instrumental, indeed, pivotal, in having such investigations shelved for at least a year. That vote had taken place the day before, and one of the reporters asked MacLoon to explain why he'd taken such a stand in favor of religious cults.

"That's the trouble with you people," MacLoon said. His cigar had gone out. He lit it again. "I did it because

I'm against the Congress of the United States poking its nose into organized religion, and because I respect the Constitution upon which this nation was built. It doesn't mean I'm in *favor* of cults. In fact, I'm not, and many things I hear about them disturb me. But the bottom line is that one of the most sacred principles of this democracy is the separation of church and state. For the government to investigate religion would be to disregard what our founding fathers, in their wisdom, bequeathed us. No, I am not in favor of cults, ladies and gentlemen, but I am in favor of church and state going their own separate ways."

He looked around the room. "Any more questions?"

There were none. He thanked them and with Rick Petrone at his side left the room and returned to his office.

"Well done, senator," Petrone said.

He nodded. "What's new down the hall?" He meant Lydia's committee office.

"Nothing much. As far as I know she's working with the MPD on preparing her report. She doesn't seem to spend too much time here any more."

"Good. Ted Proust call?"

"Yes, he said he'd meet you at the usual time and place."

MacLoon was annoyed at the way Proust had put it. It sounded too undercover, and he wondered whether Petrone had picked it up. He made a mental note to tell Proust to stop being so damned James Bondish.

"If you have nothing else for me, senator, I'd like to leave early," Petrone said.

"Who is she?"

"My mother, she's in town for a few days and wants to spend time with her favorite son."

"Give my best to her. She's a good woman, good Mormon stock."

After Petrone and other members of the staff had left for the night MacLoon poured himself a stiff shot of bourbon from his private office stock, sat heavily in his chair and thought about the evening ahead of him.

He was to meet Proust at the Lee House, a small homey hotel conveniently located only four short blocks from the White House. MacLoon used it as a place to rendezvous with an occasional paramour, and had recommended that Proust stay there on his trips to Washington. He also enjoyed a turn-of-the-century pub in the hotel called Durdy Annie's that ran old-time movies and served good food at modest prices. Wilfred MacLoon, who did not like to spend his own money, had become an expert in getting more for less.

Proust was in town with substantial sums of money. Except that MacLoon hadn't been able to come up with much of a list of those involved in the missile system decision who might also be receptive to having their palms crossed in exchange for a position favorable to Utah's cause.

He was even more worried about a meeting to take place at eight o'clock. At first he'd refused to attend, but pressure mounted and he'd agreed.

He left his office at 7:45 and stopped at a McDonald's on his way to the eight o'clock meeting. He carried a bag containing two Big Macs, a large order of French fries, a chocolate shake and hot apple pie to his car, where he quickly finished the meal, then drove toward the meeting site. "The hell with them," he told himself. "They don't own me. Nobody does."

But as he pulled into the parking lot of the Caldwell Performing Arts Center his confidence faded. In all his years of dealing with special interest groups—and there had been many—he found this one the most troublesome. It wasn't just the nature of the group that bothered him. It was the people he'd been forced to deal with. He detested them. They weren't like the men he was used to, not by a long shot.

He walked through the main entrance to the Caldwell Center. The lobby was empty, as he'd been assured the center would be that night except for a board of directors meeting in an upstairs conference room. That meeting, he was told, would go on past midnight, so no problem there.

He checked his watch. The man was late. He went to heavy double doors that led to the auditorium, opened one and looked inside. The theater was dark except for a bare light bulb that hung from the ceiling of the stage area.

He stood in the doorway, fretting, wishing things could have been better, less so damn complicated, like when the kids were younger and he even got along with his wife. His kids...an older son, now a doctor in California, a daughter who was an executive with a major airline in Atlanta, and the younger boy in his second year of prelaw at the University of Utah. He missed them, things had been different when they were young and at home. No big financial squeeze to push a man into all kinds of deals he didn't want, make him do business with disgusting characters like—

"Good evening, senator."

MacLoon turned. "Hello, DeFlaunce. You're late."

"I was detained," Jason said. They looked at each other a moment, sharing an intense mutual dislike, to put it mildly.

For Jason, MacLoon represented everything that was wrong with life in high places. Jason's own father had been a local politician in their Massachusetts hometown. He'd been a heavy drinker and womanizer, and Jason had spent his childhood and teenage years hating him for the way he treated his mother, who unaccountably more often than not defended her husband. Jason had gone on to earn a degree in theater at Northwestern University, then a master's in the same subject at NYU in New York City. Along the way he'd given up ambitions for a performing career, instead concentrating on the business side of the theater, becoming an expert fund-raiser for Broadway shows. He moved to Washington to be a bigger fish than he could ever be in the Broadway scene. In quick time he'd gained access to Washington's inner artistic circles, and was pleased to find its members willing to rely on his experience in the world's theater capital. He became, in short, a formidable art maven, to use the phrase of one of the local columnists.

From MacLoon's perspective, Jason DeFlaunce was nothing more than a swish, a fairy. Gay rights was not one of his favorite causes.

"Okay, Mr. De*Flaunce,* let's get on with this. I got places to go."

Jason, a half-smile on his lips, shrugged. "Whatever you say, *senator.*" He pushed past MacLoon and walked down the aisle of the darkened theater until he reached the stage. MacLoon slowly followed after him. "Why here?"

"Why not?" Jason said. "No one will bother us. Besides I like discussing important things on a stage."

MacLoon felt the gorge rising. He looked at the bare bulb hanging over the stage, pressed his lips tight together. "What do you want to tell me?"

Jason walked up a short flight of steps leading to the stage apron, passed under the light bulb and went to the furthermost corner of the stage-right wings. MacLoon reluctantly followed him, turning once to look out over the empty seats. Jason took two folding metal chairs from against the wall, opened them and sat on one. MacLoon, who would have preferred to stand, roughly pulled one of the chairs away from Jason and sat down.

"I met with our mutual friend recently," Jason said.

MacLoon knew who he meant but still asked, "Who's that?"

"Francis Jewel, of course."

"He should be happy the way I...discouraged the investigations in his outfit. It was a question of conscience being coincident with—"

"Oh, come off it, senator...But yes, I expect he is. People usually are pleased when they receive a return on money spent. That, however, was not what Mr. Jewel asked me to speak to you about."

"Whatever else he wants to talk about doesn't concern me," MacLoon said. "Nor your own impertinence. I did what I thought was *right* by keeping church and state separate. The money he's contributed to me through *you* had nothing to do with it, and you'd better damn well let him know that. I don't like him or his damn cult, but there is a constitutional principle involved here—"

Jason laughed. "Whatever appeases your conscience, senator."

MacLoon almost came off the chair. "Look, De-Flaunce, if there's a conscience that needs appeasing, you'd better look to your own."

MacLoon settled back in the chair, took out a cigar and lit it. "Is this all you've got to say to me?"

Jason reached up, ran his hand along one of many ropes attached to spars on the wall, almost as though the rope were a living thing being stroked. His eyes remained on it as he said, "No, this is much more important than simply influencing a congressional investigation. You are aware that the Caldwell family's interests have been threatened for a long time by the presence of a certain videotape."

"What are you talking about?"

"Come now, senator, I can't believe that you haven't heard something about the tape."

MacLoon drew on his cigar, leaned forward. "That's the problem with people like you. You get so wrapped up in playacting you have no idea what reality, or the truth is. Videotape? I don't know what the hell you're talking about."

Jason shrugged, turned his hand over in the air. "Be that as it may, this same videotape that has caused the Caldwell family so much anguish is doing the same thing to our mutual friends at the Center for Inner Faith."

"So what?"

"So *what?* Senator MacLoon, you have chosen to be very directly involved in that organization's work." MacLoon started to protest but Jason waved him off. "I know, you like to see yourself as a dedicated public servant working within Congress on behalf of Mr. Jewel's interest only because of your deep and abiding belief in the Constitution." His sarcasm was not lost on MacLoon. "But in reality, and you are very big on reality, and the truth, you have a continuing obligation to Mr. Jewel. I'm sure you would agree that it would be embarrassing to you should your distinguished colleagues in Congress, or your constituents, learn that you'd been accepting...how shall I say it, gratuities from such people."

MacLoon stiffened, draped his arm over the back of the chair and crossed his legs. "Don't try to intimidate me, damn you. I could chew you up and spit you out anytime I wanted to, and don't you forget it."

"Tough talk, senator. But you don't intimidate me either. The fact is, you've gotten pretty sloppy lately, and I don't mean just the size of your belly. I know all about Cale Caldwell having found out about some of the sources of your extra income, including the take from Mr. Jewel and his people."

"You're crazy—"

"No, I'm not, Senator MacLoon. Senator Caldwell had discovered not only that you were taking from Mr. Jewel, but he'd learned about the millions being laid on you by those wonderful folks back in Utah."

MacLoon denied the accusation, which wasn't easy. The fact was that Caldwell *had* discovered certain things about him and had directly confronted him with his findings. They'd almost come to blows once, and Caldwell had left MacLoon's office that day threatening to expose him to the full Senate...

He shifted in the chair and puffed on his cigar. His collar was tight, he ran his fingers around it. Finally: "What does all this have to do with you and with that gang of weirdos—?"

"I wouldn't call them that, senator. After all, they've contributed rather handsomely to you—"

"And you too—"

"I'm a survivor, senator. I'm good to my friends, they're good to me. That qualifies me for the Senate, wouldn't you say—?"

"No, I damn well wouldn't."

Jason stood and turned his chair around so that he could sit with his arms folded over its back. "Well, no matter...Mr. Jewel originally called me because he thought you might be of help in locating the tape."

"About that tape. Just what's on it?"

"That's not important, senator. What counts is that it exists and is of vital importance not only to Mr. Jewel but to the Caldwell family. It must be located, and destroyed. You see, when Mr. Jewel first called me he was shooting in the dark about where the tape might be. But I received a call late this afternoon from him telling me that it now appears that the tape is in the possession of Lydia James or her researcher Ginger Johnson. It's not Mr. Jewel's style to suggest breaking into Lydia's office to search for it. But there's no need for that anyway, is there? All you have to do is make the search yourself, or, if that's distasteful to you, have one of your loyal aides do it."

"I'm not a thief—"

"Ah, shades of Richard Nixon...well, I wasn't suggesting that you were. But if this all bothers you, you might view it the same way you did the investigation into religious cults, as having constitutional ramifications or, if you prefer, as a threat to national security ...come on, Senator MacLoon, your fine rationalizations are not the point. The tape must be found. That *is* the point. If you find it you'll be rewarded. Need I say more?"

The senator stood, pulled the waist of his trousers over his belly and pushed the chair against the wall with his foot.

"Mr. Jewel would appreciate having your end of things accomplished by five o'clock tomorrow," Jason said evenly.

"Tell Mr. Jewel to go to hell."

"As you wish, senator. It was good of you to come."

As Jason started to walk away, MacLoon suddenly grabbed him by the front of his cashmere sweater, wheeled him around and pushed him against the wall.

"Tell Jewel that if the tape is in Lydia James's office he'll have it tomorrow. Then, don't ever come within fifty feet of me if you know what's good for you."

Jason, slumped against the wall, watched MacLoon cross the stage, lumber down the stairs and leave the auditorium. He turned and again ran his hand up and down the ropes. He'd been expressionless during MacLoon's assault on him. Now, a sly smile crossed his boyishly handsome face.

He left the auditorium and went to the box office, where he phoned the Caldwell house in Virginia.

"Jason?"

"Yes. I just met with Senator MacLoon."

"And?"

"He'll cooperate in trying to find the tape. But something that he said concerned me. I'd like to speak with you about it."

"What is it?"

"Is Cale there?"

"Yes."

"I'd like to drive down to see you."

"Right now? I'd rather not—"

"Yes. Right *now*."

MacLoon drove back to the Senate Building, went to his office and called Rick Petrone's home number.

"Yes, senator, what can I do for you?"

"You can get your tail over here right now."

"I'm with my mother. I told you that she was in town for a few days and—"

"Then tell her, damn it, that being an aide to a United States senator is no bed of roses. Tell her what you want, but get over here."

Twenty-seven

"Hello Jason, come in," Veronica Caldwell said coolly as she greeted him at the door.

"I'm sorry, but it couldn't wait, Veronica."

She briskly led him to the study, where Cale Caldwell, Jr., was waiting.

"Coffee?"

"I'd love some." He was both annoyed and disappointed by her curt manner. It wasn't the first time she'd treated him this way. He didn't make an issue of it. He never did. Whatever his pretensions, he was a sort of Caldwell family retainer. Nobody said so, and he never admitted it to himself. But it lay there, unspoken and real.

Veronica poured the coffee, and Jason asked Cale, "How is Mark Adam's defense coming?"

Cale nodded solemnly. "Good. The attorneys I've brought in are cooperative and are in tune with my views on the best way to present Mark's case. Unless something dramatically unexpected occurs, it should be an insanity plea, simple to present and to win."

"How's Mark Adam holding up?"

"Quite well...I visit him every day. There's been a deterioration in his mental processes, which on the one hand, of course, is unfortunate, sad, but on the other hand is advantageous to his defense."

"Now, Jason," Veronica said impatiently, "just what was so important?"

Jason, who'd driven to the house with considerable confidence, had by now lost much of it. The demand he'd intended to make was now reduced to a request, made almost apologetically... "Veronica, I'd like more assurance that Senator Caldwell's letter will never be revealed..."

Veronica looked at her son.

"Mother has assured you, Jason, that the letter has been destroyed," Cale said.

"I know," Jason said, "but after talking to MacLoon I realized that *each* one of us would be... in jeopardy if that letter ever saw the light of day."

Cale went to the fireplace, opened the screen and poked at what was left of three logs. The embers came to life again and tongues of yellow light flickered over the room. "There's nothing more we can do, Jason, and you'll have to understand that. My father, sad to say, had lost his grip on reality. He knew he was very ill, and that acute knowledge of mortality did strange things to his mind. He had this need to set the record straight, as he put it, to make amends for what he considered the sins of his family, his friends, of his own life. Very sad, actually, but not unusual. Think of all the celebrities who write their autobiographies once they pass the wrong side of fifty. That was all my father was doing, actually, writing his life story."

Jason slid forward in his chair and his hand tipped over his coffee cup. "Sorry," he said to Veronica, who seemed not to have noticed. He looked at Cale. "I know all this. You explained it to me when the letter was first discovered. But you do realize, Cale, that many people's lives would be, to say the least, adversely changed by what your father claimed about them. Think of it. Because of a series of circumstances, your father could have destroyed his own son, your brother, as well as the memory of the girl he'd raised as a daughter. He held a sword over the heads of some of his colleagues too, especially that animal, Will MacLoon. And what about people outside his professional and personal life, people like Quentin Hughes, who got pulled into things because of his relationship with Jimmye, and of the Center for Inner Faith because of Mark Adam's involvement with it?"

"And you, of course, Jason, by having become involved with our family..."

"Yes, including me, Cale. Very true..." As he sat there, a familiar anger surfaced. As hard as he'd tried, as loyal as he'd been, he was still the outsider, second-class, a friend of the family rather than a member of it...

"You look upset, Jason," Cale said. "All the things my father revealed in his letter, about you, others, they're safely destroyed. We alone know them... and surely you can trust us. As you've said, you've been very loyal to us, and we *appreciate* it. As for what you chose to do for Francis Jewel...that's your business—"

Jason started to say something but Cale cut him off. "And, Jason, I must remind you that you also decided to play your own little game just as Jimmye did—"

"What little game?"

"Intimating to us that unless we took better care of you financially you just might be tempted to let out a few of what some might term embarrassing family secrets. Aside from the salary paid you for your work at the center, there was considerably more money given you, if you'll recall."

"I deserved that money for what I'd gone through. I had to deal with Jimmye, represent the family. Nobody in this family wanted to deal with that end of it. Surely that deserved *something* in return?"

Veronica was visibly annoyed. "Enough, Jason. Nobody is demeaning your contribution. The very structure of this family was threatened by the indiscreet, to put it mildly, actions of some of its members. Mark Adam's decision to join that absurd group of fanatics set off a whole chain of events that threatened at any minute to destroy everything the Caldwell name stood for." Her voice softened. "You've been a very dear friend, Jason. I consider you a son, in a sense, and have tried to treat you that way. But please don't turn our generosity back on us in this manner. Everything is going to work out if we all exercise *patience*...More coffee, Jason?"

"No, thank you. I'm sorry. It was a very upsetting meeting with Senator MacLoon. He pushed me so..."

Cale stretched, yawned. "I'm beat. I really have to go home, I have a very busy day tomorrow. Jason, thank you for coming, I trust you feel better now. Mother is right, all the problems we've had to face...Jimmye, Hughes, Mark Adam and the cult, father's death...soon they'll fall into perspective." He came over to Jason, patted his arm. "Go home, have a good sleep and forget about the letter. The minute mother discovered it she destroyed it. You can count on that. Remember, the Caldwell word has always been solid gold. That's part of the reputation we're trying to protect."

"We all must remain strong through these final days," Veronica put in. "I know you will and that I can count on you as though you were one of my own."...

Jason and Cale stood together outside the house as they prepared to get into their cars. "By the way," Cale asked, "have you heard anything new about the tape?"

"No, I haven't, but Jewel is putting on the pressure. That's why I met with MacLoon tonight, to get him to find what he could through Lydia James."

"He agreed?"

"Yes. If Mark hadn't been so stupid, none of this would ever have happened—"

"I know," Cale said. "But then again, no one ever dreamed that Jimmye would end up doing to us what she did. I suppose there's no sense crying over what people have done in the past. The important thing is to resolve it, and that means finding the tape and destroying it."

Twenty-eight

"Hello, Rick..." Lydia said as she was about to snap off the overhead light in her Senate office and leave for the night. "What are you doing around here so late? Bucking for a raise?"

The young Senate aide grinned and shoved his hands in his pockets. "The old man had me working on a project, Lydia. I just wrapped it up and thought I'd come down here and take a look at the notes on the committee report."

Lydia nodded, slipped into her coat, picked her briefcase up from a chair. "How's your mother?"

"Fine...well, good night, Lydia, have a pleasant evening."...

She went directly to Clarence's apartment. He suggested they go out to dinner but she said she was too tired, "I just wanted to come by and give you this." She reached into her briefcase and handed him the letter and videotape she'd removed from her office safe moments before Rick Petrone had arrived. "Sure you want them?" she asked.

He weighed the tape in his hands. "Absolutely. No one would ever think an aging piano teacher was in possession of such important documents. You know,

Christa's three-day grace period will be up tomorrow night. You plan to look at the tape before the concert or after?" He was referring to a concert at the Caldwell Center that they'd made plans to attend.

"After. Actually I'm not sure how to arrange to screen it. I guess I could ask one of the TV stations to use their equipment, but then I'd be in an awkward position...I don't want anyone else to see it...Anyway, please put these away in a safe place and bring them with you tomorrow night."

She kissed him, lightly at first, then paid attention and put her heart in it. He more than cooperated, then abruptly held her at arm's length. "Enough of this love-making, let's make love. Either stay the night, or leave in a hurry. You know how I vote."

"Me too, but I've really got to go...got to think, sleep...you're not the best atmosphere for either."

"I'll take that as a compliment."

"And I'll take a rain check."

Twenty-nine

Christa Jones sat on the floor of an apartment on East Sixteenth Street in New York City. It belonged to a friend, Amy Upshur, who'd known Christa from Des Moines. In fact, Amy had been the only friend Christa had in Des Moines, the only one she could turn to when things had become particularly unpleasant with Quentin Hughes.

Amy had moved to New York to chase a retailing career and had progressed through a succession of jobs with department stores and boutiques, then managed a few small shops until finally opening her own children's boutique on the Upper East Side. Not having heard from Christa in a long time, she was surprised to receive her call, then quickly sensed that her old friend was in some kind of trouble. She readily agreed to her coming to stay with her for a few days.

It was late afternoon of the third day of Christa's visit. She'd told Amy that morning that she planned to leave New York after dinner, and so Amy insisted on leaving the shop early so that they could have a leisurely dinner together.

"What's your pleasure, Christa?" Amy asked.

"Oh, I really don't care. I like most things, except Indian and Mexican."

Amy shook her head. "My two favorites. Tell you what. There's a great place up on East Forty-ninth, Antolotti's, northern Italian. A guy I've been seeing takes me there. It'll be my treat, no arguments."

Christa checked the time. It was five. "Amy, could we go now? I'm hungry and I do want to get to the airport in time for an early flight back." She'd already packed her suitcase, which sat on the floor next to the front door.

"I really can't, honey...I'm expecting a couple of phone calls, one of them from a man who's very important in my life and who's in California on a business trip. Let's do this. I'll make a reservation and tell them you're on your way now. You go in, ask for Joe, give him a big kiss on the cheek for me and gorge yourself on antipasto and have a drink. I'll catch up with you soon as I can. How's that sound?"

"Fine, except I really don't mind waiting for you—"

"No, nothing worse than sitting around listening to lovebirds on the phone, especially when it gets a little gushy. Go ahead, grab a cab and settle in. I'll be there before you know it."

Actually Christa was relieved to be able to be on her own for a while. The day had started okay but as the afternoon wore on she felt increasingly anxious. A walk would do her good, and maybe get her to the restaurant about the same time as Amy. She double-checked Antolotti's address, picked up her suitcase and left the apartment.

Darkness had fallen on the city, and a cold wave that had moved in during the afternoon had dropped the temperature considerably. Christa set down her suitcase and buttoned her coat. She hadn't brought many clothes with her, in fact owned very few. She allowed a twinge of optimism and decided she'd buy a new wardrobe soon, one that was in style, for a change. She picked up the suitcase and walked briskly along the street toward a main avenue. As she approached it, she decided to take a bus. She liked buses, and trains, enjoyed watching the people.

She crossed the avenue, went to where a large group of people waited at a bus shelter, asked someone whether a bus that stopped there would go up as far as Forty-ninth Street and was told it would. She settled into line and waited until a blue-and-silver bus fought its way through the intersection and stopped six feet from the curb. Christa noticed on the side of the bus that exact change was necessary. She fumbled through her purse in search of the right combination of coins, and luckily came up with them just as it was her turn to deposit her fare in the meter. For a moment she had an image of herself being lined up in front of a bare wall and shot for the high crime of insufficient coins...

She navigated the crush of passengers and moved toward the rear of the bus, spurred on by the driver's command, "Move to the rear." Or be shot down... The last passenger boarded, and the driver pulled away from the curb, which jolted Christa into another passenger. "I'm sorry," she said. The man didn't even seem aware of her, kept his nose buried in his newspaper.

As the bus slowly proceeded north, Christa crouched down in an attempt to read the street signs. No one else on the bus seemed to be doing that, which made her feel very much the tourist.

After what seemed forever, the bus arrived at the corner of Forty-ninth. Christa went through the rear exit door behind three other passengers, not noticing that other passengers had left through the front door, including a man who'd been the last to board at the corner where Christa had caught the bus.

She waited for a large group of people to pass, then crossed the sidewalk and stopped to look in a store window. The man stood just out of her sight, behind a bus shelter.

She looked up at the street sign to make sure she was in the right place, then turned the corner and began walking east on Forty-ninth. The man quickly left the shelter, peered around the corner and followed her. If *he* had turned to look behind him, he might have noticed another man who'd ridden the same bus, and who'd waited until Christa had turned the corner before falling in step with her.

East Forty-ninth Street was relatively free of people. A few office workers who'd returned home were walking their dogs. One of them carried an elaborate device for scooping up the dog's droppings. Unbelievable. An old woman with two dachshunds carried a piece of newspaper and a small plastic bag to accomplish the same thing.

Christa came up now to a fenced parking lot that served a small commercial building. She looked through the fence and admired a silver Rolls-Royce. She put her suitcase down to give her hand a rest, then looked up the street and saw a sign on a canopy: *Antolotti's.* It looked mighty inviting an oasis. She picked up her suitcase and was about to move toward the restaurant when a man came up behind her.

The suitcase dropped out of her hand. She turned and looked into his face. God... Quentin Hughes... She wanted to scream but nothing came out of her throat. He grabbed her arm and put her up against the fence. "Where is it, Christa?"

She felt frozen to her spot.

"What are you doing here?" was all she managed to get out.

"The tape, Christa, *give me that tape.*" He looked down at the suitcase. "Is it in there?" He decided not to wait for an answer, took the purse from her shoulder, picked up the bag and started to leave... when the man who'd been following him suddenly came up.

"What do you think you're doing, friend?"

"Who the hell are you?"

"I'm saying leave the lady alone."

Hughes tried to push by him, which was a poor idea. The man leaned his bulk into Hughes, then slammed him against the fence. Hughes lost his grip on the suitcase. The man yanked away Christa's purse from

Hughes's other hand and dropped it to the sidewalk, then rammed his hand up against Hughes's throat and held a cocked fist inches from his face. Hughes tried to bring his right knee up into the man's groin. Another bad move. "You do that again, mister, and you're dead."

Christa grabbed up her suitcase and purse and ran up the street toward the restaurant. She stopped in front of it, turned to look back at the parking lot fence. As far as she could tell, neither man had realized she'd left, too busy with each other...she hoped. She darted into the restaurant and said to the first person she saw, a man in a tuxedo, "Could I use your phone?"

"Of course—"

And it occurred to Christa that if Hughes got away from his attacker he might well look for her in the closest place, which happened to be this restaurant. "I was supposed to meet someone here," she said to the tuxedoed maitre d'. "Her name is Amy Upshur. My plans have changed and I've got to leave. Would you tell her that...?"

"Miss Upshur called. Are you sure you can't wait for her?"

Christa shook her head. *"No*, I have to go right now. Tell her I'm sorry, I'll write her."

Christa started to leave, turned. "Are you Joe?"

"Yes."

She kissed his cheek. "That's from Amy." Also from herself now.

The Eastern Airlines shuttle to Washington was full, and a second section had to be put on. Christa sat back in her seat on the 727 and tried to collect her thoughts. Having Quentin Hughes come up to her on the street in New York was still like a bad dream. She had no idea how he'd learned that she was in New York. It didn't matter. What did was that he clearly was not about to accept the loss of that damned tape. Of course he won't, she thought as the plane pushed away from the gate and the pilot increased engine power to begin his taxi toward the active runway. That tape is worth too much to him...

Unlike her mood—her life—the flight to Washington's National Airport was easy and smooth. Christa went directly to a bank of public telephones, where she dialed several numbers, all in the hope of reaching Lydia James. Each one produced nothing but a long succession of unanswered rings. She clenched her teeth, swore silently, then she rummaged through her purse until she came up with a scrap of paper another telephone number was written on. She dialed it, and Ginger Johnson answered.

"This is Christa Jones, Miss Johnson...Quentin Hughes's producer. I'm sorry to bother you but—"

"That's okay," Ginger said, "I know that Miss James was anxious to hear from you. What can I do for you?"

"Do you know where Miss James is?"

"Matter of fact I do. She told me she and Mr. Foster-Sims are attending a concert at the Caldwell Center—"

"They're there now?"

"I suppose so. I'm not sure what time the concert started but I'd think it's any minute now. Can I help you, Miss Jones? Lydia and I work together very closely and—"

The sound of a receiver being clicked into place.

"Who was that?" Harold asked.

"Somebody the committee's been involved with."

"I'll be glad when you're through with that damned committee."

Ginger, who was wearing a thigh-length blue terrycloth robe, plopped down on the couch next to him. She ran her fingertip around the outline of his ear. "I wasn't thinking about any committees, Harold. Care to fool around?"

He said he did.

Thirty

John Conegli arrived home too late for dinner,
ducked Marie's plaints, changed his shirt, slipped into
his overcoat and was about to leave the house when
the phone rang. He heard his wife ask who was calling,
then her irritated: "It's for you, your highness, some
guy calling from New York. Hal."

Conegli took the phone, and cupped the mouthpiece
with his hand. "Hal, what's up?"

Standing in a phone booth on the corner of Forty-
ninth Street and Third Avenue, collar up against the
cold, Hal said, "Damndest thing happened—"

"You got the package from her?"

"No. I've been tailing her ever since I picked her up
at Port Authority, like you told me. I never seen her
with any package like you described. Everytime she
came out of that apartment she wasn't carrying any
package, and I figured her purse wasn't big enough...
anyway, tonight she comes out of the apartment carrying her purse and a suitcase, the same one she had
with her from the bus station. So I follow her. She gets
on an uptown bus. She comes up to Forty-ninth Street,
gets out of the bus and looks in a store window. Then
she starts walking east on Forty-ninth. I followed her

too. How do I know? That's my job...right?...to know these things. She gets halfway down the street, stops and looks through a fence into a parking lot. Before I know it this other guy comes up behind her and starts to mug her."

"Mug her? I don't believe it—"

"In New York, you don't believe it? This guy, he's tall, a headful of sort of gray hair, pins her up against the fence. I thought about just grabbing her suitcase and taking off...but what the hell, I'm a lover, right? So I decide to pull the guy off. Which I did. I saved the broad—"

Johnny looked at his watch. He had to leave. "Look, what about the suitcase?"

"Well, while this character and I are mixing it up, she picks up the suitcase and takes off."

"Where did she go?"

"Beats me."

Conegli hung up and left. He drove quickly to the Caldwell Performing Arts Center...he knew Lydia and Clarence had planned to go to some concert there and had decided to follow them after it was over on the off chance that Lydia James might lead him to the package. He found Clarence's car, parked near it in a space that gave him an unrestricted view of the center's front entrance.

He settled back to wait.

To wait. The story of his life. Well, at least it gave him a chance to let his fantasies take over. Right now the lady was coming out of the water...like the one in the TV commercial. Dripping wet and all for him. And she didn't look anything like Marie. What self-respecting fantasy would...?

Thirty-one

Quentin Hughes still felt shaken as he boarded an Eastern Airlines flight to Washington at New York's LaGuardia Airport.

He wasn't certain where Christa had gone, but felt it a reasonable assumption she would go back to Washington. Anyway, he had to return to do his show.

He thought about what had just happened on Forty-ninth Street, how the man had pulled a revolver from a small holster beneath his armpit and shoved it into his stomach. Obviously he was some kind of a professional, and Hughes had come up with the best story he could...that this was his girlfriend and she'd run out of their apartment and stolen things of his...The man with the gun didn't seem much interested one way or another in his story, but had let him off, almost as though he were an afterthought. By then, of course, Christa was gone.

Finding Christa had been a hopeless job until a phone call that morning from Amy Upshur. He and Amy had been close in Des Moines for a brief time, something Christa never knew about. After some initial chitchat Amy told Hughes that Christa was at her place and acting strangely. He'd asked her what she meant and she'd said, "Well...it's crazy, but she claims you were somehow mixed up in the death of Senator Caldwell and that journalist...what was her name?...Jimmye something..."

"Like you say, that's crazy—"

"Well, that's why I finally decided to call you. For her own sake too, I thought you ought to know about it. Christa is a wonderful person, I'd never do anything to hurt her but I'm worried that in her present state of mind she'll hurt herself, and other people too..."

Hughes had caught the first flight to New York. He'd not wanted just to arrive at Amy's apartment, so he sat in a café across the street and hoped that Christa would show up. His timing had been right; he'd had to wait only an hour before she came out of the apartment carrying her suitcase...

Now back in Washington, he drove to Christa's apartment. He rang the bell. No answer. He decided to go to the studio and call her apartment from there during the night until he got her.

He told his new producer, a long-legged young woman with a degree in communications, and with such other requisites as long red hair, green eyes and a Scottish burr, that he wanted a rerun ready to go at a moment's notice should he suddenly have to leave in the middle of the show.

"Why?" she asked.

"Just do what I tell you." He went into an empty office to try Christa's number.

"I don't like to be talked to that way," she said.

"Shut up."

"I quit."

Hughes couldn't hear her—or, at the moment, care.

Thirty-two

Lydia and Clarence waited for the program to begin—it featured an up-and-coming cellist named Vittorio Pelini accompanied by an established Washington pianist, Marshall Gottlieb. Also, and which pleased Clarence, in addition to sonatas by Beethoven, Schubert and Debussy, was String Quartet No. 2 by Alexander von Zemlinsky, "a pretty adventuresome item," said Clarence.

His lecture went on with the information that Zemlinsky had been a teacher of Mahler and that his music often threatened to cross over into atonality but never quite did. Lydia smiled to herself, happy to hear Clarence being so happy in his element, but frankly not much able to concentrate on music. A videotape was too much on her mind.

They waited for the ritual of his eminence Jason DeFlaunce stepping onto the stage to announce the evening's program was about to begin. Instead, it was Veronica Caldwell who stepped through the curtains. Most in the audience immediately recognized her, and spontaneous applause rippled throughout the auditorium. Veronica waited for it to die down, then said, "I'm so delighted to be here this evening to introduce the program. I'm honored to be a member of the United States Senate but this center and the arts in America, particularly in Washington, have always been close to my heart. Like religion, they've sustained me in our family's tragedy. I was determined to be here tonight to renew my old involvement in what this center stands for. I assure you that nothing short of a declaration of war would have kept me from it."

Veronica stepped back through the curtains. The houselights went down. The curtain opened and the two musicians stepped center-stage. Lydia nervously squeezed the oversized handbag on her lap, feeling the contours of the videotape through the leather. Clarence had handed over to her both the tape and Christa's letter when he'd picked her up, in spite of his conviction that they would be safer at his apartment. Lydia, though, had insisted he give them to her, then shoved them into her bag.

Somehow she felt that more than one show was about to begin...

Well, at least her cats were okay, Christa thought when she got back to her apartment. People who said that cats were aloof and didn't miss human contact were crazy. Both animals came to her, rubbed against her legs and nuzzled their heads against her hands. She couldn't stay long. Quentin would be returning to Washington, probably that evening, and would surely come looking for her.

She looked up the number and dialed the Caldwell Performing Arts Center. After finding out that the performance was going on, she finally persuaded the woman who answered that there was an emergency and she must find Lydia James and bring her to the phone. Thanks to Lydia's recent publicity, the woman could recognize her and bring her to the phone.

"Hello, this is Lydia James. Who is this? What's the—?"

"Christa Jones—"

"Oh, well...I'm glad to hear from *you*. Are you all right? Are you here in Washington?"

"Yes, I am...Miss James, I must see you."

"All right. When?"

"Right now. Please."

"I'll leave immediately and meet you anywhere you say."

Christa considered asking Lydia to come to her apartment but was afraid to stay there any longer. "Meet me at Luigi's."

"On Nineteenth Street, Northwest?"

"Yes."

"I'm on my way."

Lydia hurried back into the darkened theater and told Clarence she was leaving to meet Christa at Famous Luigi's.

Clarence pulled her up from her seat and led her to the lobby.

"Can't you meet her *after* the concert? I'll come with you—"

Lydia shook her head. "I promised her I'd be there right away. I've got to go *now,* Clarence."

"I'll come with you."

"No, please. If I don't show up alone she might panic, even run. Stay for the rest of the concert, then go home. I promise I'll call you the moment I can. Please, Clarence, thanks for understanding—"

"Look, damn it, I'm not worried about Christa Jones, I'm worried about *you*."

She kissed his cheek. "I'll call you soon."

As Clarence reluctantly went back into the auditorium and Lydia headed for the exit door, Veronica Caldwell, who'd been observing them from an alcove at the far end of the lobby, quickly went to a phone located in the coatroom.

Joanne Marshall, Cale's secretary, answered her call. "This is Senator Veronica Caldwell. I'd like to speak to my son."

"He's sleeping—"

"Wake him."

(251)

Joanne went to Cale's bedroom and shook his bare shoulder. "Wake up, Cale. Your mother's on the phone."

"Tell her I'll call back," he said sleepily.

"Cale, she sounds angry. Please talk to her."

He sat up in bed, shook the sleep from his head and reached for the phone on the night table. "Mother?"

"Yes."

He told Joanne to hang up the living room extension. After Veronica heard her do so, she said, "Come to the center, Cale, right away."

"Mother, I'm in bed, I—"

"Cale, get here. Twenty minutes."

John Conegli watched Lydia exit the Caldwell Center. He expected her to go directly to her car, but instead she went to the first in a line of waiting cabs, which quickly pulled away from the curb. Conegli maneuvered his car out of the parking lot and followed her cab at a safe distance until it pulled up in front of Luigi's restaurant. He watched Lydia pay the driver and go quickly into the restaurant.

Pretty strange, he thought. She comes to a theater with her boyfriend, runs out on him, grabs a cab and goes to an Italian joint.

Since Lydia had no idea who he was, he could safely enter the restaurant and get a look at who she was meeting. Besides, he was also hungry.

Both the upstairs and downstairs rooms at Luigi's were near capacity. Conegli spotted Lydia seated at a table at the extreme rear of the downstairs room. She was facing the door. Across from her was another woman...wait, he recognized her...sometimes you could get lucky...he checked their table for the package, saw nothing. Both women he noted, had purses large enough to hold a package.

Conegli was about to take a table too far from Lydia's to overhear the conversation when a couple at a table next to hers paid their check and got up. Luck comes in twos, once in a blue moon, he thought.

He quickly moved to it, then ordered a black olive and anchovy pizza and a glass of red wine.

Lydia and Christa took passing note of Conegli as he sat down next to them, then returned to resume what appeared a heavy conversation. Conegli leaned to his left, but even this close the general noise in the restaurant made it impossible for him to hear more than snatches of conversation. Well, it was better than nothing. And it sure beat sitting in a car waiting for them to come out. The zesty smell of Italian food tickled his nostrils. He sipped his wine, and made a mental note to make sure the waitress gave him a blank receipt so that he could put in a hefty dinner tab for Mr. Francis Jewel.

"I still don't understand," Lydia said to Christa. They'd ordered a carafe of white wine.

"It all fits together, Miss James—"

"Please call me Lydia."

"All right... Well, you asked about the tape you saw of Quentin and Senator Caldwell. I remember the day you came to the station to screen it. You said that there were things that bothered you about it."

"That's right. One was that Senator Caldwell fiddled with a missing button on his shirt. It seemed so unlike him to make a public appearance without being perfectly groomed. I asked his wife about it and she assured me that he'd worn a brand-new shirt that day."

"I was aware of it too, but *I* knew why the button was missing. Just before the taping Senator Caldwell and Quentin had an awful row... Quentin actually grabbed the senator by his shirt collar and that's when the button popped off."

"What could have caused such an argument?"

Christa glanced at Conegli, who casually looked away and focused on his wine. She leaned across the table. "Jimmye McNab."

"What about her?" Lydia asked.

"Quentin was insanely jealous over Senator Caldwell's affair with Jimmye."

(253)

"Then it was true," Lydia said. "I'd heard rumors that the senator had been intimate with her but I never believed them. After all, he raised her as a daughter—"

"Except she wasn't really his daughter...anyway, the important thing is that Quentin was crazy in love with Jimmye, always had been. When he found out she was pregnant with Senator Caldwell's child, he became wild...I'd never seen him so—"

"*Senator Caldwell's child?* Are you sure it wasn't his son's, Mark Adam's?"

Christa shook her head, and thought back to that night when Hughes had told her that Jimmye was pregnant with Senator Caldwell's child. She'd replayed it over and over to herself, remembering what they'd said to each other, the tears, the shouts of rage, the love-making, especially the lovemaking, that was remarkably tender compared to what it usually was...

"He's the lowest," Hughes had said about Caldwell. "He was her father, at least he raised her as a daughter, and he took advantage of her." The irony of Hughes taking a moral tone escaped him, and was not something that Christa could mention.

Christa *had* wanted to point out Jimmye's less than sterling qualities, but thought better of that too. She and Hughes had sat on the couch in his apartment, actually a moonstruck, outraged, unrequited lover. Christa welcomed his unaccustomed vulnerability...for her it meant she might finally be *needed*.

"I told her to get an abortion," Hughes had said, "but she laughed. She actually laughed, right in my face. She told me that the baby was worth more than the tape had ever been."

It was the first time Christa had heard of the video-tape, and she asked him about it. Later that night they drove to WCAP and he screened the tape for her. When it was over, he told her to forget about it and said he was going to put it away for safekeeping.

They returned to his apartment and went to bed, where for the first time in her experience rough-tough

Quentin Hughes actually broke down and cried and allowed her to comfort him as she made love to him.

In the morning while she was making breakfast, Hughes also happened to mention that Senator Caldwell had cancer. Jimmye had told him. When Christa made some appropriate response Hughes shook his head, said he didn't deserve a respectable natural death...

Christa looked now at Lydia through eyes that were misted over. "I felt then that Quentin would kill Senator Caldwell."

Lydia said: "But it was Jimmye who was murdered right after she became pregnant, not Caldwell."

"I know... Quentin called Jimmye and made a date to see her. They weren't lovers any more, of course, but he'd never gotten over her. I knew they were meeting because I overheard his telephone call to her. And that was the night she was murdered. He'd worked in the office until early evening, then left to meet her. He came back and did the show, and it was in the middle of it that a bulletin came over the UPI wire that she'd been found murdered—"

"You *knew* he'd met her the night of her murder, and never told anyone about it?"

Christa looked down, closed her eyes and bit her upper lip. "No, I told no one. I couldn't be sure he'd killed her. After all, the fact that he met her didn't absolutely mean that he'd murdered her—"

"Did you ask him about it?"

"No... if I had he would have been furious. I learned a long time ago that making Quentin angry only gave him an excuse to get rid of you. I know, I know, I should have left then, but I guess my obsession with him was almost a match for his with Jimmye."

Lydia wanted to shake Christa, but at the same time felt for her. She'd obviously lived in constant fear that Hughes would dismiss her, as he'd done with so many other women in his life, and couldn't stand it when one did it to him. Lydia resisted the urge to reach across the table and touch her in a gesture of sympathy.

"But, Christa, you stayed with Hughes even though you suspected, more than suspected, that he might have murdered someone."

"I know it doesn't say very much for me, Lydia, but like I said, I've been addicted to him. I guess it started the day I met him in Des Moines. To me... and remember where I was coming from . he was *the* most exciting man, the man for me. Just being with him made me feel special, if you can understand that. He seemed to *know* so much, appeared so at ease in every situation, which God knows was the opposite of me. But there was more than the professional success that rubbed off on me, made me feel better about myself... Believe it or not, at that time there was a side of him that was gentle, a side he kept hidden from almost everybody... Well, I saw it. He could even make me laugh, Lydia. I think I know him... knew him... better than any other person on earth, certainly better than any other woman. I've spent most of my life trying to make him see that I was the *only* woman for him. I decided years ago that I'd do anything, take anything to stay close to him. I kept hoping the time would come when he'd feel the same way I did and—"

"Why now, then? What made you walk away from him now?"

A weary smile crossed her lips. "I didn't walk away, Lydia. He did."

"I'm sorry, Christa..." But what, she thought, about Christa's hinting on the phone before their meeting at the bus station that she had something important to say about the senator's murder. "Christa, what did Jimmye's death have to do with the later Caldwell killing?"

"I think Quentin finally killed Senator Caldwell just like he killed Jimmye McNab."

"Why?"

"My God, I told you... he'd been Jimmye's lover, made her pregnant..."

Lydia's attention was diverted by John Conegli, who'd been served his pizza, but who'd allowed it to cool. Now he was leaning noticeably far to the left.

Lydia's annoyed look made him quickly pick up a slice of the pie and look away.

"I think we should go someplace else," Lydia told Christa.

"I think you're right...you have the envelope I gave you?"

Lydia flushed. She drew a deep breath and said, "I opened it, Christa, right after you left, and I opened the locker and took the videotape."

"Oh...then you've seen it?"

"No. I wanted to wait for you to come back to do that." It was only a partial truth but Lydia felt it was justified. She wasn't, though, sure how to read the expression on Christa's face. "Are you angry at me?"

Christa shook her head. "I needed time to think. No more, not after New York...let's go to the station, I can play it for you there."

"Is that a good idea? You've told me that Quentin attacked you in New York, that you were afraid for your life. Going to WCAP will be walking into his hands, won't it?"

"It's a good risk...he's over on the radio side at this time of night. The TV side is quiet. We can use a vacant editing room or production studio..."

Conegli, forced to be more discreet, had not heard them talk about leaving, so he was surprised when they suddenly stood and headed for the front door. He hated to give up his pizza, but duty called. He put enough money on the table to cover what he guessed would be his check, pushed through a maze of tables and got to his car just as Lydia and Christa hailed a passing cab.

As they headed for the sprawling facility that housed the radio and television operations of WCAP, Lydia asked Christa about what she was going to see.

"I couldn't even begin to describe it to you...you'll see for yourself...Lydia, in a way I may have misled you and I apologize for that. I guess I wanted to say anything that would get your attention. I needed an ally, I was scared...The tape doesn't really prove Quentin was involved in the murders of Jimmye and

Senator Caldwell, but I think it does provide pieces of the puzzle you've been trying to put together. I hope that's enough..."

"Christa, if it does that, it's a whole lot more than enough."

The two women settled back and rode in silence. Christa told the driver not to go to the front door but to circle through a large employee parking lot until he got to a door at the rear of the building. "I have a key," she said to Lydia. "I was supposed to turn in my keys but I kept this one. Still not quite able to let go..."

As the cab pulled up in front of an unmarked metal door, John Conegli came to a stop in the employee parking lot, quickly shut off his lights. He saw the two women get out of the cab and, as it drove away, watched Christa insert a key into the door's lock, open it and lead Lydia through it.

He got out of his car, walked to the door and tried it. Solidly locked. He considered going to the front entrance but knew he'd never get through security. He returned to his car, started the engine and drove to a public telephone, where he placed a call to Francis Jewel at the Center for Inner Faith. He quickly told Jewel what had happened, listened to Jewel's instructions, hung up and returned to the parking lot, where he shut off the engine, lit a cigar, and stared at the door.

Thirty-three

Clarence had been home from the concert a half hour when Lydia called him to say she was at WCAP. She said she had no time to talk but that he should pick her up in about an hour.

He'd no sooner hung up when the phone rang again. This time it was Lydia's researcher, Ginger Johnson. "I'm sorry to bother you," she said, "but I was worried about Lydia." And then she quickly told him about the phone call she'd gotten from Christa Jones and said she wondered whether Christa had gotten in touch with Lydia at the concert.

"Yes, she did. In fact Lydia left the concert to meet her. They're at WCAP right now. Lydia is going to call me when she's through."

Ginger was silent for a moment. Then: "Do you think she's okay with Miss Jones? I mean, she sounded so...upset when she called. Somehow I have this crazy feeling that things are about to blow up and I hate to think of Lydia being smack in the middle of it."

Clarence didn't tell her he had exactly the same sort of worries. What he did say was: "Maybe I shouldn't wait for Lydia's call. Maybe I'll drive out there now."

"I'd love to come with you, if you wouldn't mind."

"I'll pick you up."

"Why don't I pick you up? You're on my way to WCAP. Give me a half hour."

He was immediately sorry he'd agreed to wait for Ginger...oh, come on, he told himself, you've been watching too many movies. He did a lousy job of convincing himself.

After Lydia finished talking to Clarence, Christa led her down a series of hallways until they reached a small dark studio in the basement of the WCAP building. The studio had been designed to handle taped interviews with celebrities and newsmakers, but received little use.

Christa snapped on a few lights, which made Lydia feel better. Two orange swivel chairs stood on a slightly raised platform in the middle of the studio. Three huge television cameras stood silently on their tripods, bizarre statues in the world of electronic communications. Lydia and Christa stepped over heavy black cables that curled across the floor like reptiles and went into a control room overlooking the studio. Christa stripped the brown paper from the package, exposing the reel of videotape. "I was going to use one of the editing rooms, like the one we were in when you screened Quentin's interview with Senator Caldwell, but I think you might as well see what's on this tape on the biggest screen possible. I can run it through the rear-screen projection system here. It'll only take a few minutes to rack it up."

Lydia watched closely as Christa deftly negotiated the array of electronic equipment in the control room. It was obvious that she took pride in having mastered it all. She gave Lydia a play-by-play of what she was doing..."We're as well equipped as any station in the country. All two-inch equipment, but we'll be converting to one-inch in a few months. Quentin is a gadget nut, he loves electronic equipment, his apartment is loaded with it. Everything here has total remote capability too. It can all be run from slave units out in the studio..."

When everything was set Christa led Lydia back to the studio and motioned to her to sit in one of the swivel chairs. Lydia did, and Christa pointed to a rack of equipment mounted on a movable console that stood next to the chair. "That's the remote panel," she said. Lydia absently ran her fingers over the panel's buttons, then returned her attention to Christa.

"I'll run it from the control room," Christa said. "It's a little easier. Besides, I think you'd probably rather be alone while you watch it. There's nothing for me to explain to you. The tape says it all. The only thing I'll point out is that it contains material from two sources. One is eight-millimeter film that was taken by someone at the Center for Inner Faith. The other footage was a videotape interview Jimmye McNab did with Mark Adam Caldwell after the eight-millimeter film had been shot. You won't have any trouble telling the two apart because the quality of the videotape is so superior to the film footage. I have to warn you, Lydia... what you're about to see isn't very pretty or pleasant."

Lydia's stomach was twisted into a knot. She realized she was about to learn something she wasn't even sure she wanted to know. For a moment she had the urge to tell Christa not to run the tape. She wanted to get out of that studio and go home and seal herself off from everything that had happened since Senator Cale Caldwell's murder. Of course, she didn't. She'd come this far, she'd go all the way. She watched Christa return to the control room and sit behind a huge console. The lights in the studio were dimmed, and a large screen suspended from the ceiling came to life.

The screen was eight feet wide and six feet high. Two massive speakers, also suspended from the ceiling and flanking the screen, gave out beeps as a series of numbers counted down from ten to one. Lydia glanced up at the glass separating the studio from the control room. Christa's face was lit by a glow from the control panel. The way the illumination came from below her chin, it turned her face into a sinister mask, reminding

Lydia of when she was a child and would point a flashlight at her face from below to scare her friends.

Now the screen was filled with crude, shaky footage of the Center for Inner Faith's main house. The person taking the film was obviously trying to establish the general location because a series of scenes of the grounds followed—quick short bursts of film that eventually ended up behind the main house.

The next scene was of at least a hundred white-robed cult members, male and female, who'd congregated along the bank of Occaquan Creek. Lydia noticed one man carrying a portable cassette tape recorder. She guessed he wasn't supposed to be in the film but apparently had walked a little too far ahead of the cameraman.

Up until this point the film had been silent. Now the voice of the cult members could be heard. Lydia leaned forward to better hear what was a chant...a long, sustained, rhythmic moan that grew louder as the camera and recorder neared.

Abruptly, the film footage ended and Jimmye McNab's face filled the screen. It had been so long that Lydia had forgotten the incongruously angelic face of the woman...incongruous in terms of what she'd come to learn of her...It was a face, somebody had once said, that would look good in a bathing cap. Lydia tried to figure out where Jimmye was for the taping...it appeared to be a motel or hotel room. Jimmye, in a chair in front of a set of heavy green drapes, faced into the camera. "Hello, this is Jimmye McNab," she said in her husky voice, also incongruous with the delicate, feminine face. "As some of you might know, I've been interested, in my role as investigative journalist, in the subject of brainwashing and mind control. That interest led me to write a book on the subject. I was obliged to research every possible aspect of the subject, including the use of manipulative techniques in so-called religious cults that have proliferated recently in our country. My research led me to the conclusion that individuals were, indeed, being controlled by the leaders of these organizations.

"Like any journalist, my personal involvement in a subject can only be as good as the contacts I'm able to establish. For this story I have been extremely fortunate. I was brought up by a very wonderful and distinguished family headed by United States Senator Cale Caldwell. In that home were two young men I learned to call my brothers, Cale Caldwell, Jr., and Mark Adam Caldwell. With me today is one of those brothers, Mark Adam."

The scene now widened to include Mark Adam, who sat in a similar chair on Jimmye's right. They were close together. He wore his cult's traditional white robe. His head was shaven, and his eyes had the same vacant haze that had upset Lydia when she'd visited him at the center.

Jimmye continued: "What you are about to see will undoubtedly shock you. It did me, so much so that I think I shall never get over it for as long as I live. But not only will you see this dreadful event with your own eyes, you will hear from its main participant exactly why it occurred and, more important, why he was involved in it." She turned and looked directly at Mark Adam. "You are my brother, Mark, and I love you no matter what." (She certainly did, Lydia thought.) Jimmye again looked directly into the camera. "Once more I must warn you that what you see will shock and anger you, but if brainwashing and its use by cults is ever to be understood, it will only be because such practices are exposed."

The screen went black, then again lit up with crude eight-millimeter footage. Lydia focused intently on the screen. The camera was in the midst of the cult members gathered at the creek. It moved jerkily through the young men and women until reaching the edge of the water. Standing there were four young men in white robes. They'd formed a box around a young woman who also wore a robe. She appeared to be no older than twenty. She had a sweet face. Her brown hair was closely cropped, like all the other females in the cult. Her hands were secured behind her back. She stared straight ahead, but in spite of an apparent calm and resolve on her face, her eyes testified to the fear she was also experiencing.

Jimmye now began to narrate the film off-camera... "One of the important ingredients in brainwashing is to strip away the individual's sense of self, to deprive him of all roots, all links to the past and then to substitute new ideas and philosophies. Generally, that's sufficient to keep members in line. Of course, it depends a great deal upon the person on the receiving end of the manipulation. My research has indicated that ultimately the capacity to be controlled is within the individual, and that those who in the first instance embrace fanatical cults have a predisposition to fall under such control. No one seems to know why one person is susceptible to such tampering and another isn't. Perhaps it's a combination of genetics, early patterning, parental influence. The important thing is that for those who do possess this heightened capacity to be controlled, the job is made very easy for those who have that as a goal.

"There are times, though, when someone will stray from the pattern expected of them. When that occurs, punishment helps to reinforce the control. What you are about to see is punishment in the extreme. It is not unlike the Arabic custom of severing a hand or a head in a public square and demanding that everyone attend. An example made, and there is less likelihood that others will deviate from the precepts set down by the leaders."

The girl's face was caught in a close-up, and the combination of resignation and fear was now even more evident to Lydia. Jimmye's words about punishment had brought Lydia to the edge of her chair. She was like someone appalled at the thought of seeing an impending disaster, yet not able to take her eyes from it. She glanced up at Christa, who sat motionless, her face empty of expression.

The four young men surrounding the girl moved closer until she was literally pressed between their bodies. One of them grabbed the neck of her robe and yanked at it. The crowd observing the event had become dead still. Now the chant rose up again from its midst, an eerie cacophony that put goose bumps on Lydia's arms and neck. She watched as the young men stepped back and completed the act of disrobing the young girl. She now stood naked. Lydia felt outraged, sickened. Then Mark Adam Caldwell stepped into the frame and sharply struck the girl in the face. The blow knocked her to the ground. He pulled the girl to her feet by her hair and hit her again. And again. The cameraman stepped closer and caught the sickening action. The tape recorder picked up her cries that cut through the monotonous din of the chant.

Eventually Mark Adam stepped out of camera range. The girl appeared to be unconscious. She was on the ground, her legs askew, her head turned to one side. Blood trickled from her mouth.

"My God," Lydia said.

Jimmye's voice came through the speakers. "It was not the intention of those who ordered the punishment you have just seen that the victim die. But that is what happened on this day. For whatever supposed transgressions she had committed against the cult to whom she had dedicated her life, she was to be punished at the hand of a fellow cult member. It was to be an object lesson for others tempted to stray from their commitment. It did not work out that way.

"Why was such a film made? One might ask the same thing about why tapes were recorded in the White House when the Watergate cover-up was being discussed. It's difficult to ever evaluate the motivations of people in high places, in positions of authority. In this case it seems the film was made as a permanent document to be shown to *members* of the cult . . . not, surely, potential members . . . as a warning not to falter in their commitment."

The film ended. Jimmye McNab appeared on the

screen. "How I became the owner of this film is irrelevant. The important thing is that you, the viewer, will now hopefully have a better understanding of the insidious hold such organizations maintain over so many young people..."

She turned then to Mark Adam Caldwell. "Why did you agree to inflict the punishment on her, Mark?"

His eyes remained fixed on some unseen object, just as they'd been when Lydia had visited him. He said in a flat, emotionless voice, "She'd sinned against our Father. It was right that I carry out his wishes."

"Who told you to do it, Mark?"

"Our Savior," he replied, still visually ignoring the fact that she was sitting next to him.

"You didn't mean to kill her, did you?"

"She died for her sins."

"But you didn't mean to kill her."

"She was evil. Satan had possessed her."

Lydia remembered what Mark had said about Jimmye McNab during her conversation with him at the center. He'd branded *her* as a woman who had sinned and whose death was justified.

Jimmye finished her commentary and the screen went black, leaving Lydia in near-darkness, though she could see Christa get up from behind the console, go to a videotape machine and rewind the tape. The horror of the killing, accident or no, left Lydia wrung out. What did it have to do with Senator Cale Caldwell's murder? Certainly Jimmye might have been murdered by members of the cult who knew she'd come into possession of their tape. God knew, it was damaging, legally and otherwise. Murder to suppress it would not be unthinkable.

But Senator Caldwell? Did he know about the tape showing his son murdering a young girl? If so, who would want to kill him because he had that knowledge? Hughes? Hardly. Christa may have been right that Hughes did it out of jealousy, but the cult was at least as likely. And was Mark Adam the cult's agent, as he had been in the punishment of the girl in the film? Maybe his compassion was legitimate after all. Maybe...

Lydia's thoughts were interrupted as Christa walked into the studio, sat down in the matching orange chair and handed her the reel of tape. "Jimmye used the tape to blackmail the Caldwell family. Later, I believe Quentin did too. Pretty, isn't it..."

Lydia looked at Christa. "It's hard to believe that. Jimmye was brought up with all the love and care that a natural daughter could ever expect. To turn on those people who'd been so good to her..."

Christa closed her eyes, hunched her shoulders. "Jimmye McNab was driven with ambition. Even Quentin understood that. He told me. When he found out that she was pregnant by Senator Caldwell, he went crazy. That's why he killed her, and like I said, I can only assume that jealousy was his reason for killing Senator Caldwell—"

Lydia shook her head.

"What does this have to do with the tape?"

Instead of Christa's voice answering, a male voice said from behind them, "I'd say it has a good deal to do with it."

Both women turned. Lydia found the voice familiar but couldn't quite identify it. The man stepped from the shadows of the corner of the studio into the dim light. Cale Caldwell...?

"Cale? What are you doing here? And what do you mean," Lydia got up from her chair and took a few steps toward him.

"Sit down, Lydia," he said.

Lydia looked hard at him, then went back to her chair. Cale came around in front of her and stood next to one of the video cameras. "Give me the tape, Lydia. After all, it involves my poor brother—"

"You've seen it?" Lydia asked as she reluctantly gave it to him.

"I never had to. It was described to me in detail."

"*Who* described it?" Lydia asked.

"Jimmye, of course. She'd been holding it over our

heads ever since she made it. Our wonderful so-called sister turned out to be neither wonderful nor a sister...she was a blackmailer who victimized our family from the first day she came to my mother and told her that if she didn't receive large sums of money regularly, she'd make the tape public."

Lydia looked at Christa. "Quentin had the tape..."

"After Jimmye was murdered, Quentin ended up with it. I suppose he took it from her the night he killed her."

Lydia turned to Cale. "Did Hughes blackmail you after Jimmye's death?"

"In a sense," he said wearily. He leaned against the camera. "Hughes never *directly* asked us for money, but just knowing the tape existed and what was on it was enough to keep going the potential destruction of the family. Hughes told my father he had the tape, never mind how...It was more frustrating dealing with him having it than Jimmye—at least with her there was an ongoing transaction to focus on. Not with Hughes. He seemed happy to taunt my father with it. He'd call him at odd times just to remind him that it existed. In fact, he brought it up just before the interview he taped with my father at this station. They actually scuffled, I was told. No, Quentin Hughes never asked for money from us. He asked, or rather extracted, much more."

Keep him talking, Lydia told herself. Cale had obviously been under intense pressure for a long time. Finally talking about it in a darkened television studio was a relief he seemed to need very badly. Maybe he'd say more than he intended. Keep him talking...

Lydia shifted in her chair, out of the corner of her eye noticed what Christa had called the remote panel. Casually she moved her right hand to it and in the dim light managed to use five fingers to press down on buttons that activated silent solenoid switches without being detected by Cale. She had no firm idea what would happen from pressing the buttons, all she could do was hope they'd activate a recording. She waited. No flashing lights, no whirring spools, nothing...

"Cale, how did you get into the studio?"

"When you're the son of a United States senator, both dead and alive, you go pretty much anywhere you please. Jewel telephoned mother at the center, I headed here. I told the security guard who I was and that I was meeting Quentin Hughes on a personal matter. He wanted to call Quentin and confirm it but I told him that it was of a very delicate nature and that Mr. Hughes would not want anyone in the station to know about our getting together. He waved me through. That's the problem with security, it depends on people."

"Are you aware of Miss Jones's claim that Hughes killed Jimmye *and* your father?"

Cale shook his head. "The important thing, Lydia, is that Jimmye is dead. My father, unfortunately, couldn't do anything to stop her. He was far more effective on the Senate floor than in real life. He met with her, tried to reason with her. And ended up sleeping with her. Made her pregnant, of all things. How's that for messing up a mess. You can imagine what it did to mother when Jimmye told her that she was carrying dad's child...and it wasn't so much that my father had slept with another woman, Lydia. We'd become quite accustomed to that. Of all of us, it bothered my brother the most. In fact, my father's weakness for the opposite sex had a great deal to do with pushing Mark Adam toward the cult. In his sad mixed-up view of life, he felt *he* had to atone for the sins of his father."

Lydia tried to sort out what she was hearing...she was hardly naive, but somehow the image of Senator Cale Caldwell being a womanizer was not easy for her to accept. She felt sorry for Veronica Caldwell. It must have been excruciating for her to keep up the front...

She glanced at Christa, then said to Cale, "I take it from what you've said that you don't believe Hughes killed Jimmye and your father. But Quentin did meet with Jimmye the night of her murder, was apparently terribly jealous of her affair with your father, not to mention that she'd become pregnant by him—"

"I didn't realize that you knew about Jimmye and my father, Lydia. You'd asked me about it, but I figured you were only responding to rumors and that my denial was enough to put them to rest."

"Well, I didn't know for sure until tonight, but now that you've confirmed it, it raises other questions."

"Such as?"

"Who *did* kill Jimmye?"

"My brother, sad to say. He's confessed to it, and—"

"I've just never been able to believe that Mark Adam killed Jimmye, or your father. Even though I realize he hated them both..."

Cale sighed and rubbed the bridge of his nose. "That's too bad, but it's the truth. Lydia, mother and I assumed you would accept that. Mother apparently assumed too much about you, including the way you would conduct yourself as special counsel to the committee investigating my father's murder."

"Did she really think I would simply go through the motions? And why push for a committee at all?"

He stepped away from the camera and his voice took on new strength, a kind of genuine urgency. "So that everything could be finally put to rest, Lydia, so that what's left of this marvelous family could get on with the important work it was put on this earth to accomplish. Have you any idea of the hell mother and I have gone through because of the pathetic weakness of my brother, and father? Can you count the sleepless nights, of tears, the fear of exposure and disgrace? It was my father's responsibility to put his own house in order. God, how my mother pleaded with him. She expected him to stand up and protect us. Well, he wasn't capable of it, Lydia, never was. It was all left up to mother to protect the Caldwell name against people who would destroy us by their indiscretions, or their greed and ambition."

"You mean Jimmye..."

"Yes, damn it, I mean Jimmye. She got hold of that film and persuaded Mark Adam to be interviewed about it. Not so hard, considering their relationship. After that she held it over our heads. We weren't the only people she blackmailed because of that tape, Lydia. She took from us, *and* from the cult. She was a taker. There was no reasoning with her. Nothing worked. I talked with her a few times and she laughed at me. I suspect she must have laughed at my father too, especially after he not only failed to persuade her to stop blackmailing us but ended up making love to her. I'm a lawyer, but if there was ever a person on this earth who deserved to leave it, it was Jimmye McNab, my dear and unlamented nonsister."

Christa, who'd said nothing through it all, broke her silence. "Maybe he didn't do it?"

"No, of course Hughes didn't kill Jimmye," Cale said.

Lydia looked directly at him. "Did you kill her?"

Cale stared at her. "Don't be ridiculous, Lydia. But for the record, being a lawyer and since a lawyer has asked, *no.*"

"Did your brother? I know he's confessed, but—"

"Yes, he's confessed. Lydia, not to seem cold-blooded, but the *important* thing is that he finally will be making a contribution to his family that will in some way make up for the pain he caused it by joining the cult and killing that young girl, in front of a movie camera, God help him. Anyway, I'll get him off on an insanity plea and that will finish it."

Lydia swiveled in her chair as though looking for someone to share what she was thinking and feeling. Mark Adam Caldwell, it seemed pretty clear now, was being sacrificed to save someone else. And his own brother knew it...."Cale, how could you possibly allow your brother to confess to murders he didn't commit? You talk about this wonderful family of yours, yet the remaining members of it, you and your mother, are willing to identify flesh and blood as a killer? Who are you protecting? Who will benefit from your brother's confession?"

"I didn't say he didn't commit the murders. You did. But to answer your question...the Caldwell name."

"And who was used to protect that name, Cale?" And then it hit her...*"Jason DeFlaunce?* Loyal, faithful Jason...?" It was logical but still a shot in the dark...or rather the dawn...

"An interesting notion, Lydia. Jason is very loyal to my mother and to the Caldwell tradition. But why must you ask so many questions? From the beginning you've refused to understand what was really important about investigating my father's death. He was about to hurt us all by telling what he knew about Jimmye and my brother, about how she died. Pregnant with his child. His reasons weren't the same as Jimmye's but they were just as dangerous. He knew he was dying of cancer...I suspect you've found that out by now...and suddenly he was filled with a rush of lofty ideals, with a need to purge himself, to set the record straight, the way he claimed to do in campaign speeches. He was such a damned fool, Lydia, so proper and upstanding to everyone except those who most deserved the best from him."

"You're referring to the letter he wrote, aren't you?" Lydia said.

"Still probing, Lydia, still trying to involve yourself in something that's truly none of your business. All right, yes, there was a letter. Not any more, thank God, because mother came across it in his study before he could deliver it to Dr. Clemow. It was quite a letter, Lydia. It would have fed you and people like you enough destructive scandal about the Caldwell family to satisfy appetites for years to come. When he discovered that mother had the letter he became irrational, threatened to tell the contents of it to his friends, even the press. We couldn't allow that to happen. It would have destroyed this family...surely you can understand that..."

"And so to protect the good Caldwell name, you and your mother used good old Jason."

Cale looked at both women carefully. Carefully weighed his mother's and his word...the *Caldwell* word...against the possibility of a court believing one very upset woman and one confused lady lawyer, more a female out of her depths than a credible professional. He liked the odds...overwhelming in his favor. And what a relief to tell it, and without substantive fear of the consequences..."Well, Lydia, I won't say you're wrong.

"You know, it's ironic, the tape brought the cult and the Caldwell family into a bizarre alliance. We were both threatened by it and worked together to find it. Eventually mother convinced Jimmye...or thought she had...to turn it over to us for two hundred and fifty thousand dollars. But when Jason met Jimmye, she demanded the money and said she'd destroyed the tape. Considering the source, that was hardly credible. Jason properly acted on his own initiative."

"And Hughes...?" Lydia asked, exhilarated and disgusted at the same time, leading him on now, but not wanting to press too hard and risk shutting him up.

"We waited for Hughes to pick up the blackmail where Jimmye had left off. Talk about your sword of Damocles..."

Lydia turned to Christa. "Why did Jimmye give Quentin the tape, Christa, and what did he actually intend to do with it? Apparently he never directly asked for money."

"I guess Jimmye was afraid for her life...I mean from the cult. And she trusted Quentin to do what she wanted no matter what. She was right. And for him the tape meant a lot of things...a hedge against failure—for all his macho act he's the most insecure man I've ever known. A day hardly passes that he isn't convinced his career, which is his life, will collapse around him."

"What else did it mean?"

"Most of all I think it was a reminder of Jimmye." She forced a grim smile. "Instead of a wallet photograph of a lost love, he had Jimmye on tape, moving, talking, almost alive." She paused, then said, "And the tape gave Quentin a way to work out his hatred of Senator

Caldwell. It was a hatred that could easily have led to killing the object of that hatred. I thought it had."

She was on the edge of tears, took a deep breath, tried to compose herself. "Anyway, I knew that taking that tape would hurt him, and that's what I wanted. I was hurt and angry, I wanted him to be."

Lydia put her arm over Christa's shoulder and held her for a few moments, then looked at Cale. "Your brother isn't the only sick one, Cale. You'll never get away with this. Now there are two of us who know that Jason killed your father and Jimmye on behalf of you and your mother. What do you do now, kill us, or have Jason do it? And then do you get rid of Jason? And you a lawyer...God..." She felt far less brave than she sounded. Take it easy, she told herself...you've drawn him out...don't provoke him...

But he seemed very calm. "Lydia, this has all been a very bad dream. The truth is, hard as it may be for you to accept it, no one would believe either of your *concocted* stories against the word of one of the most distinguished women in America, Veronica Caldwell, a champion of the arts, grieving wife, mother, a member of the United States Senate. My poor brother will be judged mentally unfit and spend the rest of his years in an institution, and a damn sight better one than that crazy one he's been in."

"Your brother...yes...you no doubt handled that."

"Well, it wasn't too difficult to convince him...he isn't lying you know. He believes he did what he says...probably *wanted* to do it for years. I would never let my brother die. Even if none of this had happened, he's still better off being institutionalized, and I'll see to it that he receives the finest of care."

My God, Lydia thought. He actually sees himself as a savior instead of the instigator of murder. He's crazier than Mark Adam, but he's also crazy like a fox. What a lethal combination...

"You know *nothing*, Lydia, only what your fertile imagination has conjured up for you. And this young lady," nodding at Christa, "has already demonstrated her overactive imagination. After all, she said it was her lover, Mr. Hughes. This night never happened, ladies. Let's all go home and get on with our lives. All that's happened is that the tape that has caused so much anguish will now be put to a positive, however painful, use."

Lydia had first thought he would immediately destroy the tape. As though sensing what she was thinking, he added, "The tape will now be turned over to the attorneys I've retained for my brother's defense. It had always been my intention to destroy the tape once I found it, but the situation has changed. But there's always been the possibility that another copy exists and will surface to haunt us again, and now that Mark Adam has confessed, shown himself sick enough to kill his own father, the tape becomes strong evidence to support an insanity plea in his behalf. I'm sure you would agree to that. And by the way, the tape also provides a sympathetic motive for Mark having killed Jimmye...he was brainwashed by the cult to do their dirty work, just as he did it at that ceremony of theirs. Rather fitting, matter of fact, in view of Jimmye's long-time interest in the subject."

All very logical, Lydia had to admit, and felt herself shiver slightly in spite of herself. She shifted through the sequence to clear her thoughts, get herself under control...Until the tape came to their attention, the Caldwells were embarrassed by Mark Adam's involvement with the cult, but there it stayed. Until Jimmye got hold of the incriminating tape, which now made a huge scandal a real possibility, especially with her threats to reveal it. When she became untenable, they had her killed by Jason, not expecting that the tape would turn up in the hands of Quentin Hughes. But at least Hughes didn't use it, only threatened to—which was bad enough but almost tolerable. Then when the senator, in an apparent fit of conscience brought on by the knowledge of his terminal illness, threatened to destroy the family reputation by telling all, Veronica and Cale felt they had to help him along the way to eternity, for the sake of the family, of course. Hughes was still a problem, but she, Lydia realized now, was a bigger one. With her refusing to play the passive role as counsel to the committee that Veronica had presumed she would, she herself more than anything else forced their hand. Now they needed a scapegoat above all else, and pitiful Mark Adam was the ideal candidate, and the tape of his terrible act at the cult now became the document to make the guilty confession stick—as a creature of the cult he did its bidding in killing Jimmye, and to avenge himself on a father who had impregnated Jimmye, he took a terrible revenge... or at least so Cale's story would go in court. And, as Cale had said so confidently, Mark would be found mentally incompetent, not able to distinguish right from wrong at the time he committed the killings, and put in an institution. Well, at least once the tape was made public the Center for Inner Faith would be severely damaged. Even Senator MacLoon's wheeling-dealing would have a hard time bailing them out of this.

Would Cale really get away with it? Was the Caldwell name, especially Veronica Caldwell's, that all-powerful, that damnably respectable? Maybe. Better than maybe, if Lydia were honest with herself. Sure she'd try, go to Horace Jenkins with Christa to corroborate her story, but would they be believed? More likely she would be the one perceived to have snapped under the press of frustrated ambitions. And Christa... an emotionally disturbed woman, who'd just been jilted by her lover...

Well, damn it, at least don't say anything more. Cale was dangerous, dangerous like a lizard—which he now looked like to her. Smooth and easy in manner but a man who had been part of such a sick conspiracy. Oh yes, they called Mark Adam sick and no doubt he was, but how much sicker, in their dissembling ways, were Cale and the redoubtable Veronica, hiding behind a facade of respectability and their own rationalizations.

Once again, as if reading her mind, or at least part

of it, Cale said, "And, Lydia, if you actually insist on telling any outlandish tale about us, I'm afraid we'll be obliged to sue you for reckless disregard for the truth—slander. That won't sit well for your future career as an attorney around these parts. Might even end it... Well, it's been instructive, ladies, all around I trust. I'll be going now, and thank you for this..." By which he meant the videotape, which he'd come for in the first place.

Casually, almost insolently it seemed, he moved to his right, taking a circuitous route to the door that led from the studio. Both women looked at each other, and seeing the dazed look on Christa's face, Lydia knew she'd get little comfort or meaningful response from the woman.

She willed herself into action, ran across the studio and out its door, rushed up a hallway to the door they'd entered through, opened it and stumbled outside, leaning against the building, breath coming in gasps—

A sound from the direction of the parking lot froze her against the building. It might have been an automobile backfire, a firecracker even. It wasn't. The *crack* cut through the chilled night air. A car door slammed shut. The sound of a man calling out, "Drop it," melodramatic, except not in this awful context of reality. Headlights suddenly lit up the parking lot to frame a car coming around the corner of the building. Looking across a grassy strip that separated the parking lot from the building, it seemed to Lydia that it looked like Ginger's car. She ran toward it, the only familiar... safe... thing in this surreal storm of deceit and violence.

It was Clarence, though, who called out her name as he jumped from the car and ran to close the distance between them. As she ran, Lydia's attention was drawn to her left, where a heavyset man had Francis Jewel pressed up against the side of a car. He was holding a gun to Jewel's head and yelling at him... something like, "What the hell did you do that for...?"

Clarence was holding Lydia now, but she could see

(277)

over his shoulder that Ginger had gotten out of her car and was coming to them. Suddenly Ginger stopped, looked down at something hidden from Lydia's view by a parked car. And then Ginger, laid-back Ginger, let out a scream that Lydia could feel down to her toes. She and Clarence ran to Ginger's side, looked down to see the body of Cale Caldwell, Jr., sprawled out on the asphalt, the videotape cartridge still in his hands. Blood seeped from a wound in his chest. He looked dead, and he was.

It was unreal, like all the rest that had happened in the last hours, and horribly real. Moments before this man had acted—and convincingly so—invulnerable. Now...Tentatively Lydia and Clarence and Ginger went to where the unknown man held Jewel against the car. Lydia asked him who he was.

"Never mind," Conegli said. "Call the police. Hurry up."

Obviously Jewel knew who Conegli was, and in fact was both pleading with him and threatening him, which was strange, considering that it was Conegli who held the gun in his face. "Damn it, you work for me...I only did what you should have done, did your job...I couldn't help doing it...he wouldn't give me the tape, started to punch me, run off. That tape is worth my life..." He meant because of what the cult would do to him for not retrieving it, ironically not even thinking of the murder charge that soon would be lodged against him. The cult's power was still, Lydia thought, in its fashion surpassingly powerful...

Conegli's only answer to Jewel was to tell him to shut up, that he might do strange things for a living but getting mixed up in a murder for sure wasn't one of them. That he had his principles.

"Let's go inside and call the police," Lydia said to Clarence and Ginger. They were moving toward the entrance to the WCAP building when the rear door opened and Christa and Hughes came through it. They all met in the middle of the grassy strip.

When Lydia asked Hughes if Christa had filled him

in on what had happened, he said she hadn't needed to. The security guard had called him and asked whether Caldwell had arrived. Hughes hadn't known what he was talking about, and when the guard told him that Caldwell didn't want anyone else to know about their so-called private meeting, he really wondered what the hell was going on. He decided to look around, and wandered into the control room right after Caldwell showed up to interrupt Lydia and Christa after they'd viewed the tape.

"Then you'll back me up when I tell what happened," Lydia said, for the first time feeling that some sense was coming into all this.

For one of the rare times in his life, Hughes smiled and meant it. "You don't need anybody to back you up, counselor, not with this..." And he held up a reel of quarter-inch audio tape. "Damned if I know why, but one of the Ampexes was taping through a studio mike. You do a passing fair interview, Lydia. You've got the secret down pat. Let the victim do the talking and hang himself. Anytime you want a job, let me know."

At first Lydia was confused, and then she remembered idly pressing some buttons. Obviously, without even knowing what she was doing, only hoping against hope, she'd activated the equipment Hughes mentioned. She leaned against Clarence, then straightened and headed for the phone to call the MPD.

Thirty-four

The flashing lights and sirens of police cars, the gawking crowds and reporters, television cameras and lights that had almost miraculously materialized at the fine old Virginia homestead of the distinguished Caldwell family, resembled a Hollywood premiere more than the grim business going on—the arrest for murder and conspiracy to commit murder of one of America's foremost patrons of the arts, the Honorable United States Senator from the sovereign state of Virginia, Veronica Caldwell, descended from the best and most aristocratic traditions of the nation, and of charming Jason DeFlaunce, lesser patron of the arts and fancy handyman to the mighty.

They came out and were rushed into separate police cars. Veronica, head high, still trying to look the perfect Caldwell, was almost a touching figure, until one reminded oneself of what she had done. Jason, the hired hand, somehow came off better, looking the way he felt, dazed, disbelieving, pale as chalk. The police cars taking them, one presumed, to MPD headquarters took off with a screech of tires and sirens. Even now, Jason was separate from the family. Whether he would be, finally, equal, if only in crime, was yet to be seen.

Thirty-five

Lydia and Clarence sat at Peng's, one of their favorite Chinese restaurants in New York, treating themselves to sweet-and-sour shrimp, beef with snow pea pods and chicken prepared in three different styles. They'd arrived in New York that morning and checked into the Carlyle Hotel. That night they had tickets to the concert by the New York Philharmonic, conducted by Zubin Mehta.

"Come on, honey," Clarence was saying. *"Relax,* or at least try to. It's over—"

"I'm trying, Clarence, but you know it really isn't over. Not until Veronica's and Jason's cases are dealt with. And for me...well, I'm not sure I'll ever get over it..."

"Hey," he said, "what about me? I had a damned mike planted in my apartment. My bedroom, yet." He smiled when he said it. "I just hope we weren't too noisy."

And now she was able to smile, even laugh. "I'd say we better try to get our own tape or whatever it is of that one. What was the guy's name...Conegli? Tape, tape, who's got the tape...the case of the missing tape. Sounds like an Erle Stanley Gardner mystery. Well,

I doubt I'll be reading any mysteries for a long time. I've had enough of the real thing..."

"What do you think will happen to Veronica?"

"Well, at first, after I found out everything that was said by Cale at the studio had somehow been recorded, I thought it would be pretty open-and-shut. But that was really the elation or high of the moment. A little while later I knew it wouldn't be that simple, once I reminded myself about who Veronica is, who the Caldwells are, and the sympathy of her case, the sympathetic motives behind what she'd done. When I saw Chief Jenkins I *knew* it wouldn't be simple. He was grateful for the help, you remember, but warned me that there were a few miles between arraignment, indictment and conviction. He's right. Veronica was smart enough to try to defend Jason, which makes her look good, even though I doubt it will do him any good. He's cooked, poor guy. He wanted so badly to be a member of the Caldwell family. Well, he finally made it, but not the way he wanted."

"Okay, counselor, enough. Get into that terrific food and—"

But once started Lydia wasn't about to be diverted. Not yet. "You know, I once mentioned the Harris case. I think I compared that woman to Christa at the time. But it also reminds me a little of Veronica. I mean, people felt sympathetic about Mrs. Harris's reasons for what she did, she was a woman badly used, that sort of thing. Well, Veronica was badly used, God knows, too. A husband that carried on with their adopted daughter, who threatened to ruin the family reputation she so desperately cared about. And a girl she raised like a daughter turning on her, the family, and blackmailing them. God, Clarence, it's really not too surprising that she cracked, took leave of her senses... I'm not excusing her, please understand. That's what she did for herself. But I am trying to understand. I'll testify for the people, and accept the jury's verdict. Don't expect me, though, to take any satisfaction in it coming out guilty. That's a human reaction, and I apologize for it, but—"

"Lydia, of all the people in this thing, *you* have the least to apologize for. And as for you being human, frankly, my dear, I wouldn't have you any other way. In fact...and don't die of shock...I just had a very human idea. Why don't we skip the concert, finish up here and get us to the Carlyle for the evening. You get my point, lady?"

"I do, sir. And I approve. This case is closed."